INSURRECTION

A MEDIEVAL ROMANCE

BY KATHRYN LE VEQUE

PART OF THE GUARD OF SIX SERIES

Another Guard of Six adventure as a powerful knight, with a sword known as *Insurrection*, faces his own demons.

But will his friends be so forgiving?

Epic Medieval Romance on a grand scale as sworn enemies live and love… with explosive secrets to be revealed!

Kent de Poyer is part of the powerful Norman de Poyer family from Netherworld Castle. He was raised on the Welsh marches, a knight who has been at the forefront of Welsh rebellion against the English. Therefore, it's little wonder when Henry sends Kent to the Welsh marches because of some trouble between an English family and a local Welsh warlord that threatens to ignite the entire border into a blaze of battle.

Kent and the Guard of Six head to Wales.

Madelaina ferch Bryn is the daughter of the apothecary from the village of Penderyn. The mighty castle known as The Narth anchors her peaceful valley, and when the English sack the castle, it's a valley of apprehension. The Welsh warlord has fled, helped by the villagers, and when Kent poses as a Welsh traveler to discover the whereabouts of the warlord, he finds himself in the dark world of a spy game.

One that involves the sweet Madelaina.

He's intent on using her for his own purposes, but never planned on falling in love with her.

The Welsh marches are building up to an explosive battle between the Welsh and the English, but not for land or money. This one is about revenge and threatens to disrupt everything Kent's career has stood for. Will his Guard of Six brethren support his stance? Or will Kent be on his own as he battles for Madelaina's love?

Insurrection means rebellion… but does it represent Kent's personal rebellion against everything he's ever known? Or Madelaina's?

GUARD OF SIX

Fortitudo in unitate
Motto: Strength in Unity

We are protectors.
Defenders.
The shield between the king and those who threaten him.
We are the Guard of Six.
Fortitudo in unitate
Strength in unity.

Author's Note

Welcome to another book in the Guard of Six series!

If you're a loyal reader, then you may know where this series stemmed from and what book—it actually came from the de Lohr Dynasty series when I wrote about David de Lohr and his sons, Daniel and Chadwick. In particular, we met the Guard of Six in Chadwick's novel, *Silversword*. In the story, they were looking for the woman Chadwick was protecting and, of course, he wasn't going to give her over, but as I wrote about the Guard of Six, I thought it would be so cool to give these guys their own story.

And here we are!

The Guard of Six aren't just a normal group of royal bodyguards. As I explained in the first book, these guys are kind of Henry III's death squad. They do whatever he wants them to do. If Henry says jump, they jump, and each one of them has a bit of a dark secret that Henry holds over them. They're really a bunch of misfits, unlike other groups I write about. These guys have secrets and scandals in their past. The Guard of Six comprises (their families/house name in parentheses):

- Torran de Serreaux (*The Unholy Hour—a contemporary novel*)
- Aidric St. John (*The Warrior Poet*)
- Dirk d'Vant (*Tender Is the Knight*)
- Jareth de Leybourne (*Lady of the Moon*)
- Britt de Garr (*Lord of Light*)

- Kent de Poyer (*Netherworld*)

These are all families from some of my older or lesser-known books, so I love that they're coming to the forefront again. Do you recognize them? The names of the books their families are originally featured in have been put in parentheses. If you haven't read these books yet, they're a must. *The Warrior Poet* was, I think, about the fourth or fifth Medieval Romance I ever wrote.

But on to the men collectively known as the Six…

In this book, you're going to meet a few new members—or potential members, including the bastard son of an original de Wolfe Pack knight. Gasp! Also, to be clear, the Earl of Hereford and Worcester mentioned in this novel is, at this point in time, Christopher "Chris" de Lohr, eldest son of Curtis. Chris also makes an appearance in *A Wolfe Among Dragons*, as do his sons, as does Corbett Payton-Forrester, whose brother is a secondary character in this book. This book is set about the time of *Nighthawk* (Sons of de Wolfe) and the older sons of William and Jordan de Wolfe, toward the end of Henry III's reign and after the fall of Simon de Montfort.

Another little Easter egg in this story is the mention of Cilgerran Castle and the le Mon family. That comes from *The Whispering Night*, a book that is part of the Executioner Knight series. That book was written about twenty years ago, and the very first book of mine where William Marshal, Earl of Pembroke, appeared as the leader of a band of spies, assassins, and agents. The sequel, *Netherworld*, took its hero from *The Whispering Night*—Keller de Poyer. Now, we have Keller's grandson, Kent, as the hero of this novel.

One of the things that is becoming prevalent for this series is the focus on brotherhood and the relationships between men who serve together. Of course, all of my books have those themes, but with the Guard of Six, the emphasis on the strength of bonds seems to be greater. I really love how they have one another's backs—and they're not related by blood—so it has been fun to introduce these guys and the strength of their ties. There are just some friendships that are unbreakable, and that's what you find with the Guard of Six, so beyond this being a romance series, it's also a series of love between friends. And what are we without the love and support of good friends?

Now, on to the usual pronunciation guide:

Celyn—SEE-lyn
Madelaina—Mad-uh-LANE-uh
Tyr—Teer

And with that, welcome to *Insurrection*, which has some interesting moments in it—and some really great characters. This book is setting up some plot points for the rest of the series, so full steam ahead.

Happy Reading!

Hugs,

PROLOGUE

Year of Our Lord 1240
Welsh Marches

"Y**OUR MOTHER IS** a frog!" Giggles followed. "Do you hear me? Your mother is a frog and your father is fish and you smell like stinky baby fish-frogs!"

It was a threat but, evidently, not a serious one. Serious threats weren't usually followed by laughter or snickers or titters, which was exactly what was coming from behind the rock about twenty feet away.

But he wasn't going to let his friend get away with it.

It was a bright day, unusually mild, on the gentle hills of the Welsh marches. This area was remote and lush, known as "The Wilds" to the English. The grass was greener than any grass, anywhere, and the scattered trees were filled with birds. Perhaps laughing at the lads below.

One lad in particular who was preparing to hurl an insult.

"Your mother is a… a sow!" he said, popping up from his hiding place and launching a pebble in the direction of the giggling rock. "She's a sow because her son is a piglet!"

"Is that so?"

"It is!"

"Fight me!"

He did. Fistfuls of pebbles began to fly between the pair. Both boys were all of six years of age, but they were mortal enemies. Sort of. One was English, the other Welsh, because this was the Welsh marches, after all. It had been ingrained in them that they were enemies, so they acted the part. *Acted.*

The truth was much different.

In reality, they were the best of friends.

They'd met one another a couple of years earlier when the Welsh lad had run away from what he perceived as his mother's nasty punishment and ended up on the English side of the border. A patrol from Nether Castle, the largest bastion between Gloucester and Hereford, had found the lad, cold and hungry and lost, and taken him back to the castle for warmth and sustenance.

That was how they had met.

Kent de Poyer was the eldest son of the Lord of Tyr Castle, Caledon de Poyer, and his father had asked him to comfort the young Welsh lad who found himself at their table, weeping and scared. Kent had been so young that he hadn't realized he was sitting with the enemy, a young boy who had a funny way of speaking and who shoved bread into his mouth until Kent's mother had to pull some out so the lad wouldn't choke. He was hungry and thirsty and frightened and exhausted, and after much bread and hot food, he'd fallen asleep on the floor of the great hall, using one of the dogs as a pillow, curled up in front of the hearth. Jealous that the lad was permitted to sleep there, Kent waited until everyone was in bed before dragging his blanket down to the great hall and falling asleep next to the Welsh boy.

And that was how their friendship had started.

Ivor was his new friend's name, Ivor ap Yestin, and Caledon had discovered that the boy was the son of one of the most powerful warlords in southern Wales. He lived in a great and mighty castle with the odd name of The Narth just across the border and, concerned that Ivor's father might think the English had abducted his son, Caledon sent a messenger to The Narth to relay the message that Ivor had been found wandering and was safe. That message had brought a hundred Welshmen to Tyr Castle, seeking to claim that which had been lost, but it had taken time for them to come.

Time in which Kent and Ivor had cemented their alliance.

Kent had two younger brothers at the time and the three of them, plus Ivor, had a marvelous time whilst waiting for Ivor's father to arrive. They played with little wooden carts, chased chickens, stole bread from the kitchen, and other naughty things. When the younger boys got too tired and surrendered to their nurse, Kent and Ivor went on to chase each other, startling horses and the guards. They'd even run circles around an old sergeant and ended up stealing his coin purse, right off his belt, as he bellowed at them.

They ran away laughing.

But Caledon forced Kent to return the coin purse about the time the Welsh began to show up in search of their lord's son. Before the lad was taken away, Kent whispered in his ear—

Hen Gastell.

Old Castle.

That was where Ivor had been found. Kent knew that because he'd heard his father talking about it. He knew exactly where it was because he'd been there, and not wanting their playtime to end, Kent told Ivor to meet him at *Hen Gastell* in twenty days, indicated by holding up his hands with fingers splayed. Ivor nodded emphatically. He understood the assignment. Twenty days later, he wandered over to Old Castle, which was really just a mound and a pile of old rocks, a fortress from before the age of the ancient *Kymry*, and for the two young lads, it became the hill they guarded, or fought against, or surrendered on.

It became their home.

Now, two years later, it was still their home. They were still quite young, however, so there was always the chance that someone was out looking for them, and, too many times, they'd found them playing at the old castle. It was on the Welsh side of the border, which Caledon didn't like, and he'd punished Kent more than once for straying away.

But that didn't stop the lad from meeting his friend every twenty days.

They could count that on both hands and feet.

Today had been that day. The twentieth day, to meet with his friend and play that they were the lords of the castle, only they were bigger now, so the games became a little more daring. Rocks and pebbles were flying at each other because the game today was King of the Castle—whoever could keep the other one off the hill would be the king.

Kent intended that it should be him.

But it might be his last time.

"I call a truce!" he shouted as more pebbles came flying at him. "Do you hear me? A truce!"

Behind his rock, Ivor brushed off his hands. "What for?"

"I have to tell you something."

"What?"

Kent stood up from behind the dirt pile that was protecting

him. "My father is sending me away."

Hearing that, Ivor stood up also. "Where?" he said, concerned.

Kent came out from behind the pile and went to sit on it, despondent. "Arundel."

Ivor came to sit down next to him. "Where's that?"

Kent lifted his shoulders. "Somewhere south," he said. "Papa says it's near the sea. A very big castle where I am to learn how to be a knight."

Ivor pondered that. "And teach you how to fight the Welsh?"

Kent looked at him. "I will never fight you," he said. "And they can't make me. They can torture me and cut my toes off, but I won't fight you. Will you fight me?"

Ivor shook his head. "Nay," he said. "Not if they stick me with a thousand red-hot daggers."

That made Kent feel a little better. "What are you going to do when I am gone?" he asked.

Ivor shrugged, looking around at the landscape, at the sky. "I don't know," he said. "Stay here and learn my lessons. The old priest from Abergavenny comes to The Narth twice a week to give lessons to me and my younger sister. Does he give you lessons, too?"

Kent shook his head. "Nay," he said. "My mother gives us lessons. I can write my name and I can read a little."

"They'll teach you more at Arundel?"

"Aye," Kent said. "They'll teach me everything."

"And then you'll come back?"

Kent nodded. "I have to, sometime," he said. "When Papa dies, Tyr Castle will be mine. So will Nether Castle, where I was born."

"Where's that?"

"Far to the north, in Wales."

Ivor's features scrunched with confusion. "Why do you live here, then?"

"Because Tyr is part of my grandfather's properties and my father commands it," Kent said. "But when the castles are mine, I'll make it so we don't fight the Welsh anymore, but you have to make sure you don't fight the English anymore."

Ivor nodded solemnly. "I won't," he said. "I'll make sure all of my people know we don't fight the English from Tyr and Nether."

"What about other English?"

"If they fight me, I have to fight them."

Kent thought that was logical enough. "I'll help you," he said. "If they attack you, I'll cut their heads off."

"Good!" Ivor declared. Then he leapt to his feet. "Come along! We have to finish our battle before you go, so let's make this the greatest battle ever!"

Kent stood up as Ivor ran down toward the River Mynwy, which slithered gently through the countryside like a blue snake. He followed, but at a slower pace.

"We must fight now?" he called after him. "We have the rest of the day to do this!"

But Ivor shook his head. "I am going to the other side of the river and we will pretend this is a great border," he said. "I will launch projectiles at you and if all of my projectiles land and do not fall into the river, I win."

"Win what?"

"Hen Gastell!"

That didn't sit well with Kent, who was clearly the superior warrior here. He was English, after all. Scowling, he watched

Ivor rush off toward a series of rocks that constituted the river crossing at this location. Truthfully, the river wasn't usually hazardous at all. It was low most of the time, with sandbars in the middle of it, and very easy for young lads to cross back and forth.

But today was different.

There had been a good deal of rain as of late, and the water had swelled the river to nearly twice its size and depth. Gone were the sandbars. Mostly gone were the rocks used to cross the river. The banks on either side, thick with foliage, were muddy and soft. In fact, some of the small saplings lining the riverbank had already partially tumbled in, leaning into the water because their roots had pulled up in the mud.

Kent stood on the bank and frowned.

"I don't think you should go across the river here," he said. "You can hardly see the stones and it will be slippery."

But Ivor, brave as he was, waved him off. "I made it across before," he said. As he located the first rock, about three inches below the surface, he began to sing in an off-key voice. *"Summer days and summer stars, and a deep blue sea that glistens like silver."*

"What are you singing about?"

Ivor pointed at the water. "It's like a deep blue sea that glistens like silver," he said. "Don't you know that old song?"

"Of course I know that song," Kent snapped. "Everybody knows that song. My nurse sings it."

Ivor stopped pointing at the water and waved toward the bank on the opposite side. "Once I cross over, I'm going to find a tree branch and make a bow," he said. "I can make arrows to shoot at you!"

He was enthusiastic about continuing their war. Kent was,

too, but he was afraid of the river. That was the truth. He'd never particularly liked water, and he didn't even like baths, so Ivor's movements had him nervous.

He stood there and fidgeted.

"I don't want to play by the river," he said flatly. "Come back to the castle. We still have a war to fight there."

Ivor ignored him. He was already at the edge of the river, looking at the stones that were just below the surface. Frustrated, Kent turned away from him and headed toward the castle, hoping Ivor would take the hint and give up on the river idea. He always had such silly ideas, anyway. As Kent stomped his way back to the mound that was once a castle, he heard something behind him.

Something deadly.

Splash!

He knew what had happened before he even turned around. But turn around he did, and he ran at top speed back to the river where Ivor had fallen in headfirst. In fact, he didn't even see his friend until the lad's head finally came up and he began to howl.

"Kent!" came the sputtered cry. "*Help!*"

Kent was in a panic. The river wasn't moving swiftly, but his inherent fear of water had him frozen and indecisive. But only temporarily, because he was more terrified of his friend drowning in front of him than he was of his own phobia. Since the flow of water was slow, he had a little time, but it was also freezing, so he knew he had to act fast.

"I'm coming!" he shouted. "Try to swim to the bank! Swim toward me!"

Ivor was trying but the river was just a little too deep for him to get his footing. If he let himself go under a little, he could push off the bottom, and that was what he did, trying to push his way toward Kent, who had grabbed a broken branch by this time. He was holding it out to Ivor, but the lad couldn't quite get to it. The river was moving a little swifter now because there were some rocks ahead that were causing the flow to quicken.

Kent knew he had to get to Ivor before the rocks did.

In he went.

He was a little taller than Ivor so he was able to get his footing once his head came out of the freezing water. His ears hurt like mad because of the shock of the cold water, but he managed to grab Ivor and half push, half pull the boy toward the muddy bank. Ivor was starting to stiffen up because of the water temperature, so Kent gave a hard shove and pushed him right into the muddy bank. A sapling was drooping down, and he grabbed Ivor, and the tree, and began to pull on them both.

"Take hold of the tree, Ivor!" he cried. "Pull yourself out!"

Ivor was so cold that he could hardly get a grip, but he managed to do it after a couple of tries. Kent was starting to freeze up as well, so he pulled himself out, pulling Ivor with him, and somehow the two of them ended up on the riverbank, lying face down in the mud.

Kent rolled onto his back.

"Did you hurt yourself?" he asked Ivor, his teeth chattering. "Ivor, say something!"

Ivor flipped onto his back, his entire body trembling with cold. "I… I'm not hurt," he said. "But my hands are freezing."

Kent sat up and grabbed Ivor's hands, rubbing them briskly between his own. But it wasn't much help because they were both soaked through.

They had to get moving and find some help.

"Get up," Kent finally said, pulling on Ivor's hands. "Stand up. We have to move. We have to get warm."

Ivor sat up unsteadily as Kent finally pulled him to his feet. Together, they staggered their way back toward the old castle. They were just coming through the trees when they caught sight of men on horseback over near the mound. It didn't take Kent long to see that it was his father and several of his father's soldiers. Rather than run from the man, as he'd done in the past, he realized that he was very glad to see him.

"Papa!" he screamed, waving his arms. "Here!"

One of his father's men heard him and called over to Caledon to alert him. The entire contingent came racing over to the soaking boys who were struggling to walk.

Caledon, tall and blond and handsome, was the first one off his horse.

"Kent!" he gasped, seeing the state of the muddy, soaked boys. "What happened?"

"I fell in," Ivor said, lips blue and teeth chattering. "Kent pulled me out."

Caledon looked as if he wanted to scold them, badly, but only for a brief moment. Even he realized the need to get the boys dry and warm quickly.

"Hurry," he said to the man next to him. "Build a fire. A big one. We have to get them dry before the chill kills them."

The soldiers began to move swiftly, finding kindling and fuel and moving to build a fire right in that very spot. Meanwhile, Caledon and another soldier began to strip the boys out of their wet clothing while still another soldier stripped off both of his tunics, turning them over to Caledon to put on the boys to somehow try to keep them warm. It was a swift operation with men trying to build a fire as Caledon tried to keep his son from succumbing to frigid temperatures.

But he'd never been so angry in his life.

"I told you not to come here again," he said as he pushed Kent onto his bottom and began to unlace his shoes. "I told you to stay away from this place. What on earth possessed you both to go to the river? You know you should not play there."

Kent wasn't sure how to answer. It wasn't his fault, but Ivor's. Still, he wasn't going to blame his friend. He was willing to take the punishment. Seated next to him, Ivor was having his shoes yanked off him in the most undignified way and spoke before Kent could think up a plausible excuse.

"I was going to make an arrow and a bow," Ivor said, sounding feeble. "We were going to fight for the castle."

Caledon sighed heavily as his attention shifted to the Welsh lad. "Ivor, what has your father told you about playing at the old castle?"

"Not to play there."

Caledon cocked an unhappy eyebrow. "Now you've fallen in the river," he said. "How would he feel if you drowned? Worse still, you pulled Kent in with you. What if he drowned, too? Do you know how terrible that would be?"

Ivor did. Tears stung his eyes and he turned his head so the English lord wouldn't see him weep. Not that Caledon was wrong, but Ivor just didn't want the man to see his tears.

Tears are only for the weak, his father would say.

He wasn't weak.

But he was cold and naked until the English soldier wrapped him in his tunic. When the fire began to blaze, Caledon put both boys close enough to it to singe their eyelashes, but they warmed quickly and their clothes dried well enough. Stiff with the mud still, but dry. When that was finally accomplished, Caledon had the boys dress in their clothing again and Ivor was put on the rear of one of the soldier's horses and taken all the way back to The Narth, where Yestin, Ivor's father, was informed of his son's actions that afternoon.

The day did not end happily for Ivor.

And Kent never saw his friend again.

Life had a way of taking up his time, and his training at Arundel had been intense. As the years passed, he thought of his old friend once in a while, but by the time he became a full-fledged knight, memories of Ivor ap Yestin had mostly faded into the mists of his past. The fiery little Welsh lad with the stiff black hair and the strong-willed English lad with his grandfather's dark hair had gone their separate ways in a world that wouldn't allow for such friendships.

And they accepted that, long ago.

For Kent and Ivor, Hen Gastell was no more.

But it was sure fun while it lasted.

CHAPTER ONE

Year of Our Lord 1270
The Month of June
Tower of London

Summer days and summer stars,
And a deep blue sea that glistens like silver.
All at once, the past has turned to shadow,
And the future gleams like diamonds.
~ Welsh folk song, circa 14th century

S UMMER DAYS AND *summer stars,* he was humming to himself as he took a swing at a novice soldier who had only recently arrived in London as part of a contingent of men contributed by the Earl of Rutland. The young soldier was terrified of the big, seasoned knight and took to cowering rather than fighting back, as he was supposed to.

This was training time, after all.

Whoosh!

The knight's sword met with no resistance. Bored, he kicked out a booted foot and caught the soldier squarely in the chest.

Down he went.

Thump!

The knight had been so bored that he'd been thinking of that song from his youth, from his carefree days as a child growing up on the marches. Kent de Poyer hadn't thought of those times, those easy times, in years. The song had been taught to him by an old Welsh nurse who had coddled him and his siblings, babied them, and then tried to poison them. She'd ended up with her head on a pike and her body thrown into the moat surrounding Tyr Castle.

In her case, it was a fitting end.

Strange he'd thought of that at this moment.

"That is how you do *not* fight when in battle against a knight," he shouted to the one hundred or so new soldier recruits around him. "We have been practicing battle tactics for the better part of a month, and if you idiots do not start learning something, I'm going to send the lot of you back where you came from."

The group was properly subdued by the scolding. Given the fact that they were at the Tower of London, a more inelegant and military locale than Westminster Palace a couple of miles downriver, they were surrounded by the might of England perhaps more than any other location in the country. The Tower reeked of history and death, the remnants of the energy of men who had fought, and died, there. Here they were, surrounded by greatness, and the knight in command—one of six that comprised the king's personal guard—was telling them that their fighting abilities, and the basic ability to learn, were shite.

Given the demonstration they just saw, the man wasn't wrong.

It wasn't as if Kent didn't know what they were thinking simply by the expressions on their faces. A lot of fear, but also some determination. A knight was only as good as his instincts and training, and as he looked at the individual faces, he could see those who were willing to learn. Willing to fight. Those were the men he wanted for the royal troops.

He pointed to one of them.

"You, there," he said to a young man in the front row. "What's your name?"

The lad, tall and skinny with a thatched pile of blond hair on his head, looked terrified that he'd been singled out but, to his credit, quickly responded.

"Alvis, my lord," he said.

"Where are you from, Alvis?"

"Uppingham, my lord."

"What is your father's vocation in life?"

The young man cocked his head curiously. "Vo-vo…?"

"Vocation," Kent said. "It means trade. What does he do to put food on the table?"

The young man understood. "My father was a knight."

Kent lifted a dark eyebrow. "Oh?" he said, puzzled. "Then what are you doing here?"

"My lord?"

"Why are you with the commoners and not following his path?"

"Because he died a long time ago," the young man said. "I was a babe. I was sent to live with a cousin of my father's, a man who tends cattle for Rutland. This is as good as it will be for me, in the king's army, so I will do the best that I can with it. I will be a good fighter, my lord. I will work hard at it."

That changed Kent's opinion of the young man, just a little.

He wasn't afraid to look him in the eye and tell him about his life without sadness or drama. Simply facts. Kent appreciated the straightforward approach without any complaint. He looked the young man up and down, studying him. He was tall but on the lean side. He also had enormous hands, indicative of the strength in that slender body. Though he'd cowered from Kent, with the size of those hands and feet, he could probably be taught and taught well. Especially if his father had been a knight.

Kent pointed to a small group standing several feet away.

"Go stand with them, Alvis," he said.

The young man did. He moved quickly. That left Kent standing with dozens of other recruits, men he'd been teaching the basics of warfare to, but they'd been slow to learn. As he was pondering his next move, he caught movement out of the corner of his eye, seeing more seasoned knights in protection and mail coming up behind him. They had other recruits with them, instructing them to join the group that was in front of Kent.

It was a gathering of more men, donated by more warlords loyal to the king, men who would go on to comprise the king's army. As was usual, those closest to the king were tasked with assessing the recruits and sometimes even training them. They usually had sergeants for this kind of thing, but there had been some military action lately and they were down several basic commanders. Therefore, the elite group of knights known as the Guard of Six were in charge of the recruits for the moment.

These were the crème de la crème of warriors, men hand-selected by the king himself. Torran de Serreaux was the first man who caught Kent's eye. The unofficial leader of the Guard of Six, or the Six as they were commonly known, Torran was a big man with hazel eyes and a brilliant intellect. He also happened to be the Earl of Ashford, a recent title, and he smiled at Kent as he came to stand beside him. Following Torran were two more members of the Six—tall and blond Aidric St. John was gazing at the group of recruits critically while Jareth de Leybourne, the diplomat of the group, seemed a little more amiable about new men hoping for a position in the royal army.

"Ah," Jareth said, running a seasoned eye over the rather ragtag collection. "Rutland's contribution, I presume?"

Kent nodded. "Aye," he said. "Farmers and peasants mostly, except for that group over there."

He was pointing to the group that Alvis was part of, and four heads turned in that direction. "What makes those men special?" Torran asked.

"Smithies and those who have already fought with Rutland's army," Kent replied. "That tall, slender lad with the blond hair said his father was a knight. If that is true, he may have more potential than most."

"What is his father's name?"

Kent shook his head. "I've not asked," he said. "That is why I had him stand aside, so he can be more thoroughly investigated."

Torran nodded, his gaze lingering on the slender lad before he returned his focus to Kent. "Speaking of potential," he said. "That is what I came to tell you. We may have a new knight joining our ranks."

"Who?" Kent said. "Are you referring to de Lohr? He has been with us for months now, Torran. Our king has declared that he wanted a de Lohr in our ranks, so the Six is about to become the Seven."

He was speaking of Stefan de Lohr, a son of the Earl of

Canterbury and an extremely capable knight. Stefan had spent a good deal of time in London, on behalf of his father, and he'd assisted in some skirmishes, something the king had been impressed with. A de Lohr had served the Crown, closely to the king, for more than sixty years, and Henry very much wanted Stefan to be part of his personal guard if he could wrest him away from his father.

It was just a matter of time.

But Torran shook his head to Kent's assumption. "I am not referring to Stefan," he said. "There is… another."

He waggled his eyebrows as if it wasn't, perhaps, the most ideal situation, but Kent didn't know what he meant.

"Who else is there?" he asked, confused.

"This is an interesting situation," Jareth said, entering the conversation on a subject he knew something about. "It seems that we are to be joined by a knight who fought with Simon de Montfort."

That was a distinct surprise, and Kent's brow furrowed. "By whose command?" he said, incredulous. "Does Henry know about this?"

Jareth nodded. "The command comes from Henry himself," he said. "It seems that this knight has quite a story. He is one of the great elite who served the king several years ago, but when Henry's sister, Eleanor, requested the protection of a skilled knight, Henry gifted this knight over to her."

Kent still wasn't following. "Eleanor was married to de Montfort and he had an entire stable of skilled knights," he said. "Why did she ask this of Henry?"

Jareth shook his head. "This, I cannot know," he said. "But in speaking with the king on this subject, he mentioned a couple of things that led me to believe Eleanor didn't actually ask Henry for the knight. I suspect that Henry simply sent him to Eleanor."

Kent's frown deepened. "Why should he do that?"

Torran leaned over and lowered his voice. "Because the knight was with Margaret, Henry's eldest daughter, when she married the young King of Scotland," he said. "The knight was part of the delegation, and rumor had it that Margaret, even at her very young age, was infatuated with him. That gave fodder for the Scots to spread rumors about Margaret, and she wrote to her father telling him how poorly the Scots were treating her, which caused quite a bit of upheaval. Henry must have heard the rumors about Margaret's infatuation, so he sent the knight to Eleanor to get him out of Scotland."

"And away from Margaret," Jareth said.

"And the man ended up serving de Montfort," Torran finished.

Now, the situation made a little more sense. "If I remember correctly, Margaret was ten or eleven years of age when she married Alexander," Kent said. "Are you telling me that a grown knight had an affair with a child?"

Jareth shook his head. "Nay," he said. "Not at all—and that was Margaret's problem. The more he ignored her, the more infatuated she became. I seem to recall hearing about the situation back when it happened and also remember hearing the knight was not at fault, in any way. But he was sent to Eleanor and, by virtue of that post, ended up serving de Montfort. Something he did not wish to do."

Kent shook his head at the sordid tale. "And Henry wants him to serve as a personal guard," he muttered. Then he shook his head as if the entire thing were ridiculous. "This ought to be interesting."

Torran nodded. "The man has impeccable lineage," he said. "His father is one of the greatest knights in the north of England, but it is a complicated tale. Britt and Dirk have been with him today, at Henry's request, and they are to bring him out here at some point. I will tell you the rest of the knight's story later because I do not want him to hear us talking about him if he comes around whilst we are in discussion."

He started looking around to ensure Britt de Garr and Dirk d'Vant, the last of the Six, weren't somewhere nearby with this mysterious knight, and Kent didn't ask any further questions. The situation seemed strange enough with a new knight who had once served the king's greatest enemy.

Things were indeed changing.

"Considering what we all went through in the battle against de Montfort, I'm not exactly sure how comfortable I am at the prospect of serving alongside a knight who was once my enemy," he muttered. "But I suppose that does not matter now. I will continue to serve at the pleasure of the king and do as I am told. That includes assessing these recruits before we finally turn them over to those who will properly train them, so let me get on with it."

Aidric, a tall man with shoulder-length hair, came out from behind Torran and put his hand on Kent's shoulder. "And I will help you," he said, sensing Kent's frustration. "Truthfully, I think we've done all we can with this group, but I am interested in the ones you have pulled aside. Given the seasoned soldiers we've lost over the past several years to de Montfort wars, discovering men with some command ability would be helpful."

Kent nodded. "Agreed," he said, letting Aidric soothe his irritation. "In fact, let us—"

He was cut off by a messenger wearing royal silks. The king

had a small legion of messengers and the man approaching was very much out of place in a military situation. Either a clerk or an academic, the man dodged men and horses as he shouted again.

"De Poyer!" he called. "I seek Kent de Poyer!"

"Here," Kent said, heading in the man's direction. When he recognized the older man with the closely shorn hair who smelled heavily of perfume, he lifted a disapproving eyebrow. "What is it, Orly? I'm very busy at the moment."

The messenger could see the situation for himself. "I know, my lord," he said, distaste in his expression. "Better you than me, I must say. I detest the Tower. So… uncivilized."

Kent found himself fighting off a grin at the snobbish messenger. "I am sure it detests you, also," he said. "Did you come here just to insult this mighty bastion?"

Orly shook his head. "Nay," he said. "I come from the king, my lord. He has summoned you."

"Now?"

"*Now*," he confirmed. "I have also been sent to fetch Ashford."

He was referring to Torran, who heard him. He'd only just left Henry that morning and had been hoping for a little reprieve, but it was not to be. Knowing he couldn't get out of a direct summons, Torran moved to follow Kent as Aidric and Jareth stepped in to take charge of the recruits. Aidric immediately began shouting orders, whipping the group into a frenzy. He believed that a man's body should be fit and strong, so the vast majority of his role with the recruits was assessing physical strength. He ordered the entire collective to begin running, and shortly the bailey was full of hustling men. With Kent and Torran on their way to Westminster Palace, the recruits were in the hands of new masters.

The truth was that Kent's busy day was about to take a dramatic turn.

CHAPTER TWO

Westminster Palace

"IT IS *INFURIATING*. Gaspard de Russe has evidently laid siege to the castle, chased the Welsh into the mountains, and now he claims this castle. The man has started a war!"

The royal solar of Westminster Palace had heard much worse shouting over the years. Kings tended to be excitable creatures, by habit and by trade, so the old stone walls had learned to absorb the volume and the anger. In this case, it was coming from a man of average stature and a head of hair that had turned gray long ago. A man who had been king since he'd been nine years of age and, truthfully, never knew anything else. He was England and England was him, the two of them blended into one creature that lived and breathed, rejoiced and wept.

Henry, King of England, had a problem.

"Is that what my father said, your grace?" Kent asked. "He is the one who sent you the information?"

Henry was frowning and had been ever since he read the missive from Caledon de Poyer. It had come for Kent but Henry, as he often did, read it first because he assumed any information from the Earl of Talgarth, a title that he himself had bestowed upon Caledon's father, would be meant for him as well. That meant he was the first one to get the bad news on a very volatile section of the Welsh marches.

"Aye," Henry replied. He pointed to the opened vellum, lying on a table a few feet away. "You can read for yourself. Evidently, de Russe, who is an extremely unpredictable man himself, was forced to take up arms when his son got into a skirmish with a local Welsh warlord. I can only imagine what happened, since the House of de Russe from Clearwell Castle is, and always has been, ready to go to war against any infraction, no matter how small."

Kent was already over at the table, picking up the vellum and reading his father's careful handwriting. Caledon liked to write his missives himself to keep private information from spreading, and Kent was barely halfway through the message but could see what had the king so enraged.

"Treyton," he muttered, then spoke louder. "I know Treyton de Russe, my lord. We were not only neighbors, but we briefly fostered together."

Henry waved him off. "I know Treyton as well," he said, snapping his fingers at the nearest servant as a demand for wine. "The man is enormous and strong and a fine knight, but he thinks every man in England and Wales and Scotland is out to challenge him. I have no idea what happened with this Welsh warlord, but I am not surprised. The problem is that Gaspard took his army into Wales and expelled the Welsh from a castle that has historically been extremely unstable. The Welsh are going to want it back."

Kent had been watching the king, listening to his concern, before returning his attention to the missive. When he got to the bottom of the message, he was able to discover the Welsh castle in question.

The Narth.

Startled, he must have made a sound because Torran, a few feet away, looked at him with concern. "What?" he asked. "What is it?"

Kent struggled to overcome his surprise, handing the missive over to Torran so the man could read of the situation. "The castle that has been sacked," he said. "I've not heard that name in many years."

Henry, cup of wine in hand, heard him. "You know this place?" he asked.

Kent nodded as he turned to him. "I do, your grace," he said. "At least, I used to. Very long ago."

"What about it?"

Kent simply shrugged. "When I was a child, I knew the son of the warlord of The Narth," he said. "Believe it or not, he was my playmate before I was sent to foster. How strange… Only today I remembered a song from my youth, a song that my friend would sing. How very strange I would think of that just as my father sent this missive."

Henry took a big gulp of wine. "Kent, how much do you keep up with the current situation on the marches where your father's property is?"

"As much as anyone else, I suppose," Kent said. "I've not been home in a few years and my father only sends me missives as he sees fit."

Henry regarded him a moment. "Your father still has not forgiven you for not returning home to assume your rightful place beside him, has he?"

Kent smiled weakly. "I am his heir, your grace," he said. "Of course he wants me home. He wants me to know the land, the people, that I will one day preside over. I will return someday, of course, but not now. Serving you has been more fulfilling, I think."

Henry grunted. "As if I would release you to your father," he said. "You have four brothers, all of them still at Nether Castle, I think."

Kent nodded. "My brother, Henry, has command of Tyr Castle, our outpost on the marches," he said. "It is usually commanded by the heir, but clearly, I am not there. However, my father and my other brothers are, indeed, at Nether Castle."

"Henry, Clarke, Everett, and… and…"

"Owen, your grace."

"Owen," Henry repeated, reminded of the one he forgot. But he wagged his finger at Kent. "I will lure that one into my service. I seem to remember a beastly lad with blond hair and black eyes."

"Owen is a big man, your grace," Kent said. "Taller than I am, and that is saying something."

Henry chuckled, clearly calming down from his earlier tirade. But he noticed Torran setting the vellum to the table again and that reminded him why he'd been so angry.

"I do not know what skirmish young de Russe entered into, but his father should not have been so hasty in laying siege to a Welsh castle," he said. "And especially not that castle."

Kent looked at the man, knowing he probably wouldn't like the answer to his next question. "Why not, your grace?"

Henry turned back to his wine. "You should know the area," he said. "That is where your family's home is."

"I know the area, your grace, and I know The Narth," Kent said. "But I was very young when last I had any contact with anyone from The Narth, or heard anything about it, truthfully. But, clearly, you are concerned with it."

Henry grunted unhappily. "Concerned, indeed," he said. "The warlord that rules The Narth these days has gone deep to his family's roots and has brought forth all of the legends about true Welsh blood and Welsh pride. His family is descended from the rulers of Elfael, a small kingdom that eventually became part of Gwent when his grandmother, many times over, married into the Gwent royal family. Oddly enough, he seems to make more war on fellow Welsh than the English, which is good for your father considering how close The Narth is to Tyr Castle. But Ivor ap Yestin is a powerful man with a good deal of sway along the marches, much more than his father ever had, and now he has been driven out of The Narth by de Russe. That means his focus will turn toward the English now, and that is what your father is worried about. With The Narth so close to Tyr, he is afraid that Tyr will now be attacked by angry Welsh."

Ivor ap Yestin.

Kent closed his eyes, briefly, as he heard that name. He hadn't heard it in years. He hadn't thought of the man in years. It was simply something that never came up in conversation with his father, not even on those occasions when he'd come home to visit. It simply wasn't part of their daily lives. Kent had his life to live and Ivor had evidently had his, and the two never crossed, not since those days of their youth. As Henry said, Ivor's attention had evidently been focused on other Welsh, and that realization brought something to mind that Ivor had said to him once, long ago.

I'll make sure all of my people know we don't fight the English from Try or Nether.

My God... Did he actually mean it? Even after all these years?

But something in the pit of his stomach told him that that was about to change.

"Your grace, I must be perfectly honest with you," he said, watching Henry accept more wine from a servant. "When I was four years of age, Ivor ap Yestin got lost on our lands and my father's men brought him to Tyr. Ivor and I became fast friends and continued to play together, in the hills of the marches, until I was sent off to Arundel. I've not seen him since, nor spoken to him, but I did know him as a child. He was my best friend."

Henry looked at him with interest. "Your father made no mention of that."

Kent shrugged. "It was possible he forgot," he said. "Or he did not think it relevant."

Henry didn't share that opinion. "It could be *quite* relevant," he said. "Your father is asking for help. He wants de Russe removed from The Narth and a royal occupation force to take control. He does not ask to have The Narth returned to ap Yestin."

Kent knew that. "Probably because with de Russe holding The Narth, that will bring half of Wales down on the castle, and when de Russe calls for reinforcements, my father will be obliged to respond."

"And that puts him at war with the Welsh."

"Exactly, your grace," Kent said. "My grandmother was Welsh. We have always enjoyed a peaceful existence with them for the most part. And I do not want to find myself in a war because Treyton de Russe acted like a fool and pulled the southern Welsh marches into his actions."

Henry couldn't disagree. "Idiot," he muttered. "I do not know what the circumstances are and I do not care, but I agree with you. And your father. Kent, if I send you to the Welsh marches to negotiate peace with Ivor ap Yestin, will you go? If the two of you were friends, mayhap ap Yestin will be more apt to remain calm."

"And give him back The Narth, your grace?"

Henry hesitated. "The Narth is an enormous castle of great strategic advantage," he said. "Although I do not agree with de Russe's tactics, the fact remains that we now control The Narth, and that means we control a portion of South Wales. I am not entirely sure I want to lose that advantage."

Kent could see trouble brewing. Henry was angry with de Russe, that was true, but now that he had The Narth, he wasn't sure he wanted to give it up. But the Welsh would want it back.

Ivor would want it back.

That put Tyr Castle in the line of fire should a border war erupt.

Damn…

"Why not send Chris de Lohr to negotiate with ap Yestin, your grace?" he asked. "He and his family control most of the Welsh marches. If you want to keep The Narth, you will need the strength of the de Lohr war machine behind that stance. The history of warfare between de Lohr and the Welsh warlords is well established, and Nether, and my family, have always managed to keep peace. I cannot go to Ivor and ask him for peace but not offer to return his castle."

Henry knew that very well but was still unwilling to return something the English now held. He eyed Kent stubbornly before turning away, hunting for his most comfortable chair.

"White Castle, Grossmont Castle, and Monmouth Castle already belong to me," he said. Then he shrugged. "I suppose they really belong to de Lohr, but de Lohr serves me. Having The Narth would close a large gap that exists between my southern castles and my northern holdings."

"Then ask the Earl of Hereford and Worcester to attend this negotiation, your grace," Kent said again, more firmly. "I am the son of an earl, after all. I am not a powerful marcher lord. It would mean more coming from de Lohr."

Henry sat heavily in a cushioned leather chair, grunting as he tried to get comfortable. He set his cup down on the table next to the chair, lifting his feet onto a small footstool. Kent watched the man closely, hoping he would see his point, because the last thing Kent wanted to do was confront a man he'd not seen in many years and tell him he wasn't going to have his castle returned to him.

"Torran?" Henry finally said. "What say you to all of this?"

Kent turned his attention to Torran, who had been leaning against the wall, arms crossed, listening to the entire conversation. When he saw Kent's gaze upon him, shadowed with concern, he lifted a hand discreetly as if to ease the man.

"I say that Kent has a good point," he said. "He is not a diplomat. He is one of the finest knights I have ever served with and his judgment is impeccable, and someday he shall make an astonishingly good Earl of Talgarth, like his father, but he is correct when he says de Lohr should handle this. The man is in a better position to do so. But I also suggest he wait until we can remove de Russe, because if we do not, that might damage his alliance with de Russe."

Henry pondered the advice. "Very well," he said. "Kent, you will be going to Wales. I will send you with a thousand royal troops and several knights because, should this situation burst forth like sparks on kindling, you will need the reinforcements. More than that, I want my army to replace de Russe at The Narth. I will send you with a royal decree demanding Gaspard de Russe vacate the castle, so, hopefully, he will not put up a fight."

"And if he does, your grace?"

Henry turned to look at both Kent and Torran then. "If he does, you use any means necessary to get him out," he growled. "And then you bring him and his idiot son to London to face my good judgment. Is that understood?"

Kent and Torran nodded. "It is, your grace," Torran said.

"Excellent," Henry said. "Torran, leave Aidric, Britt, and Dirk here with me, but take Jareth. I also want you to take a few royal knights that have been serving in various capacities for me around England. In fact, one of them—Bennet de Bermingham—was a garrison commander at Chepstow Castle long ago, serving the Marshal family. He should be a great help on the area and the politics."

Torran's brow furrowed. "De Bermingham," he repeated slowly. "Why do I know that name?"

"Because the man was caught in a scandal at Chepstow, and when Roger Bigod inherited the castle from the Marshal family, he didn't want de Bermingham around," Henry said. "Something about compromising a Welshwoman, as I recall. Her father was a local magistrate, a man of importance, but de Lohr assured me that de Bermingham is not the kind of man as was suggested of him. Therefore, I took him into my service because no one else on the border wanted to deal with the rumors that followed him around. I sent him to Richmond, to other places, as a simple knight. He's very good at what he does. The rumors died down, eventually. But not entirely. Some people remember."

Torran was nodding because he now recalled that he had heard something about de Bermingham long ago. "Isn't he the son of an earl, your grace?"

"Aye," Henry said. "The Earl of Louth."

"Irish?"

"Very much so," he said. "But I like the man. In any case, you will take him with you. You will also take Stefan de Lohr. And another."

"Who?"

Henry simply looked at Torran, who had no idea why the man was staring at him so until it finally dawned on him. Quickly, he nodded his head.

"I understand, your grace," he said. "You want Payton-Forrester with us."

Henry shrugged. "He must be evaluated for my service," he said. "What better circumstance than to have him working closely in a situation such as this?"

"Whom are we speaking of?" Kent asked. "What knight is this?"

Torran looked at him. "The one I told you about earlier," he said quietly. "The mysterious one."

Kent understood. "I see," he said, not entirely thrilled. "A knight who has fought for de Montfort must now be allowed into our inner ranks?"

He said it in front of Henry, which was essentially challenging the man's decision, but Henry didn't take it personally. He knew that his Guard of Six was extremely protective of him, but they also knew that Henry tended to take on men with pasts and secrets, something he would then hold over them. Only a little. Henry viewed it as insurance, men he would bail out of trouble or keep secrets for in exchange for their loyalty.

That meant Payton-Forrester had a secret.

Yet perhaps his secret in serving de Montfort had already

been revealed.

… but perhaps not.

"It is not as bad as all that, Kent," Henry said, leaning back in his chair and getting comfortable. "Orion Payton-Forrester comes from a fine family. Very fine. They are the lords of Beverley Castle in the north, one of the finest armies I have against the Scots. Orion's father, William, has been fighting them for decades alongside other notable castles like Northwood and Questing."

"Warenton and Teviot, your grace?"

Henry nodded. "William Payton-Forrester is a good friend of the Earl of Warenton, William de Wolfe, and the Earls of Teviot at Northwood Castle. Their association goes back many, many years and they are my triple defense on the Scots border. They were all quite close, but about thirty years ago, Payton-Forrester had a falling-out with the Lords of Teviot. A long time. In any case, they still remain allies, but relations are strained. Orion is one of Payton-Forrester's younger sons, but by all accounts, his most talented. So talented that he came to serve me at a young age."

Kent couldn't understand why the king didn't seem more concerned about a knight who had served Simon de Montfort being in the inner circle. "I was told that you gifted him to your sister, the Countess of Leicester, your grace," he said. "The man served Simon de Montfort."

"He did."

"In battle."

Henry nodded. "Again, he did," he said. "He was at every major battle."

"He fought against us, yet you want him to join your personal guard?"

Henry looked at him. "You do not trust my judgment?"

Kent backed down. "Your judgment is beyond contestation, your grace," he said. "But the men we have within the Six are men we all trust completely. With our very lives."

Torran took over at that point because they had touched on a delicate subject. "Kent's concern is valid, your grace," he said. "I had the same concern, and I told you so. But you assured me that Payton-Forrester's service to de Montfort was only because he was sworn to Eleanor, not because he believed in de Montfort's cause."

Henry nodded. "That is true," he said. "He sent me several missives asking to return to royal service during his time with my sister."

"Return as a spy," Kent muttered.

"What did you say, Kent?" Henry said.

Kent took a deep breath, clearing his throat as he realized he'd been caught voicing his concerns. "I said that, mayhap, he would return as a spy, your grace," he said, louder. "Forgive me, but I shall not trust him completely until I come to know him. And I believe that goes for Torran as well. Our position in your court is dedicated to serving you and ensuring you live a long and healthy life."

"And?"

"And if I do not deem this man worthy of my trust, I will resign my post before I serve alongside him," Kent said without hesitation. "I will not knowingly, and willfully, jeopardize your life by serving alongside someone who could just as easily slit my throat *and* yours."

Instead of growing angry at what could be perceived as a rebuke against the king's wishes, Henry smiled weakly. "You are a fearsome protector, Kent," he said with quiet satisfaction.

"And your concerns are understood. But I have a reason for wanting Payton-Forrester to serve me."

"What is that, your grace?"

There were a few servants in the chamber, as there usually were when the king was around. They catered to his every whim. But he chased them out, insisting they shut the door behind them. When they were gone and it was only him and Torran and Kent in the chamber, he motioned the knights closer.

"Allow me to explain my position before you think I am a complete fool," he said quietly. "It is a king's duty to pay attention to his more powerful warlords. In this case, I speak of the Northerners."

He was referring to the warlords in the north, in Northumberland and Cumbria, men who had traditionally been somewhat separate from the rest of England because of the special needs and politics of the Scots border. They were a very powerful group, as Henry's father, King John, had experienced for himself. John had habitually butted heads with the Northerners during his reign because they were not in support of the king and his policies. Henry had a somewhat easier time with them, but they still tended to live in their own world at times and rule their earldoms and fiefdoms like little kings.

Kent and Torran understood that.

"Indeed, your grace," Torran muttered. "Having Payton-Forrester's son in your ranks keeps you allied to his father and hopefully his father's allegiance."

Henry nodded, but it was faint, as if he wasn't sure that was the true reason. "There is more to it," he said. He hesitated before continuing. "I know a secret about Orion Payton-Forrester."

Torran's brow furrowed. "May I ask what the secret is, your grace?"

Henry drew in a long, deep breath. It was a sound of satisfaction, as if he were in possession of something quite earth shattering.

"I have spies in the north at all of the major houses with the exception of Warenton's fortress," he said. "I had two at Castle Questing, but William discovered them and put them on a boat to Bergen because he has allies in the Northmen who will keep those spies and use them as slaves. He thinks I do not know what he's done, but I do. In any case, the point is that I have spies everywhere and have it on good authority from Beverley Castle that Orion is not his father's son."

That didn't clear anything up. Torran and Kent passed puzzled glances. "He is a bastard, your grace?" Torran said.

Henry nodded. "The result of an affair between Payton-Forrester's sister and a knight with the Earl of Teviot," he said. "Evidently, the sister was unmarried and died in childbirth with Orion, so William and his wife decided to raise the boy as their own."

Kent didn't think that sounded much like a deep, dark secret. "Surely people would know that he was not their natural son, your grace," he said. "They would know that Payton-Forrester's wife was not pregnant if an infant suddenly appeared. They would know it was not their natural child."

"You would think so," Henry said. "But the sister was sent away to a convent during her confinement, where the child was born. After her death, Lady Payton-Forrester also went away for several months—and when she returned, it was with the infant. William Payton-Forrester told everyone his wife had given birth in Scotland."

The story made a little more sense of how a birth could be passed off from one woman to another. "So they claimed the lad as their own," Kent said. "But why the secrecy?"

Henry shrugged. "To preserve the sister's reputation, I would suspect," he said. "And also because the true father does not know he has a son."

Torran could see that this little tale was leading somewhere. "And you want to keep Payton-Forrester's secret?" he said. "Why? More importantly, how does this help you with the Northerners?"

Henry looked between his two knights. "Because the father of Orion, I am told, is none other than the captain of Northwood Castle's army, Paris de Norville," he said. "The falling-out I told you about between Beverley and Northwood? It is because of Orion, only Orion does not know that Paris is his father and Paris does not know that he has a bastard son. That is my secret to keep, because if either one of them found out, I suspect an all-out war in the north between Beverley and Northwood might erupt. And I need my warlords focused on the Scots, not each other."

Now, the situation was making a great deal of sense. Torran and Kent were starting to catch on. "But why would a war erupt after all these years, your grace?" Kent said. "Surely sufficient time has passed that it is not as critical as it once was."

Henry looked at him. "If Paris de Norville finds out that Payton-Forrester has kept a son from him, the man will be furious," he said. "More than that, do not forget that de Norville and de Wolfe are the closest of friends and allies. If Paris goes to war, then de Wolfe will. Payton-Forrester will find himself fending off two major houses, and he cannot do it. Not Northwood and Questing, both."

Torran was clearly pondering the ramifications. "And that is why he's not told de Norville?" he said. "To keep the peace?"

Henry shrugged. "I am certain that's what it is," he said. "That and the fact that if he tells the man, it will all come out that the sister was compromised, and I go back to my assertion that Payton-Forrester wishes to keep his sister's reputation intact."

It was a tricky situation, to be sure, but it was also clear what Henry was doing by wanting the bastard knight near. "Then by keeping Orion Payton-Forrester close, you can also keep abreast of anything happening in the north between Beverley and Northwood," Torran said. "But why now? What makes this point in time more important than the rest of Orion's life?"

Henry grunted. "Because I've heard rumor through the commander at Bamburgh Castle that Paris de Norville is soliciting suitors for a granddaughter," he said. "He has evidently sent word to Beverley, in an effort to heal the rift in their relationship, that he would be interested in Orion for his granddaughter. Clearly, that cannot happen."

Torran shook his head in disbelief. "God's Bones," he muttered. "What if Payton-Forrester denies him and tells him why? That could start this battle you are so concerned with."

Henry took a long drink of his wine, draining the cup. "That is why I want to keep Orion close," he said, smacking his lips as he set his cup down. "I want to know what happens with this potential betrothal, but more than that, if William Payton-Forrester decides to tell Paris de Norville of Orion's true parentage, I want to know that as well. It is an extremely volatile situation."

That was an understatement. It made Henry's support of

bringing Orion into the royal inner circle quite plain, but in a strange way, it also made Torran and Kent trust the knight just a little. But *only* a little. Kent finally ran his fingers through his dark hair, digesting the situation surrounding a man he hadn't even met yet.

"It seems that Orion Payton-Forrester has led a most eventful life," he said. "Whether or not the man knows about his true parentage, there is a tempest surrounding him."

Henry began looking around for more wine. "You speak the truth," he said. "I only tell you this so you understand why I want Payton-Forrester in our ranks, so you do not think I have become mad in my old age. It is true that he came into my service as a young knight and he was quite skilled. It is true that I sent him to Scotland with Margaret, but what happened there was not his fault. It is also true that I sent him to Eleanor to get him out of Scotland, and we all know what happened after that. Now, he has come back to the royal fold and I intend to keep him here. Are we in agreement?"

Torran and Kent nodded seriously. "We are, your grace," Torran said.

"Good," Henry said. "Now, we must return to the subject at hand and the situation at The Narth. Kent, form the army you will take with you. Torran, gather and prepare the knights. I want everyone moving to the Welsh marches by the end of the week."

The knights facing him nodded. "Aye, your grace," Torran said. "We will be ready."

Henry nodded and dismissed them. As the knights headed out, Henry found more wine and poured it into his cup, but his mind was elsewhere. He had enough trouble on the Welsh marches without worrying about northern warlords going to war against one another over a bastard that was born more than thirty years ago. Still, it was a possibility.

When love or sex was concerned, *anything* was possible.

Time would tell if the north would explode before the Welsh did.

God help them all.

CHAPTER THREE

Penderyn, Wales
The Month of August

S HE'D BEEN WAITING all morning for this moment.

A little hand, sneaking underneath the fence, grabbing for one of those fat purple berries on the vine.

Snatch!

She had the hand, but the owner of the hand was howling like a banshee. A cute banshee, no doubt, but also with the streak of evil that a banshee possessed. Holding the wrist with one hand, she slapped the little hand that had managed to grab a berry.

"The next time I catch you pilfering berries, I'll send the dog after you!" she called, standing up to peer over the fence as the small child, in dirty clothing and an old cap, raced away. She grinned, leaning on the top of the wooden slats. "If the dog catches you, then you know what will happen!"

The boy, and evidently his gang as they came out from behind bushes and sheds, continued to run. Laughing softly, she turned back to the garden she kept for her grandfather, tucked back behind his apothecary shop on the main road through

Penderyn. It was a big shop, with living quarters overhead and in the back where the kitchen was. But the yard behind it—the fenced yard—was the most valuable thing of all.

A garden like no other.

A garden that was fenced with a stone and wood fence, taller than a man, and a gate that was locked with a heavy iron lock. A thorny vine grew up all over the fence and clustered around the gate so that anyone thinking to break into the garden was deterred by those thorns. It was heavily protected, but there was a gap near the gate where the blackberry vine grew, a gap where the little hoodlum and his friends had stolen blackberries. It had taken her a couple of weeks to figure out they were doing it, and she'd lain in wait for three days before they finally returned to the scene of the crime.

Hopefully, they would think twice before coming again.

Turning back to her magnificent garden, she took a moment to gaze upon the flowers, the herbs, the vines, and, in the middle of it, a small pond her grandfather had dug, which held small fish that kept breeding. There always seemed to be new fish. A butterfly flew past her face and she smiled, watching it land on a small yellow flower.

"Madelaina!"

Madelaina ferch Bryn's focus came away from the butterfly, and she caught sight of her older sister as the woman stood at the rear of the kitchens and waved a wooden spoon. From Madelaina's earliest memories, Celyn ferch Bryn always seemed to be waving a spoon at her. Sometimes the spoon was for the pot, but sometimes it was for Madelaina's backside.

"Where is the rosemary?" Celyn asked. "The bread is ready for the oven!"

Madelaina turned to the prolific growth of rosemary bushes

off to her left. She had to move through other bushes to get to it, but she stripped several sprigs off and carried them back over to Celyn. The woman took the offered pieces before pointing to bunches of hyssop.

"And that," she said. "The hyssop. The Bryn needs them for his compound."

The Bryn. That was what everyone called the head of their household, including Madelaina and Celyn. An elderly man with strong arms and dark eyebrows that arched dramatically over his piercing eyes, Bryn ap Rhys was a man with a secret. He was a big man, with big hands, and when he first came to Penderyn, he'd appeared sorely out of place. He and his wife, Brigid, had not looked like the usual peasants. There was something cultured about them, educated, and that wasn't missed by anyone in the village. Whispers flew about the pair, that they were royalty in disguise, which wasn't far from the truth. But the months and years passed and people stopped whispering about them because they were genuinely good people who did a great deal of good in the village. Bryn had only given his name as Bryn, so people began addressing him as *The* Bryn.

And it stuck.

Even his daughters often referred to him as The Bryn. Not Papa, not Father. The Bryn.

He was the most famous man in town.

He was also a man with a temper, however, and Madelaina harvested some hyssop and entered the structure through the back. Her big black dog, Arthur, followed along behind. Wherever Madelaina was, Arthur was. He loved her like the other Arthur hadn't.

The man who, years ago, had broken her heart.

But that wasn't something she dwelt on these days. She didn't even think of Arthur ap Gryffudd, but right after he'd left her for another and Celyn brought her the little puppy, she took delight in saying things like "naughty Arthur" and "stupid Arthur." Silly things that meant something to a girl who had given her heart to a man who'd stepped on it. She'd learned the lesson so well that she'd never given it again.

And she didn't intend to.

"Here's the hyssop," she said, entering a small chamber that The Bryn used to make his compounds. "Do you require more?"

The Bryn was bent over his table, lit by two big tapers. A thick piece of glass, very precious, magnified the work on the table because his eyes weren't like they used to be. It was difficult for him to see things close up.

"Nay," he grunted, looking closely at the purple flowers that resembled lavender. "This is sufficient."

Madelaina stood behind him, her hands on his shoulders as she watched him carefully cut the flowers off the stalk. "What are you making?"

The Bryn was focused on his delicate work. "The smithy's wife is feeling poorly after delivering her child," he said. "This will help her regain her strength."

"Would you like me to deliver it to her?"

He paused and turned to look at her. "Nay," he said flatly. "I told you that you are not to stray from home. As long as the English are at The Narth, you are to remain inside and hidden. I'll not have the *Saesneg* soldiers leer at you, or worse. 'Tis not safe, *fy merch.*"

My girl. That was what he always called Madelaina. But that wasn't the answer she wanted. "You let me go where I pleased when Ivor and his men were there," she said unhappily. "They were always in the village, calling to me and demanding I go to the tavern with them. You know this."

The Bryn grunted. "At least they were good Welsh boys."

Madelaina rolled her eyes. "And that makes a difference when they try to grab me?"

Of course, he couldn't give her a straight answer. "The English are dogs," he said. "Why did you have to give your dog a Welsh name? You should have named it Henry. That way, you can order the English king around. Tell it that it's a stinking bastard and kick it!"

He was deflecting, as he usually did when a conversation didn't go his way. Pushing one of her father's many cats aside, Madelaina sat on the edge of a cluttered table.

"I will not say such things to my dog, nor will I kick him," she said. "You must face facts, Papa. The English occupy The Narth and I am not going to remain confined to this cottage for the rest of my life because of it. Nor is Celyn."

As if on cue, Arthur, who had wandered in after his mistress, had now found comfort and companionship on The Bryn's leg and was quite happily trying to mate with it. Feeling the motion, he looked down at the dog and shook his head in resignation.

"Maddie," he said, pointing, "find this dog a wife."

Madelaina could see what her dog was doing and swiftly chased him off. "Dogs do not have wives," she said. "And do not try to change the subject."

The Bryn wasn't too tolerant of her demands. "Then find that dog another leg to jump on," he said, waving her off. "I am far too busy to let that dog woo me. He tries every day."

Madelaina was having a difficult time keeping a straight

face, mostly because her father was right. Arthur loved his legs and took every opportunity to mate with them.

"Simply chase him away," she said. "It is not that difficult. But what is difficult is the fact that you want me to become a hermit as long as the English are occupying The Narth. It is no different than when the Welsh princeling was occupying the castle. Soldiers are the same in their behavior, no matter where they are from."

The Bryn couldn't really disagree with her on that point, but rather than butt heads with her, he motioned for her to sit on a nearby stool. Butting heads never worked with Madelaina, anyway, so he had to try another tactic.

The subject matter was far too serious for her not to understand it.

"I want you to listen to me," he said as she sat down on a sturdy three-legged stool. "Maddie, I am not trying to be cruel or difficult with you. I hope you understand that."

Madelaina faltered a little. "I do know that," she said. "But you cannot expect me to remain hidden for as long as the English occupy the castle. Surely you cannot."

The Bryn sighed heavily, reaching out to take one of her hands. "If you will not stay hidden, then you at least must be prudent," he said. "Do not go out unnecessarily. If you see English soldiers, hide from them. Do not make yourself a target."

"I will not, I promise."

"We've had experience with English soldiers and it was not pleasant. You know what happened to…"

He trailed off, unable to voice the experience their family had suffered at the hands of an English knight. *Celyn.* It was something The Bryn couldn't bring himself to speak of, not even after all of these years. Usually, Madelaina was very quick to go head to head with her father, but even she knew how much this subject affected him, and the understanding of it subdued her.

After all of these years, The Bryn still felt guilt.

"I know what happened," she said softly. "But it was not your fault. Celyn's assault had nothing to do with you and she has never blamed you for it. The blame lies with the English knight who woke up that morning with hatred in his heart and a need for violence. It just happened to be Celyn. It could have been anyone, but it happened to be her."

The Bryn shook his head as he looked away. "Say what you will, but I should have protected her," he said. "It is my duty to protect her, but I failed. Madelaina, I do not want to fail with you, so please… do as I ask and stay away from the English at The Narth. It would destroy me if something happened to you."

She couldn't very well dispute that. After a moment's hesitation, she simply nodded her head. "As you wish," she said quietly. "But there are still things I must do during the day, business I must conduct."

"I know. But be discreet."

"I will," she said. "But do not worry about me. I can take care of myself."

He looked at her sharply. "Can you?" he said, his voice lifting. Then he jabbed a finger in the direction of the enormous castle on the hill. "Do you know who has taken control of The Narth?"

"The English, of course. What have we been talking about?"

"Aye, the English," he said, growing angry. "But not just any English. De Russe from Clearwell. Do you know anything about them?"

Madelaina shook her head. "Nay," she said. "What should I know?"

His eyes narrowed. "They're beastly," he hissed. "Nasty and aggressive and beastly. They attacked The Narth, a castle that is, by all accounts, extremely difficult to breach, but they purged the princeling and his men in little more than a day. As Ivor retreated to Pentwyn Castle, his mother's home, de Russe raised their red dragon over the castle. Not the dragon of Wales, but the de Russe dragon. It is an abomination, my girl, so do not think you can easily handle these men. If Ivor ap Yestin could not, you certainly cannot. Do you understand me?"

He was deadly serious. Madelaina wouldn't be so arrogant as to announce that she could easily handle such men. The truth was that she'd never had to. She'd led a relatively idyllic life in Penderyn. Ivor ap Yestin's men blended in with the village, found wives there, and Ivor had even come around to The Bryn's apothecary shop on occasion, perhaps lingering and trying to start a conversation with her, but she'd turned her nose up at him. She had no interest in the warlord whose family ruled the eastern end of Brecon Beacons, where the mountains were as dark as Ivor's eyes. Perhaps he had interest in her, but he spent all of his time at The Narth, trying to keep the English on their side of the border, so there wasn't any time for him to genuinely try to court her.

And she was glad.

But the reality of the situation was this—there was no longer a friendly Welsh contingent at The Narth. Now, the enemy was there, and given what happened to her sister those years ago, an attack that brought her such shame that no decent man would marry her, perhaps Madelaina was the least bit agreeable with her father.

She didn't want to end up like Celyn.

"I understand," she said quietly. "I will stay away from them, I promise."

The Bryn still had her by the hand. Any talk of the English riled him, so he had to force himself to calm. He forced himself to smile at a daughter who should have been married years ago. He'd long accepted that his lot in life would be to have two spinster daughters, both of them quite beauteous, but both of them somehow without good fortune when it came to husbands.

The Bryn didn't want Madelaina to end up like her sister, either.

"Good girl," he said after a moment, letting go of her fingers. "Now, go about your business."

He'd got what he wanted. He had her promise to stay away from the English, so he was content. For the moment, anyway. Madelaina stood up, her thoughts lingering on the Welsh that had been chased away from The Narth, the English that now inhabited it, and the fact that the world had changed for them all. There was uncertainty in the future and The Bryn was reacting to that. He had a business to protect and two daughters who depended on him, after all.

And a world of secrets he was sitting on.

Secrets that not even Madelaina knew.

With her thoughts on her vow to her father, she headed back out into the garden, where plants needed to be weeded and watered. It was her job to tend it, after all, and she took pride in it. She did an excellent job. As Madelaina entered the garden once again, she turned to look at the castle in the distance, the one with the gray walls and towering, cylindrical keep.

A Welsh castle now occupied by the English.

And a father who was afraid of what the future would bring.

CHAPTER FOUR

The Narth

I F ANNOYANCE COULD take human form, it would have taken the form of the knight riding to Kent's left.

Orion Payton-Forrester.

In the week that it had taken for the royal contingent to travel from London to Wales, Kent had come to know the young knight that he'd heard so much about. The truth was that Orion wasn't so young, but in fact, rather seasoned by the standard of society. He didn't have a wife, but he considered himself quite a connoisseur of fine women.

Not that the guy didn't have what it took.

In fact, he looked like a Viking god. With his blue eyes, handsome face, and flowing blond hair, it wasn't the mere fact that he appreciated women, but the fact that they clearly appreciated him in return. Every night since leaving London, the army had stopped outside of various villages or cities because the knights wanted to sleep and eat inside a tavern, with a regular bed and a full fire. If they didn't have to sleep in the open, they wouldn't by choice. The army, however, set up an encampment and the soldiers slept beneath the stars and had no problem with doing so, but the knights and their higher stations dictated that if there was a bed to be had, they should sleep in it.

Orion had made that very clear.

Kent was not in command of this particular foray, but Torran was. He seemed to tolerate Orion more than he should have, and that included indulging the man every night when it came to food and drink and sleep. Kent simply did as he was told, and he had to admit that the first couple of nights on the road, he had seriously contemplated tying Orion to a tree and leaving him there for the birds. By the third and fourth nights, the irritation had worn off for the most part because Orion was actually a humorous and personable man. Some men could be quite pretentious when it came to meeting new people and making new friends, but Orion never came across like that. He was honest to a fault, and demanding, and perhaps that was where Kent's sense of annoyance with the man stemmed.

Or perhaps it was the fact that the man was extraordinarily boisterous.

Whatever the case, by the fifth and sixth nights, Kent was getting used to Orion and his opinions and the fact that he believed he was the smartest man in the entire group, which clearly was not the case, but he didn't seem to notice that. Kent had to admit that he admired a man who didn't notice his flaws and who had enough self-confidence to fill an ocean. By the time they finally arrived at The Narth, Orion had no sense of tact when it came to spouting his opinions about Wales and the Welsh and what barbarians they were. Nothing he said was untrue, but that wasn't the point.

They were in enemy territory and needed to be careful.

Less talk, more vigilance.

Torran finally told him as much, and, to his credit, Orion never said anything about the Welsh again after that. He kept his mouth shut and his eyes focused, and for the first time since being introduced to the Guard of Six, he seemed to settle down and try to blend in.

That settled down the Six, too.

No one had been particularly sure about Orion. Torran, Kent, and Jareth simply listened and observed as the knight prattled on or told jokes that sometimes had everyone grinning. The man was an entertainer. He liked attention. But there was another knight with them, a much older knight of scandalous reputation, that didn't like attention at all.

Bennet de Bermingham.

The man hardly said a word the entire journey. He was diligent and dutiful, doing everything that was asked of him without hesitation, but he kept himself away from the knights for the most part. He wasn't rude, and seemed eager to be part of a conversation if someone included him in it, but he never made any attempt to start dialogue himself or otherwise insert himself into a situation. He was, simply put, an obedient, strong knight who was excellent when it came to managing the army, so Torran put the man in charge of it. He had a booming voice that could be heard halfway to Scotland, something that served him well with troops who didn't want to listen.

The last knight rounding out their crew, of course, was Stefan de Lohr. Son of the Earl of Canterbury, Stefan was an unofficial member of the Six, but soon to be an official member because that was what Henry wanted. The Six had more or less accepted him as one of their own. He was everything a de Lohr knight should be—big, blond, powerful, congenial, highly educated, and wildly talented.

But he was also a man going deaf.

It was something he'd been born with, evidently, something that had been most noticeable when he was in training. His teachers thought he was dimwitted and obstinate, when the truth was that he simply couldn't hear commands very well. When they figured that out, they made a special effort to yell louder at Stefan, but his concerned parents had taken him to every physic they could find in the hopes that someone could help him. It was a physic from London who told them that Stefan was beyond help, that his hearing loss would only grow worse until he was completely deaf. Though he'd not reached that point yet, he was fully deaf in his left ear and had minimal hearing in his right.

That simply made the Six yell louder in his presence.

No one blamed him for his deficiency, nor did anyone judge him for it. He'd found a brotherhood of acceptance in Henry's misfit bodyguards because, God only knew, they all had something they weren't hugely proud of. Perhaps that was what made men like de Bermingham fit in, as well.

Not one of them were perfect.

And that included Kent.

His imperfections were too many to list, he felt, but he also knew he was in good company with his Guard of Six brotherhood. In fact, that very brotherhood was spread out on the front of the column of a thousand men, animals, and wagons, and after all of that travel on the road from London, they'd finally reached their destination.

"Kent, where is your home from here?" Jareth, riding to Kent's right, turned to him and lifted the visor of his helm. "Are we near?"

Kent lifted his visor as well. "Aye," he said, pointing off to the east. "Tyr Castle is on the other side of those hills, perched on a rise. The land is clear for miles around it, so any approaching army is seen for days before they actually arrive. Did I ever tell you that?"

Jareth shook his head. "You did not," he said. "Will you send word to your father now that we've arrived?"

Kent shrugged. "My father is probably at Nether Castle," he said. "It is our family seat and it is far to the north, in Powys. It is where I was born, but Tyr is where I lived in my childhood. I have fond memories of it. But, at some point, I should like to go north and visit personally. I've not seen my parents in quite some time."

"Let us push de Russe out and get settled before you do that," Torran said. Riding several feet in front of them, he'd heard the chatter. "At the moment, I need you with me in case the de Russe men decide they do not wish to leave."

"Do you have the missive from Henry?" Kent asked.

Torran nodded. "I do, but if they are resolute, that will not make a difference," he said. "They will accuse me of forgery."

Kent turned, noting the army behind them bearing the scarlet and gold royal colors. "An entire army with Henry's standard is a forgery?"

Torran shrugged. "You never know what men of greed will think," he said. "We must be prepared."

Kent glanced at Jareth, who seemed to have the same mindset as Torran. The closer they came to that imposing castle, the more uncertainty they felt, until Torran finally sent out two riders to announce their approach. The castle probably already saw them, but it was good manners to announce themselves. As the pair of soldiers rushed off, Orion reined his horse in next to Torran.

"Would you like me to go with them, my lord?" he asked. "It is possible that they will refuse the soldiers or otherwise create a problem. I would be pleased to avert any issues in that regard."

Torran glanced at the man. He was being eager, perhaps even trying to prove his worth, but having not served with him, Torran didn't really know or trust the man's judgment. But he had a good point—those at the gatehouse could easily turn away two soldiers.

They might think twice before turning away two knights.

"Kent?" he called over his shoulder. "Take Orion and follow the soldiers. Announce our arrival and demand entry."

Kent spurred his horse next to Torran. "And if they refuse?"

Torran sighed faintly. "Let us hope they do not," he said. "But if they do, tell him de Lohr is approaching and he'll not refuse the Earl of Hereford."

"*Is* de Lohr approaching?"

"Not yet," Torran said. "Not until we remove de Russe completely, but I do believe Henry has sent word to de Lohr about the situation. At the very least, he knows he may be needed here. But let us hope it does not come to that."

Kent didn't ask any more questions. He dug his heels into his horse's flanks and charged off with Orion right behind him. The road to The Narth flanked a rather large village, which was down the slope and nestled in a small, lush valley. As he was riding toward the castle, he glanced at the village below, noting the block-shaped church steeple and many other cottages and businesses. But that was the only look he was afforded, for his attention was focused ahead. Orion was beside him as they reached the gatehouse, where the two soldiers were in the midst of a shouting conversation with the gatehouse sentries above.

Reining his steed to a halt, Kent looked up at the second floor of the gatehouse, which was built into the wall that, as Kent could now see, encircled what looked like a small hill. The rest of the buildings were on the top of the mound inside and the hill itself seemed to be long and skinny. The walls encircled the base, ending at a drop-off at the rear of the castle when the hill became a cliff into the valley below. In all the time Kent had known Ivor, those many years ago, he'd never visited The Narth, so this was the first time to see his old friend's childhood home.

It was quite impressive.

"I am a knight in the service of Henry, King of England," he yelled to the men on the gatehouse. "Bring de Russe to the gatehouse immediately. We bear a royal summons."

The men at the gatehouse were perhaps willing to argue with mere soldiers, but they were not willing to argue with a knight. Especially one bearing the king's standard, with an army behind him as well. More than that, he was heavily armed, laden with sharp weapons, and he clearly meant business.

So much for dismissing the king's lowly soldiers.

Someone headed off on the run.

"Do you think they'll really summon him?" Orion muttered, inching his horse closer to Kent so he could speak quietly. "Surely it cannot be this easy gaining access to this place."

Kent grunted softly. "We shall see."

Orion had been looking at the gatehouse but now was looking at Kent. "I heard you tell Jareth that your home is nearby," he said. "You must be pleased to be back home again."

Kent's focus was still on the gatehouse. "I will be when I can see my family again," he said. "But we must first get through this tribulation."

Orion had tried to engage Kent in conversation since leaving London, several times, but Kent didn't seem too sociable. He was focused and dedicated, and not one to waste time on trivial things like conversation.

But Orion wouldn't give up.

"I was raised near the Scots borders," he said, returning his gaze to the gatehouse also. "I would like to see my mother and father again, soon. I envy you that you shall soon see yours."

"How long has it been since you've been home?"

"Five years."

"That is a long time."

"It is," Orion said. He paused because someone in the gatehouse yelled something, but he continued when he realized the shout wasn't meant for them. "I remember my father saying something to me once. He said the days move slowly but the years move quickly. I never knew what he meant until I grew older and realized how time moves very swiftly. Yesterday, I was a new knight. Today, I was a seasoned one. It seemed to have happened in the blink of an eye."

"I would agree with that."

Orion was prevented from commenting further when the great wooden and iron gates behind the portcullis began to open. Men were pulling them back, securing them, and still more men were stepping forward to get a look at the royal knights on their doorstep. One man in particular seemed to be eyeing Kent and Orion closely.

"Who are you?" he finally demanded.

"Kent de Poyer," Kent said without hesitation. "This is Orion Payton-Forrester. We bring a summons from Henry, so open the portcullis and admit us."

This was the moment of truth. They'd stated their names

and asked for admittance. Kent held his breath while the man who had spoken turned to confer with those behind him. After a few moments, he made a circular motion to the gate guards and the portcullis began to lift.

"Kent de Poyer," the man said, ducking underneath the portcullis as it lifted. "I know you. Or, at least, I did. Your father is Caledon."

Kent nodded. "He is," he said. "Who are you?"

"Treyton de Russe."

Kent's lips twitched with a smile before he dismounted his horse. "I think the last time I saw you was at a feast," he said, handing his reins off to Orion before approaching the very tall knight with shaggy, dark hair and a piercing gaze. "The feast was at Gloucester's. We were five or six years of age, I think."

Treyton's brown eyes glimmered with some mirth. "We were very young," he said. "I do remember we formed a gang with some of the other young guests and fought each other with sticks we'd broken off from the rushes in the hall."

Kent laughed softly. "Someone got an eye poked and started screaming."

"That would be me."

Kent continued to chuckle. "Any lasting damage?"

"Thankfully not," Treyton said. "I remember hearing that you went to serve Henry. You've been with him for many years, haven't you?"

Kent nodded. "Several," he said. "You returned to Clearwell after your training?"

Treyton shrugged. "My father wanted me home," he said. "I have four brothers, all of whom serve different houses, except for my youngest brother, Hugh. He has become a prince of the church."

"Priest?"

"Much to my father's sorrow, he is."

"But your parents are in good health?"

Treyton nodded. "Excellent, thank you for asking," he said. "And yours?"

"Very well, thank you."

"That is good to hear," Treyton said. Then he eyed Kent. "What's this about, Kent? What does Henry want?"

Kent didn't hesitate. "The Narth."

That wasn't the answer that Treyton was expecting to hear. His features tightened, as if he were about to start shouting, but just as quickly, he controlled himself. It wouldn't do to argue with a man who was only the messenger.

"Are you serious?" he asked.

"I am."

"Then you'd better come in."

The portcullis went up all the way.

❧

"Do you know *why* we attacked The Narth? Does Henry even care to hear our reasons before he tries to take the castle from our control?"

The shouting had commenced.

Only in this case, Treyton was shouting at Torran, who was the senior knight. Kent might have been in command of the army overall, but Torran was in command of the knights. That meant he outranked Kent at the moment, so Treyton's anger was focused on the head of Henry's personal guard.

Situated in the enormous entry of The Narth's round keep, the chamber served as a hall that could seat two hundred men easily. It ran the entire width and depth of the keep, with a tall ceiling that rose two stories. It also smelled of smoke and piss and rotten food, which was how the de Russe army had found it. Treyton hadn't cleaned it up. Now he was glad he hadn't.

If Henry wanted this place, then he was glad to leave them the stink.

But Torran wasn't rising to his anger. In fact, the angrier Treyton became, the cooler Torran became. He watched the man pace around in front of him, throwing his arms wildly to emphasize his points.

"We were told that there was an incident between you and the Welsh from The Narth," Torran said steadily. "We were told your father laid siege to the castle and sacked it because of your actions."

"Aye, he did," Treyton snapped. "But it wasn't because of something I did. It was because of something the Welsh did."

"What?"

Treyton's body twitched menacingly to that very simple question, mostly because it wasn't simple to him. It was a question with a devastating answer. "Because my sister was returning from Shrewsbury, where she was visiting my father's sister," he said. "She was attacked on her way home, robbed and beaten, and we tracked the robbers to The Narth."

Torran's brow rippled. "But how did you find them?" he said. "What proof did you have?"

That only seemed to make Treyton angrier. "Because there is a merchant in town who was selling my sister's ring," he said. "The ring the robbers took from her. They took anything of value into the village and sold them or used them to pay their debts at local taverns. *That* is why we attacked The Narth, de Serreaux. Because my sister is lying at home in a stupor and we made sure the bastards who did it paid with their own blood."

Torran couldn't argue with him. Given the shocking circumstances, they would have all done the same thing. But it made him question taking The Narth from the House of de Russe at all. From what he was hearing, it sounded as if they rightly deserved the castle as spoils of a war the Welsh started. He glanced at Kent, who seemed distressed by the tale, before continuing.

"My sympathies for your sister," he said quietly. "Truly, I mean that. We were told it was because of something you did, but clearly, that was not the case. Given that this was a retaliatory attack for something the Welsh did to your family, it makes much more sense now. Did you share this circumstance with any of your allies?"

Treyton nodded. "The House of Wellesbourne was part of the attack," he said, struggling to calm himself. "You know them?"

"I know *of* them," Torran said. "They have a formidable reputation."

Treyton nodded. "My sister is pledged to one of their sons," he said. "Truly, de Serreaux, we did not wake up one day and decide to make war with the Welsh. They did that when they beat my young, delicate sister with a club and were so rough in tearing rings off her fingers that they broke two of them."

"*Who* did this?" Kent finally asked. He found he couldn't remain silent any longer. "Do you have the names of the individuals?"

Treyton looked at him. "Nay," he said. "I wish we did. It would have made it easier on the Welsh. Initially, all we asked for were the culprits to be turned over to us, but they would not do it. They chose to stand together. And they fell together. The last we saw, they were fleeing north. Someone said they went to a castle near Brecon called Pentwyn."

Kent was silent a moment as he digested that. "Do you know much about the Welsh in this area, Treyton?"

"Not really," Treyton said. "Our holdings are further south. We are well allied with the Welsh in our area, but up here… these are wild lands with wild people. Kent, I have to ask—since your father's holding is not far from here, do you know these men? Have you had dealings with them?"

Kent couldn't lie to him. "I've not lived on the marches since I was a child," he said. "But—"

"It does not matter if he knows the men from The Narth or not," Torran said, interrupting him. "What matters is that your actions to punish those responsible for harming your sister have now created a difficult situation on the section of the marches controlled by Caledon de Poyer and, further north, the Earl of Hereford and Worcester. What about the village nearby, de Russe? Have the villagers given you any cause for concern? Because you have to know they would support the rebels turning back for The Narth and trying to regain it any way they could."

Kent was still trying to figure out why Torran wouldn't let him tell Treyton that he'd known the rebel leader as a child, but he kept his mouth shut. Perhaps he thought it would only cause problems. In any case, Torran was there to represent Henry's interests. In fact, they all were. Henry wanted The Narth, but given the circumstances of why the House of de Russe had seized it, it was possible that Torran might have to consult with the king before removing Treyton and his men.

Possible… but not probable.

Even Treyton seemed to sense that.

"We've not had a terrible lot of trouble from the villagers,"

Treyton said. "But when we found the merchant with my sister's ring, we turned the place out looking for anything else that was stolen. I'm certain they are not fond of us at the moment."

Torran thought that might have been the man's answer. He scratched his forehead, deep in thought.

"I'm in a difficult position now," he said. "I've come to take this place from you and send you back to Clearwell. Henry feels that having you here is like having a spark in the middle of a haystack. The Welsh attacked you, you attacked them, and now they *will* retaliate. It is only a matter of time. Therefore, he wants royal standards to fly over this place."

Treyton snorted rudely. "As a deterrent?"

"As a threat."

"And you think de Russe standards do not send enough of a threat?"

"I think the King of England has more power, aye," Torran said steadily. "If you do not think so, then you and I will have a problem."

Treyton was starting to get angry again but held himself in check. "Of course I do not think we have more power," he said. "But we have a mighty army."

"I know," Torran said. "And because this circumstance is a delicate one, I'm not going to remove you right away. I am going to permit you to remain, but I want the de Russe standards taken off the battlements. We will fly Henry's crimson and gold. Mayhap that will ease the villagers a bit and also give any rebel spies a moment of pause should they think to retake The Narth. Where is your father, de Russe?"

Treyton gestured in a general southerly direction. "Home," he said. "He left a few days ago to return. Shall I send for him?"

Torran nodded. "I think you'd better," he said. "Have him return immediately. We have a situation here that must be handled… carefully. You deserve vengeance. There is no doubt. But we do not want to start another large-scale war with Wales."

Treyton really couldn't disagree with that. "I only want to see those who injured my sister brought to justice," he said with far less anger in his tone and far more concern. "Talia did not deserve what happened to her. She is a kind, sweet lass and has a Wellesbourne suitor who is quite in love with her. He is devastated by all of this."

Torran wasn't without sympathy. "Given that I have a wife I adore, I understand completely," he said. "And if someone did such a thing to my wife, I would erase him from this earth. So I am in complete agreement with what you've done. But there is a bigger concern here, Treyton. May I call you that?"

Treyton nodded. "Of course," he said. "And I do understand the bigger concern. But I am not leaving Wales without those who harmed my sister."

"If we were to get those men to you, then you would relinquish the castle?"

Treyton shrugged. "I would go home," he said. "But the question is if Henry would relinquish it. You are here to not only remove me, but to take it from me."

There was a glimmer of mirth in his eyes as he said it, and Torran grinned. Even Kent smiled. All around them were knights who had been listening to the conversation in silence, and now that the tension was broken a little, they were relaxing as well.

"I cannot answer for Henry," Torran said, glancing over at Jareth, the diplomat. "What do you think?"

Jareth had been sitting with a dog on his lap, a big black dog that had come over to him and laid his head on his thighs. Jareth was still petting that big head as he spoke.

"I think Henry would relinquish it to prevent another war," he said. "But, then again, I am not the king."

"True," Torran said, returning his focus to Treyton. "In any case, I suspect the Welsh aren't going to return tonight, so let us eat and rest and then resume this conversation on the morrow. We have been on the road for the better part of a week and could use some sustenance and sleep."

Treyton nodded, but he seemed subdued now that the burst of fury had subsided. "If you have a better cook than we have, send him over to the kitchens," he said. "All our cook makes is mutton and beans."

Torran laughed softly. "Do you want me to take over the kitchens?"

"God love you if you do."

Torran motioned to Orion, who had been standing back by the door with Bennet. The two knights headed out at Torran's direction.

"Done," Torran said. "Anything else?"

Treyton sighed wearily, glancing around that enormous chamber. "You should have your army set up camp inside the bailey," he said. "I would not leave them outside of the walls. There are about thirty chambers in this keep, so you and your knights can select chambers to sleep in. I've only got one other knight with me, so it is just the two of us in the cavernous place."

Torran nodded. "Very well," he said. Then he looked at Kent. "Why not do some scouting in the village before the sun sets? Remove your armor, anything identifying. Blend in if you can. You speak Welsh, do you not?"

Kent nodded. "My grandmother was Welsh," he said. "She insisted all of her children and grandchildren know the language."

"Good," Torran said. "At least get a look at the village and the villagers."

"I will," Kent said, but he turned his attention to Treyton. "Have your men done any reconnaissance while you've been here? Anything I should know?"

Treyton shook his head. "We've not left the castle except when we first arrived and rousted the village," he said. "They will probably be suspicious of strangers, so be cautious."

"Indeed."

"And the man who seems to lead the town is the local apothecary," Treyton said. "They call him The Bryn. Someone told me that he's a witch, but who really knows."

Kent frowned. "The Narth?" he said. "The Bryn? Can't the Welsh come up with more original names?"

Treyton smiled weakly. Without another word, Kent headed out of the keep, out into the afternoon. Clouds were forming to the south and the smell of rain was on the air, but the weather was still good. He still had a couple of hours before the clouds would be upon them and he would need to seek shelter. As he headed in the direction of the stables where he'd left his horse, he caught sight of Stefan.

The big blond knight was bent over a horse, inspecting a hoof. Kent called to him a couple of times but Stefan didn't hear him, so he came up behind the man and put his hand on his shoulder.

"What are you doing?" he asked in a loud speaking tone.

Stefan was a congenial man, well liked by everyone. He

dropped the hoof and stood up, brushing his hands off. "This is one of the horses the Welsh left behind," he said, slapping the flank of the dappled horse affectionately. "He seems in good health, but he also seems to have a bit of a limp."

Kent looked the horse over. "Tendon?"

"Hoof," Stefan said, pointing. "He has a crack."

Kent had to take a look himself, seeing the crack in the lining of the hoof. "The smithy needs to fit him with a special shoe," he said. "I've seen our smithy construct one to take the pressure off the crack."

Stefan nodded. "I think I can make him one," he said, eyeing the hoof again before focusing on Kent. "What went on in there? De Russe did not look pleased to see us."

Kent shook his head. "He wasn't," he said. "Care to join me in some covert action?"

Stefan's face lit up. "Always," he said. "What are we doing?"

"Going into the village and taking a look around. Like a wraith."

Stefan understood. "Good," he said. "Let me get out of this armor and I'll join you."

As Stefan began to strip off, Kent found his horse and did the same. Protection came off, down to the linen breeches he wore beneath the mail. He ended up stripping those off, right in front of everyone, and donning the leather breeches he was much more fond of wearing.

However, he knew the shorter tunic would give him away, so he began hunting around for something longer, heading into the gatehouse and speaking to the soldiers who were there to see if anything had been left behind. Fortunately, some possessions had remained when the Welsh fled, so he found a couple of long, rough tunics as well as woolen cloaks used by the men on guard. Returning to Stefan, he gave the man one of the tunics, and the cloak that wasn't so horribly dirty and worn. Between the two of them, they very much looked like native Welshmen.

It was time to go into the village.

Departing the gatehouse of The Narth, and making sure the gatehouse guards knew what they looked like so they would not be denied entry when they returned, the pair headed down the road. The village could be seen from the castle, so it wasn't far in the least. But the pair of them hurried down the road and lost themselves in the bramble that separated the road from the village down in the vale, so by the time they emerged from the trees, they were covered with leaves and grass and their feet were muddy.

The perfect look for Welsh travelers.

The wind was starting to pick up as they entered the southern end of the village. It was actually quite a large settlement, with cottages and even farms tucked off toward the west into the valley. As Kent and Stefan discovered, there was a main road through the village, but several smaller roads and alleyways, like a spider's web, completed the layout of the town. There were people and children and dogs roaming the streets at this hour, still conducting business, and Kent and Stefan were cautious as they headed into the main hub of the village.

Suddenly, Kent ducked into an alleyway and took Stefan with him.

"It would be best if we split up," he muttered up against Stefan's good ear so he would hear him. "I'll head into the center of town and observe while you skirt the perimeter. Look for anything strange."

Stefan nodded. "Like what? Armed men?"

"Exactly," Kent said. "A group of armed men or even one armed man. Where there's one, there is possibly more. Ap Yestin's men are possibly watching the castle from the village, and if they are, we must know."

"I'll stay out of sight," Stefan murmured. "Where will I meet you?"

Kent stuck his head out from around the corner of the building before returning his focus to Stefan. "I am not certain, so do not wait for me," he said. "Return to the castle and I will see you there. If I am not back by sunset, come looking for me."

"Agreed," Stefan said. "Where are you going first?"

Kent gestured toward the village square. "That way," he said. "I'm going to look around at those businesses and see if any of them have armed men, or men working in them. Armed men would indicate merchants, or even rebels who are keeping an eye on the castle under the guise of working for a merchant."

"Be cautious, then."

"I will."

With that, they parted.

They were men on the move.

CHAPTER FIVE

T HEY'D COME BACK.

More little hands were reaching under the fence, grabbing for the blackberries, and Madelaina turned the dog loose on them. Arthur ran at those hands, barking and nipping at fingers, and the boys those fingers belonged to started to run. All except one boy, because Arthur had one entire finger in his mouth and wasn't letting go.

The child howled.

"I told you I was going to send the dog after you," Madelaina said, peering over the top of the fence. "Now he shall eat you for supper."

"Nay!" the boy cried. "I need my hand! Please!"

Madelaina really didn't intend for Arthur to eat the boy's hand. And he wasn't even drawing blood as he bit because the dog thought it was a game. He was playing. He didn't have a mean bone in his body. Quickly, she called the dog off, opened the gate, and watched the dark beast charge out after the boys, thinking this was all great fun. He ran about ten feet when one of the boys picked up a rock and threw it at him, which dampened Arthur's fun when it made contact with his skull.

As Arthur came to a confused stop, Madelaina grinned and stepped back into her garden. She assumed the dog would return to her, as he always did. Arthur was, if nothing else, a needy creature. As she bent over the pilfered blackberry vine, noticing that the boys had torn a branch off in their haste, she heard someone out in the alleyway.

"Arglwyddes," a man said. "Gallwn i ddefnyddio eich cymorth."

Lady, I could use your assistance.

Puzzled, Madelaina came out of the garden again, looking in the opposite direction that the boys had run. A man stood about twenty feet away, swathed in a dirty cloak and traditional Welsh clothing, as Arthur humped the man's leg furiously.

"Arthur!" she shrieked, rushing over to her naughty dog. "Stop that at once! Go home. *Go!*"

Panting, but obedient, Arthur scooted back home, encouraged by a swat to his backside from his mistress. When the dog disappeared into the yard, Madelaina turned to the man, mortified by her dog's behavior.

"My apologies," she said. "He really is a good dog. Did he ruin your clothing? If he did, you must let me fix the damage."

The man was smiling at her in a way that made her heart leap. Truthfully, she'd never seen such a handsome man. His dark hair was short, surprisingly neat. His eyes were dark, and his face… Well, it was perfect. Perfectly formed. Perfect lips, a perfect jaw, and when he flashed his teeth, those were perfect also. He was also quite big, with impossibly broad shoulders and equally enormous arms. When he lifted his hand to brush off the cloak, she could see that his hands were enormous, too.

She'd never seen anything like him.

"No harm done," he said, shaking off the cloak where the

dog had latched on. "But he is rather… friendly."

Madelaina wasn't finished being mortified. She also wasn't finished being astonished by this beautiful man lurking in her alley. But she shook off her surprise, focusing on his words.

"He is excellent at protecting the garden and shop from inside," she said. "He barks a great deal. But once confronted, he becomes everyone's best friend. I swear he would let an outlaw take everything we own and stand by, wagging his tail."

The man laughed softly. "That is a good companion," he said. "Do not punish him for his good nature. That is rare."

She shrugged. "I suppose," she said, but her gaze lingered on him. Somehow, she didn't want this conversation to end so soon, so she quickly sought something to say. "Are you traveling through the village?"

He nodded. "I am," he said. "I am going home."

"Where is home?"

He pointed off to the south. "On the coast," he said. "But you clearly live here."

He was subtly changing the subject away from him, but Madelaina didn't notice. "I do," she said, gesturing to her garden and the building beyond. "My father is the apothecary."

The man looked over at the lush garden and the stone building beyond. "Now that elaborate garden makes sense," he said. "No wonder those lads were determined to get to it."

She snorted. "They try to steal blackberries under the gate," she said. "Truthfully, they're not bad children. Just hungry. And curious."

"Do you let them have the berries?"

"Sometimes," she said.

"And you also save men from your passionate dog," he said, watching her smile. "You are a very busy woman. May I have your name to properly thank you for your assistance?"

"I am Madelaina," she said. "My father is The Bryn. If you spend any time in this village, you will hear that name."

His eyes lingered on her. "The Bryn," he repeated. "A curious name. Is that the name he was given at birth?"

She shook her head. "Nay," she said. "But it is the name he is called by."

He nodded in understanding, but didn't reply. He was simply looking at her garden, at the cottage it was attached to that was perhaps the largest cottage in this section of the village. He didn't seem to sense that she was staring at him, though he should have. She couldn't seem to look at anything *but* him.

"And your name, traveler?"

Now, he was finally realizing that she was interested in him. Kent pondered her question, but only for a moment. He'd had no real intention to do anything more than blend in with the population and pose as a Welshman, simply as an observer. But Madelaina's question opened a door, and he thought that he might be able to move about easier, and gain more information, if he made a connection with the daughter of the village apothecary. Someone who would know nearly everything about the village around her. He hated to use her like that, but he couldn't pass up this opportunity.

It was a chance he was willing to take.

"Trevyn," he said after a moment. "D'Einen is the family."

She cocked her head. "That does not sound Welsh."

He grinned. "It is," he said. "Somewhere back in the bloodlines, a Norman married one of my ancestors and the family took the name. But I promise that we are more Welsh than you are."

That was true. Trevyn d'Einen was the name of his paternal

great-grandfather, a full-blooded Welshman from the family who had once owned and occupied Nether Castle. His paternal grandfather had married that man's daughter and that was how the castle had become an English property. It was still an English property because his father was English and his mother was also English, from the prestigious le Mon family of Cilgerran Castle. But Kent wanted Madelaina to think he was all Welsh. Thanks to his fluency in the Welsh language, he sounded like it.

He could only hope Madelaina did, too.

"Are you traveling home, then?" she asked. "Most people who travel through our valley are heading deeper into Wales."

Her questions were giving him ideas, and he began to think quickly on how he could turn this conversation to his advantage. "I was hoping to," he said. "Truthfully, mayhap you can help me."

She nodded. "If I can," she said. "How may I be of help?"

Kent gestured to the enormous castle on the hill. "The Welsh no longer occupy the castle, so I've heard."

Madelaina's gaze moved to the shadowed bastion in the distance. "Nay," she said quietly. "The English live there now."

"What happened?"

She shrugged. "A battle of some kind," she said. "A big English army came and sacked the castle. Then more English came just today."

Kent grunted, pretending to be distressed. "That is what I have heard," he said. "I was hoping I had heard wrong."

"You did not," she said. "Why do you ask?"

He sighed sharply. "Because I have information for the Welsh that were there," he said. "Ivor ap Yestin and his men. Do you know where they've gone?"

She shook her head, but she was pointing off to the north. "They left under cover of darkness," she said. "I heard the men in town say that they'd gone north, into the mountains, to Pentwyn Castle. You must know where it is if you are part of Ivor's teulu."

Teulu. That meant family, or group of men, and that was exactly what Kent wanted her to think. That he was part of Ivor's group. He knew enough about Ivor that he could keep up a reasonable façade and not be questioned unless someone from his actual group of warriors was around and could refute his story.

That was an important point.

"Have they all retreated?" he asked, looking around. "When I came into the village, I did not see anyone I recognized. Does that mean they are all gone?"

Madelaina nodded. "I've not seen anyone that I know in the village," she said. "It is surely not safe, which means you are not safe if you remain here."

"Why? Have the English been to town yet?"

"Nay, but I am certain they will be," she said. "You should leave immediately."

Kent pretended to consider her suggestion. "I think I would be more use if I remained for a few days to see what the Saesneg are doing," he said, using the Welsh word for the English. "I can report that back to Ivor. He will want to know."

Madelaina's focus moved to the north once more. "You must not wait too long," she said. "The snows will come in a couple of months."

"I am aware."

"Do you need a place to stay whilst you are gathering information?"

He looked at her, perhaps with some curiosity that she would propose such a thing. "Are you a woman sympathetic to the Welsh princes and their causes?"

She shrugged. "I am a Welshwoman who loves her people and her land," she said. "I am not sure what Ivor did to incur the English wrath, but I would be willing to believe it was possibly nothing at all. The English like to show us how strong they think they are."

He was careful in his reply. "How well do you know Ivor and his men?"

Madelaina averted her gaze. "They came into the village often," she said. "They purchased things from my father and my father gave them advice."

"Did he?"

"Aye," she said. "The Bryn is a Welsh prince with deep ties to this land. He is very respected. He was always glad to confer with an Elfael son and share wisdom."

Elfael. Kent knew all of that. Henry had discussed it with him. During the course of his education, he'd learned about the Welsh kingdoms because of the location of his family's properties, so he knew about the country of his paternal ancestors and he was aware of how Elfael played into the history. Truthfully, he didn't recall remembering that Ivor was from those bloodlines until Henry had mentioned it, but upon reflection, he seemed to remember his father speaking about those at The Narth being Welsh princes. Evidently, that was something Madelaina knew something about as well. So far, she was turning out to be a wealth of information.

But he didn't want her to get suspicious if he asked too many questions.

"Then mayhap I will pay a call on your father sometime, as

a friend of Ivor's," he said. "As for you, I thank you for the conversation and for removing that amorous dog from my leg. It has been an honor to meet you, Madelaina."

Madelaina smiled, a flush coming to her cheeks. "And you," she said. "I do not recall ever seeing you around here before, but I shall remember your name. You are welcome anytime. Arthur will welcome you, too."

"Arthur?"

"The dog."

She had a mischievous gleam to her eye when she said it, and he snorted, shaking a finger at her as if she'd said something naughty. Which she had. With a lingering glance at her, he finally turned and headed off into the village as Madelaina watched him go.

What he didn't see was the smile on her face.

What *she* didn't see was his.

CHAPTER SIX

"I S THAT WHAT we are relegated to now?" Orion said. "Seeing to *food*? Our domain is now the kitchen?"

He was in the stable brushing down his horse, an expensive piece of horseflesh that had cost him plenty. Dust and hair were billowing into the air, illuminated by the streams of light coming in through a roof that needed repair. His movements were jerky and angry, but his companion, sitting on a stool and repairing part of a stirrup, remained calm and composed.

That was Bennet's usual demeanor.

"Think about it," he said, focused on a broken strap. "If you wanted to render an army inert without bloodshed, poisoning their meal would be the smart way to go about it. Therefore, the kitchens are very important. Torran is not wrong in sending us to ensure the safety of our meals."

He had a point, but Orion didn't want to admit it. He was still offended that he'd been asked to oversee the kitchens of The Narth, a vast and imposing place from what he'd seen. He saw himself on top of the battlements as an immovable force, not down in the kitchens with an apron over his chest. Frustrated, he continued to brush the rump of his steed.

"There is going to be a power struggle," he said, avoiding comment on Bennet's statement about the kitchen. "Mark my words. De Serreaux against de Russe. You can tell that Treyton does not wish to relinquish control, not even to Henry."

Bennet didn't look up from the stirrup. "Would you?"

"Absolutely not," Orion said. He paused in his brushing, his focus moving to the stable entry and the cluttered bailey beyond. "But I am not certain I like this land. The black mountains, the constant mud, the smell… It reeks of darkness. It feels like doom."

Bennet glanced up from his stirrup. "It is the season you are sensing," he said. "This time of year always feels dark. In the summer, Wales is quite lovely."

"You know this for certain?"

"I do."

Orion looked at the man. "You and I have only just met," he said. "Two weeks ago, I did not know you existed. Now, we are managing kitchens together. Where are you from, de Bermingham?"

Bennet smiled weakly as he turned back to his work. "Can you not guess simply from the way I speak?"

"Nay," Orion said. "Where?"

"Louth."

Orion's eyebrows lifted. "Ireland?"

Bennet nodded. "My family is Norman, of course, but we have Irish lands," he said. "We have since the days of the Duke of Normandy, who gave over Irish property to my ancestor. The bargain that was struck with the duke is that every male in my family line would serve the English king or in English armies, and we have. For over two hundred years, we have."

Orion thought that was rather interesting as he went back

to brushing his horse. "Have you always served Henry, then?"

Bennet shook his head. "Nay," he said. "I served the Marshal family as garrison commander of Chepstow Castle for many years."

That brought Orion pause. "*You* were garrison commander of a major border castle?"

"I was."

"Chepstow."

"Aye."

"That giant fortress on the Wye?"

"Is that so hard to believe?"

Orion leaned on his horse, looking at the man in disbelief. "Truthfully, it is," he said. "Because you now serve Henry as a secondary knight. You are not even in command of this contingent, and you should be. Why did you ever leave Chepstow?"

Bennet didn't look up from the stirrup. "Because Bigod took command of it and wanted his own men in control," he said evenly. "There is no great mystery. I came to serve Henry and am honored to do so."

Orion stared at him a moment, wondering if the man had lost his mind. Going from a position of great responsibility to being subservient to Henry's personal guard didn't make any sense to him. Bennet had the look of a commander, too—he was older, with gray hair peppering his temples, and a face that was lined with stress. He was a handsome man, but it was clear that the years had taken their toll on him. He seemed… weary. But he also had a presence about him that was evident when he handled the army or the kitchen servants. He was quiet, firm, and efficient. He was a man who was used to command.

But he *wasn't* in command.

He was part of the rank and file.

That understanding piqued Orion's curiosity.

"What about your family, de Bermingham?" he said, resuming the brushing. "Do you have a wife? Sons?"

Bennet shook his head. "No wife," he said. "No sons."

Orion simply nodded his head as he continued to brush, unsure where the conversation should go from here. He'd already asked many questions. Contrary to his usual behavior, he didn't want to become too annoying to de Bermingham. He had a good deal of respect for garrison commanders and men in positions of power.

Even former positions of power.

"I am not married either," he finally said, setting the horse brush aside. "I am not certain if there is a woman out there who can stand me. I can be a lot to handle."

"I hadn't noticed," Bennet muttered, glancing at Orion with a shadow of a smile on his lips. "Were you an incorrigible child?"

Orion could sense the humor in the question. "What do you think?"

"I think you needed to be beaten often and weren't."

That brought laughter from Orion. "You've been talking to my mother."

"If I did, I did not realize it," Bennet said, fighting off a grin. "But I know your type."

"What type is that?"

"Talented, educated, and arrogant."

It was a statement that could have easily offended, but surprisingly, Orion didn't take it that way. It was truth. Even he knew it was truth.

But it didn't bother him.

"You're an honest man," he said. "I can appreciate that. I

think we shall be friends, Cheppy."

Bennet stopped what he was doing and looked at Orion in confusion. "*Cheppy?*"

Orion nodded confidently as he moved to the front of his horse. "That is my name for you because you commanded Chepstow," he said. "Cheppy."

"Please do not call me that."

"Why not, Cheppy?"

"Because I'm not fond of it."

"That makes me sad, Cheppy."

Bennet could see that he wasn't going to get anywhere with his protests. In fact, he'd probably made it worse. He wasn't a man to let things irritate him, but Orion irritated him. He didn't particularly want to remember his days at Chepstow, and Orion's irreverent nickname didn't sit right with him when he'd asked him not to use it.

"Very well," he said. "Call me Cheppy. I suppose I can call you Monty, since you served de Montfort when the rest of us did not."

It was a cutting comment, one that speared Orion where it hurt, and it brought the mood between them down to an unexpectedly icy level. Orion's playful manner was gone as he faced him.

"You may," he said slowly, "providing you do not speak the name with the contempt I just heard in your tone."

"It was not contempt you heard. Simply fact."

Orion lifted a blond eyebrow. "I would get to know a man before I insulted him like that."

"And I would get to know a man before giving him a moniker that may not invoke good memories."

Once again, Bennet was right. Orion had started the whole thing. He was a conceited whelp at the best of times and usually didn't care what anyone else thought. When that attitude was turned against him, however, he didn't like it. Especially as his service to de Montfort, through no choice of his own, was a sensitive subject.

Before further words could be spoken, however, Stefan entered the stable. The blond knight blew in, seemingly rushed. He pulled off the dirty cloak he'd been wearing, hanging it up on the nearest peg.

"Has Kent returned yet?" he asked the pair.

Settling back down to his stirrup, Bennet shook his head. "I've not seen him," he said calmly, as if moments before there hadn't been a conflict. "Where did he go?"

"What did you say?"

That question reminded Bennet that Stefan was nearly deaf. They'd all spent the journey coming to Wales practically shouting when Stefan was involved in a conversation, so he spoke louder.

"I've not seen him lately," he said. "Why do you ask?"

Stefan threw a thumb in the direction of the village. "Because we went to scout the town for any signs of rebels," he said, removing his gloves. "It is possible that even if ap Yestin fled, his men are still in town, so we were poking around."

"Did you discover anything?"

Stefan nodded. "Possibly," he said vaguely. "Are Torran and Jareth inside the keep?"

"The last I saw, they were."

"Then you two had better come with me," Stefan said. "You'll want to hear this also."

Bennet and Orion dropped what they were doing and, alongside Stefan, headed for the keep.

The evening was about to get interesting.

CHAPTER SEVEN

"I T IS SURPRISING what one can discover from a buxom wench with a few coins."

In the great entry hall of The Narth's keep, Torran watched Stefan as the man itched and pulled at the Welsh tunic he was wearing.

"What is the matter with you?" he said loudly.

Stefan finally pulled the tunic off and tossed it aside. But then he pulled his padded tunic off as well, leaving him bare-chested.

"That clothing has vermin," he said with disgust, scratching his arms. "It wasn't infested when I went into the village. It must have come from that damnable tavern."

"What tavern?"

Stefan couldn't stop scratching. "The one at the northern end of the village," he said. "There is a wooden panel over the door with a moth burned into it. At least, I believe it is a moth. I think it was advertising for vermin to come and feast off the patrons."

"But you were able to discover something?"

Stefan nodded and finally stopped itching. "Aye," he said.

"A serving wench there, the daughter of the man who owns the establishment, was able to tell me more than I'd hoped for, but I had to promise to return tomorrow and see her again."

Before Torran could continue the conversation, the entry door suddenly lurched open and everyone turned to see Kent enter. He closed the door behind him, removing his cloak as he approached the group at the far end of the entry hall.

"Kent," Stefan acknowledged the man, waving him over. "You've come at the right time. I was just about to tell Torran what I was able to discover."

"Good," Kent said, tossing the cloak onto the nearest table. But he noticed Stefan's state of half dress and gestured to him. "Why are you without apparel?"

Stefan rolled his eyes. "Because I spent time in a tavern that had vermin, and they got into my clothing," he said. "They are probably in my breeches, too, but those will stay on for the time being. Were you able to discover anything?"

Kent nodded. "I was," he said. Then he looked at Torran. "It seems I have become a spy, after all. I met a young woman, daughter of the town apothecary, and she thought I was Welsh. I could not pass up the opportunity to be one, since she seemed willing to speak freely to a Welsh traveler. I think this will be an excellent opportunity for me to infiltrate the village a little. The more information we can get on Ivor and his men, the better."

"Your Welsh must be excellent," Treyton said. He'd been sitting near the hearth, listening. "Do not forget that Clearwell is near the marches as well. I learned the language, though I evidently do not speak it like a native. You must."

Kent shrugged. "My paternal grandmother is Welsh," he said. "I've been speaking it since I was a child. Treyton, do you know a man called The Bryn?"

Treyton immediately nodded. "Aye," he said. "I know of him. He practically rules the village."

"What else do you know of him?"

Treyton stood up and went for the pitcher of stale wine that was on the table and had been since last night. "I know he is feared and respected," he said. "One of the kitchen servants grew up in the village, and one night, after much ale, she told me about him."

"What about him?"

Treyton drank out of the spout of the pitcher before speaking. "He's a prince," he said. "I know there seem to be a good many princes in Wales, but in his case, his royal line seems to be true. That was also confirmed by another servant, a man who takes care of the horses and did not wish to leave when the rebels fled. He confirmed The Bryn's background independently when I was kind enough not to kill him in exchange for his telling me everything he knew about the rebels and the villagers."

"What did he tell you about The Bryn?"

Treyton cocked his head thoughtfully. "That he is the brother of Maredudd ap Rhys, one of the last princes of Gwyneth, a man who still rules a portion of Deheubarth," he said. "Why he makes his home in this little village, I do not know, but clearly he rules the village. The stable servant said that he was a regular visitor to The Narth and gave counsel to ap Yestin."

"I think I can answer that," Stefan said, entering the conversation. "The serving wench at the vermin farm told me a little."

Kent looked at him strangely. "Vermin farm?"

Stefan scratched his arm unhappily. "Where I picked up the latest friends in my clothing."

Kent chuckled. "Understood," he said. "Continue."

Stefan did. "The girl, named Canella, said that she'd heard that The Bryn fell in love with an Englishwoman from the marches," he said. "His family disowned him and he settled into his life as an apothecary, assuming a quiet life away from his family. He married the Englishwoman and had two daughters, though his wife died when the youngest daughter was quite small."

"The Bryn *married* an Englishwoman?" Bennet blurted. The usually quiet knight was quiet no longer. When everyone turned to look at him, it was clear he hadn't meant to speak. "My apologies. I simply meant… Welsh princes do not usually marry Englishwomen unless they are princesses themselves. Forgive me for interrupting."

Stefan had only heard a few words of that explanation, but it didn't matter. He continued with what he had been saying. "The Bryn was an advisor to Ivor ap Yestin," he said. "What Treyton said was true—he was evidently at The Narth quite often, and Ivor was fond of his youngest daughter. There are rumors that he was to marry her before all of this happened."

Kent wasn't sure why he felt disappointment at that statement. That beautiful woman that he'd had that conversation with was spoken for? She'd never mentioned it, but then again, the subject really hadn't come up. Perhaps he should have brought it up, just to keep her talking, because he could have listened to her voice forever. It was sweet and soft and almost childlike in a way, but it was also very intriguing.

As was the rest of her.

He thought back to the moment he first laid eyes upon her. She had cascades of blonde hair, slightly curly, and eyes the color of a cat's-eye stone. A pale brown that was beautiful and enchanting. She had an upturned nose and big dimples when she smiled, something he found utterly charming. In fact, there was nothing about her that wasn't exquisite, from head to toe. For a man who had essentially given up on women, *all* women, the fact that he was attracted to her was both surprising and unwelcome.

He was too old to entertain a romance.

… wasn't he?

"It sounds to me like The Bryn is someone to know," Torran said. "Kent? What do you think? Somehow get to know the man?"

Jolted from his train of thought, Kent nodded. "I think it would be wise," he said. "I've already told the daughter that I am one of Ivor's men and that I am in Penderyn to deliver a message to Ivor, only to find him gone. That is all she knows."

"Then that is what you tell her father," Torran said. "But if he is close with Ivor, he will not recognize you. Meaning he will not have seen you at The Narth before."

Kent shrugged. "I can simply tell him I am one of Ivor's scouts," he said. "My task is to watch the English and report back to him."

Torran waggled his eyebrows. "Then let us hope he believes you."

"I will do my best."

"And find out who attacked my sister," Treyton said, not to be left out. "That is why I am here, why we are all here. Because ap Yestin's men attacked my sister. Mayhap The Bryn knows who did it."

Torran looked at him. "Did you ever ask the man yourself or try to find out?"

Treyton shook his head. "Nay," he said. "Our time in town

was rather violent, spent trying to find more of the possessions that were stolen from my sister. I doubt The Bryn would tell me anything at all because of it."

That made sense. Torran turned his attention back to Kent. "You heard the man," he said. "See if you can discover what The Bryn knows about the perpetrators."

Kent nodded. "I will," he said. "You can depend on it."

That seemed to satisfy Treyton a great deal. In fact, Torran let his focus linger on the man a little, simply to make sure there was nothing else he wanted for the wrong done to his sister, before turning back to the group.

"I think that is all we can do tonight," he said quietly. "De Russe, I will be putting my men on the walls alongside yours. Have you told them we intend to assume our roles here?"

Treyton nodded. "I did," he said. "I told them when we pulled the de Russe standard down and raised Henry's."

"Good," Torran said. "Since there are two armies here, essentially, communication and coordination will be para-mount. You will remain in command of your men, Treyton, but I will assume overall command along with Kent and Bennet. Jareth, you will deal with communications. Any communique will come through you. Your first order of business will be to send word to de Lohr on the situation here, but tell him not to come—yet. With good fortune, we may not need him at all."

Jareth nodded. "I shall," he said. "I require use of the solar of this place if I am to do such work."

Treyton pointed to a small room toward the front, near the entry. "That is a chamber that seems to have been used as an administrative center," he said. "There are books and writing implements and the like."

"It is my chamber now," Jareth said.

As he moved toward the room to get a better look at it, Torran continued his conversation by looking to Treyton once more.

"Will you man the gatehouse?" he said. "Keep the de Russe men up there, on guard, and I will put my men on the walls and grounds."

Treyton nodded. "With pleasure," he said. "There is also a small, secondary entry, a barbican over near the postern gate."

"You will guard that as well."

Treyton headed out, feeling as if he were still part of The Narth and not cast aside by Henry and his men. Given what they knew of the reasons behind the de Russe presence, it was clear that Torran wasn't going to make the man vacate. At least, not at the moment. In fact, Torran and the others were watching Treyton walk away, pondering that very thing.

It was a difficult situation.

"Well done, Torran," Kent muttered. "That man has more of a right to be here than we do."

Torran nodded. "I know," he said. "But I am going to have to send a missive to Henry explaining why I did not send him home. Did he send word to his father yet?"

Kent shook his head. "I do not know," he said. "I've been gone all afternoon. But Jareth should know."

"I will ask him," Torran said, but his focus quickly shifted to Stefan. "You have the eyes of an eagle, lad. Go to the wall and watch. I want a report when the night watch settles in."

Stefan was scratching his scalp. "Can I at least wash the vermin from me first?"

Torran chuckled. "I suppose that is reasonable," he said. "But get to the wall when you are done."

Stefan turned and departed the chamber, leaving Orion,

Bennet, and Kent. Torran's attention shifted to Orion.

"I need eyes in the village tonight," he said. "Are you willing?"

Orion's features lit up. "Aye, my lord."

"Stay out of sight, make no contact with anyone," Torran said pointedly. "You are to observe only."

"I will, my lord."

"Report back to me immediately if you see anything concerning or suspicious," Torran said. "But if you do not, remain until before dawn and then return with a full report."

Orion nodded sharply and was gone, preparing to be a spy for the night, which thrilled the adventure seeker in him. When he was gone, Torran rubbed his eyes wearily.

"Ben," he said quietly, "you will have command of The Narth. You have some experience with big fortresses, so I would feel better if you were in charge."

Bennet nodded. "Aye, my lord."

"That also means the kitchens. I think we could all do with a good meal."

"Of course, my lord."

With that, Torran stood up from the end of the table he'd been sitting on. "And now, I'm going to see to my steed," he said. "I sent him off with a stable servant when we arrived, but he's a sensitive creature. I should rub him down and reassure him. Oh, Kent?"

"Aye?"

"Do not forget to send word to your father tonight," he said. "Tell him where we are and why. He may have information on ap Yestin that will help."

Kent grunted. "I am not entirely sure I want to write that down," he said. "It could fall into the wrong hands. I'll send it with a messenger, verbally."

"Agreed," Torran said. "How long will it take to reach Nether Castle?"

"At least two or three days."

Kent pondered that for a moment. "Very well," he said. "Then waste no time."

With that, he headed out, leaving Kent and Bennet alone. Bennet, who had been seated, stood up without a word and had begun to leave when Kent stopped him.

"De Bermingham," he said. "Wait a moment."

Bennet paused, turning to Kent politely. "My lord?"

Kent cleared his throat softly as he approached the man. "Forgive me," he said. "But something tells me that you know The Bryn."

Bennet's brow ripped with confusion. "Why would you say that?"

Kent smiled faintly. "I am many things, de Bermingham, but unobservant isn't one of them," he said. "I saw how you reacted when Stefan mentioned The Byrn. Given the fact that you were the garrison commander at Chepstow for several years, and it is only a day's ride from here at the most, I think you know, or knew, The Bryn. Am I right?"

To his credit, Bennet's features didn't change expression. He held Kent's gaze steadily for several long moments before taking a deep breath and nodding his head.

"Aye," he finally said. "I knew him."

Kent could see something in the man's expression that suggested the association wasn't a good one. "And hearing his name again displeases you? Why?"

Bennet seemed to falter then. No longer able to maintain his steady gaze, he turned away and returned to his seat, lowering his body wearily. When he spoke, it was low and quiet.

"I will make you a bargain, my lord," he said. "If you tell me why Torran would not let you speak on your knowledge of Ivor ap Yestin when we arrived, I will tell you of my association with The Bryn."

Kent should have known that what Kent saw in Bennet, Bennet had seen in Kent. The former Chepstow commander was older, experienced and seasoned, and he had realized the moment Torran had not permitted Kent to tell Treyton of his relationship with Ivor. It was a moment that Treyton clearly missed, and perhaps others, but Bennet hadn't. Not strangely, Kent hadn't spoken of his friendship with Ivor on the journey to Wales. It had been something Torran knew, and they'd told Jareth in private, but that was all. The fewer that knew, the better. But now Bennet was asking. Given that Kent had been prepared to tell Treyton, he didn't have any reservations about telling Bennet.

"Very well," he said after a moment. Like Bennet, he went to find a seat, across from the man as he faced him. "You already know that I grew up on an outpost not far from here. When I was very young, before I went to foster, I was friends with Ivor ap Yestin. He was my best friend, in fact. We used to play at the ruins of an old castle and throw rocks at one another. Whoever cried first from a rock injury was the loser and the winner would be the King of the Castle. But I've not seen the man since I was about six years of age, so I will be of no help when it comes to knowing his plans or why he's done what he's done. I am in the dark like everyone else."

Bennet nodded in understanding. "And Torran did not want you telling Treyton this for fear the man would turn his anger on you because you were once friends with his enemy."

Kent cocked his head. "You are intuitive," he said. "I'm sure that's exactly why."

"Treyton seems very angry about his sister's attack," Bennet said. "God knows, he has a right to be."

"I agree," Kent said. He paused a moment, his gaze on the older knight. "Now, I have answered your question. You will answer mine."

Bennet didn't speak right away. He seemed to be contemplating how to phrase whatever it was that he seemed to be hiding. After several long moments, he met Kent's eye.

"What I am about to tell you is something only a few people know," he said. "I would appreciate it if you would keep it to yourself."

"If you ask me to, I will. You have my oath."

Bennet accepted that without reserve. "Thank you," he said. "My situation is a bit different from yours. To begin, I do know The Bryn. I know him very well and he hates the sight of me."

"Why?"

Bennet leaned forward, resting his elbows on his knees as he spoke softly. "May I ask you what you were told about me, my lord?"

Kent's brow furrowed. "Please do not address me formally," he said. "I think we are beyond that. I hope we are."

Bennet seemed grateful. "As do I," he said. "But I would like to know what you were told about me before I answer you fully."

Kent cocked his head thoughtfully. "Henry said that you were relieved of your command at Chepstow over a scandal," he said. "He said it had something to do with compromising a warlord's wife."

Bennet averted his gaze. "That is the rumor."

"Is it true?"

"It is not."

Kent watched the man's lowered head. "I believe you," he said. "But what does it have to do with The Bryn?"

"He was the one spreading the rumors."

Kent frowned. "But why?"

Bennet sighed heavily. "I am the bastard son of the Earl of Louth," he said. "I am, in fact, his only son. The earl treated me very well. The finest training, the finest education. In fact, I trained at the Blackchurch Guild. Have you heard of it?"

Kent's eyebrows lifted. "Of course I have," he said. "That is where the elite of the elite train. It is difficult to be accepted and even more difficult to finish their program. Isn't the saying that one does not simply finish Blackchurch, one survives it?"

"I survived it," Bennet said. "Christ, you should have seen me, Kent. You think Orion is arrogant? I could have put that lad to shame. The world was mine. I could serve any liege I wanted to. The Marshal family ended up the victors in that contest, and at twenty years and two, I was put in command of Chepstow Castle. I thought I was a god."

Kent was smiling by the time Bennet was finished. "At that age, what knight does not believe he is a god?" he said. "And being put in command of mighty Chepstow indeed made you a demigod of sorts."

Bennet smiled weakly. "So I thought," he said. "I pranced around like a peacock. I'm sure some of the older knights wanted to throttle me, but I was Blackchurch trained. They would take their lives in their hands by even attempting such a thing."

"True."

"But even the mighty can fall," Bennet continued. "Four

years into my command, I was in the town of Chepstow because there was a smithy from Madrid who was very talented in making swords. That day in town was the day my fall began."

"Why?"

"Because I saw the woman who would take my heart."

"Ah," Kent said in understanding. "Who was she?"

"The Bryn's daughter."

Kent was puzzled. "Not the lass I met today," he said. "She is not old enough."

Bennet shook his head. He averted his gaze, but not before Kent could see a rather pained expression on his face. Something soft and aching, a silent testament to his buried sorrows.

"Bennet?" Kent said, gently. "What troubles you?"

Bennet's head came up. "I knew The Bryn was married, but I did not know his wife was English," he said hoarsely. "Oddly enough, I was never told. You see, I fell in love with Celyn, his daughter. I wanted to marry her very much, but The Bryn refused because I was English. That was the only excuse he would give. When Celyn and I agreed to run away to be wed, he discovered the plot. He also discovered that she was pregnant. That is how the rumors of the rape got started—The Bryn started them. He had to explain his daughter's pregnancy, and I became the villain in that tale. He would not give permission for us to wed, so he had to explain the child somehow. I accepted his lies because I wanted to protect Celyn's reputation. If the village believed I attacked her, then she would receive sympathy and understanding. But if they knew she'd fallen in love with an English knight, then her life would be ruined."

"So you took the blame," Kent said. Everything suddenly became clear to him, and he rolled his eyes. "Christ, Bennet, is *that* what happened? You loved a woman and were ruined for it?"

Bennet smiled weakly. "Better my ruin than hers," he said. "The girl you saw today—what was her name?"

"Madelaina."

"That is my daughter."

Kent's eyes widened. "*Her?*" he said. "But… but she told me her father was The Bryn."

Bennet shrugged. "That may be what she's been told her entire life," he said. "She may believe it. I truthfully don't know. I only had contact with Celyn once after the scandal erupted, and that was when she smuggled a missive to Chepstow to tell me my daughter had been born. She named her Madelaina, after my mother. I… I do not know anything more about Celyn's life since I left, and I do not want to know, but when Henry told me to accompany the army to The Narth, I knew where the castle was located. I knew we would be at Penderyn. I honestly didn't know if The Bryn was even still alive, or what had become of Celyn or Madelaina, but I knew I would probably find out."

Kent was watching the man carefully. "And how do you feel about it?"

Bennet simply shook his head in a bewildered gesture. "I do not know," he said. "I am trying *not* to feel, if that makes sense."

"It does."

"I've returned to the scene of the worst time in my life, a time that ruined my great career, and I'm trying very much not to feel anything at all."

Kent genuinely felt sorry for the man. "Wales is a big land," he said. "How ironic that you would return to the very place you did not wish to go."

Bennet grunted unhappily. "Believe me when I tell you that the irony has not been lost on me," he said. "But here we are.

And there is nothing I can do about it."

That was true, but something else occurred to Kent. The entire ride north, Bennet had never shown any angst or bitterness in his manner. It was true that he kept to himself for the most part, but after what Kent had just heard, he could understand that.

But nothing to belie the apprehension he must have felt.

"You never hinted at what you were returning to," Kent said. "During the ride from London, you showed no hint through your manner or through your words. You are concealing a great and probably painful secret, yet none of us knew. I must say, I admire your restraint, Bennet. It takes a strong man to hide something so profound."

"Blackchurch training," Bennet quipped, trying to lighten the mood. "In any case, now you know."

"Now I do. And your secret is safe."

"Thank you."

Kent couldn't help but feel closer to the man. Bennet had kept himself in the shadows, being as unobtrusive as possible, which made the fact that he was returning to the scene of the crime that much more remarkable. Kent didn't make friends particularly easily due to the nature of his job, and also the quirks of his brooding personality, but after this exchange he felt as if he and Bennet could indeed be friends.

He felt honored that the man should confide in him.

"You are welcome," he said after a moment. "But I do want to say one thing about this and then I'll say no more."

"What is that?"

"The Bryn seems to be heavily involved with the Welsh rebels," he said. "We will be trying to solicit his trust, and it is possible that, at some point, he might end up here at The Narth.

He may even recognize you. What then?"

Bennet shook his head. "I do not know," he said honestly. "I shall have to deal with that situation when it happens, I suppose."

"You may have to tell Torran what you've told me," Kent said. "He is the commander, after all. He has a right to know."

"You're probably right, I'm sure."

Kent thought about it for a moment longer before reaching out to put a hand on the man's shoulder. It was a moment of sympathy, of camaraderie. A moment that suggested they'd moved beyond simple acquaintance.

"Thank you for telling me," he said. "This duty is going to be understandably difficult for you."

Bennet seemed to be disbelieving of the hand on his shoulder. Perhaps because he'd spent the past twenty years living with a rumor that wasn't true and not clarifying it so it wouldn't damage the reputation of the woman he loved. As a result, not many men had been kind to him. That sort of sentiment was unfamiliar but, as he quickly realized, most comforting.

"I still love her, you know," he said softly. "Celyn. I never stopped loving her. I simply try not to think about her, pushing her out of my mind, but now that we're so close to her… it is going to be difficult to keep the mindset."

Kent stood up, removing his hand. "I will make this offer only once, and if you decline, I will not ask you again," he said. "Do you want me to tell you what I find out about her? If I am to infiltrate The Bryn and his family, I am going to learn things. Do you wish to know?"

That was a horrible question because there was no right answer for Bennet. After a moment, he shook his head sadly. "Of course I want to know," he said. "But do not tell me. As long as Celyn is still young and beautiful in my mind, she still belongs to me. But the reality is that she is probably married and has been for many years. She is another man's wife. If I knew that for certain, I could not bear it. As long as I do not know, she is still mine."

Kent understood. "As you wish," he said. But his gaze was on the man, perhaps with sorrow. "What you have done all these years is nothing short of heroic. Truly, Bennet. I mean that."

Bennet shrugged and stood up beside him. "Truthfully, there was nothing else I could do," he said. He could see the sympathy in Kent's eyes and forced a smile. "Many men go through worse. At least I had the opportunity to experience love. Some never do."

"I never have," Kent said, an ironic smile on his lips. "In that respect, you are far richer than I."

"You still have time."

"I do not think so."

There wasn't much more to say after that. The two of them had made an unexpected connection this day and there was something valuable in that. Something worth respecting. Kent was about to suggest that they go about their duties when the entry door flew back on its hinges and Orion appeared. Unhappy and frustrated, he caught sight of Bennet immediately.

"Cheppy," he said urgently, "you'd better come. The cook hardly speaks anything other than Welsh, and I do not speak that language. Come and speak with the woman or we'll be eating mud pies tonight."

With that, he stormed back out again, and Kent turned to Bennet, puzzled. "Cheppy?" he said. "Who is that?"

Bennet sighed heavily. "Me," he said. "He has decided to call me Cheppy because of my command at Chepstow."

Kent snorted in understanding. "Ah," he said. "Well, it could be worse, I suppose."

"Not really," Bennet said. "I'm afraid I may have to kill that man before the night is through."

"Does he know you're Blackchurch trained?"

"Nay."

Kent fought off a grin. "Tell him," he said. "But do it when I am there to watch his expression. I want to see the fear that rolls through him. I want to see him sweat."

Bennet looked at him for a moment before he broke down in laughter. That brought laughter from Kent also, and together, they headed out into the coming evening, prepared to take on the world.

Orion included.

CHAPTER EIGHT

Pentwyn Castle

I T WAS SUCH a tiny place.

Compared to The Narth, Pentwyn Castle was, indeed, a tiny place. It was perched on the top of a hill in a vale that had been occupied for thousands of years. Therefore, the castle itself had been built upon an earlier fortress that had been occupied by the Welsh since the country was broken up into small tribes. This particular location had been occupied by the Elfael, the tribe that Ivor directly descended from.

The blood of his ancestors saturated this ground.

Like a holy site, Pentwyn had an aura about it. From the grass on the rocky ground to the sky above, and the walls of the mountains that reached for the heavens, the castle was situated in an area that was someplace between God above and the devil far below. Even now, Ivor stood on the top of the steps leading into the small, round keep, watching his men below, smelling the rain upon the air and feeling this land to his very bones. Bones that, not a week before, had been located at The Narth until the English came and took it away.

We are looking for outlaws, they'd said.

Ivor had had no idea what they were talking about.

Of course, they hadn't believed him. From the moment the English army arrived until the moment they laid siege, the span had been less than a day. They had come for war and that was exactly what they did—create war. It rained down from the war machines they'd brought with them and in the flaming bolts that were fired over the walls of The Narth, burning anything that was worth burning. Outmanned and without an abundance of materials to fight back with, the Welsh had lasted longer than they should have, and that could be attributed to pure rage. Rage that the English had come, rage that they were intent on destroying men who were confused by their very presence.

Fleeing The Narth had been an act of self-preservation.

The rage faded into bewilderment, and bewilderment to indignance. It had taken a few days for them to regroup, but they had. The Welsh were, if nothing else, resilient. Resilient against an English king who kept trying to rule over their country, using knights and armies that numbered in the tens of thousands. Ivor felt as if he'd spent his entire life battling the English at one time or another, and the truth was that he had. He was born during an age when battles were normal. There didn't seem to be a good deal of peace in Wales, if not because of the English, then because of petty warlords battling each other. Welsh-upon-Welsh hatred was something that was accepted because Wales had been divided into several minor kingdoms for a thousand years before Welsh princes tried to unify it. There were always men who held a grudge against fellow countrymen.

But it was different when the English came.

That gave them all something to focus on and unite against,

so in a sense, the English and their aggression against Wales had done wonders for national pride and harmony. Every Welshman could agree that he hated the English, and that gave them a common cause. It was that common cause that bonded Ivor and his men together.

It would carry them through to victory.

"Has he returned yet?"

Train of thought interrupted, Ivor turned to see his second-in-command coming up behind him. Dai ap Cadell was a good man, dedicated, but perhaps a little too thirsty for English blood at times. That clouded his judgment as far as Ivor was concerned, because the man used hatred as his primary motivation, not logic. And logic was something that was needed desperately if they were to survive. Even so, he'd do anything for Ivor without question, and that made him an excellent second.

One Ivor could control for the time being.

"Nay, I've not seen him yet," Ivor said in answer to Dai's question. "He passed through our outer posts less than an hour ago, so he should be here any moment."

Dai came to stand next to him, his dark-eyed gaze moving over the trees and gaps in the foliage much as Ivor's was. They were awaiting a scout that had been south, into Penderyn, and their patience wasn't limitless. When it came to the English activities, they needed to know what was happening.

Dai sighed heavily.

"Fud always moves slowly," he complained. "The man is big and ungainly, like an ox. He moves like one, too. You should have let me send Davey or Gwil. They are faster on their feet."

Ivor snorted softly. "They are also young and foolish and would probably walk right up to the gatehouse and get themselves killed," he said. "Nay, we need a man like Fud. He may not be the brightest star in the heavens, but he is deliberate and careful. He will tell us what we wish to know."

Dai knew that. Well, *mostly*. The man they called Fud was big and stupid, but Ivor was right—he was older and seasoned. He would make sure he was concealed, listen to the chatter of the villagers around him, watch the castle as much as he could, and then report back without fail. Younger men might be distracted by ale or a fight or pretty women.

But not Fud.

"I hope so," Dai said, frowning as he watched the base of the road that led up to the walls of Pentwyn. Suddenly, he perked up. "There he is, Ivor. He's coming."

They could both see a man riding a raggedy horse at the bottom of the hill, moving slowly but picking up pace as they headed up the incline. They left their perch by the keep and headed toward the gate, through the bailey, pushing past men who had made an encampment on that rocky ground. By the time they reached the gate, Fud was just entering through a sea of curious soldiers. Men were grabbing at him, grabbing at his horse, and Ivor had to intervene. He boomed at his *teulu*, his men, and chased them away to allow Fud to enter the bailey. When the wooden gates closed behind him, Fud slid wearily off his horse.

"Well?" Dai demanded. "What did you see?"

Fud wasn't fond of Dai. That was clear in the way he eyed the man. He didn't even answer him.

His focus was on Ivor.

"More English," he muttered. "They fly Henry's flag."

Ivor looked at him, horrified. "Henry?" he repeated. "The king?"

"Aye."

Ivor's jaw dropped. "Are you telling me that England's king has taken over my castle now?"

Fud nodded. "I saw the standards with my own eyes," he said. "They pulled the de Russe dragon down and replaced it with the golden lions. Many more men came also. There must be two thousand English at The Narth now, Ivor. Too many for us to fight."

Ivor was beside himself. "Christ's Bones," he muttered. "De Russe must have sent for him. But he came so quickly!"

"He was coming before our battle was even over," Dai said. "He had to. Henry's army's arrival was planned long ago."

Ivor sighed heavily. "Mayhap," he said. "But one thing is for certain—we are paying for the crimes of someone else. We never attacked the de Russe girl. But someone wants de Russe and Henry and everyone else to think we did."

"What do you want to do?" Fud asked quietly. "Do we fight back?"

"Of course we fight back," Dai said angrily. "Why would you ask such a question?"

Fud ignored him, his focus still on Ivor. "We cannot fight two thousand English," he said. "We do not have enough men. If we were to tell Henry that we did not attack that girl, mayhap he would listen and leave us in peace."

Ivor looked at Fud. The man had a simple view of the world, but it wasn't usually naïve. Just… simple.

He shook his head.

"Nay," he said. "They would not leave us in peace. We cannot prove that we did not attack her, and therein lies the problem. We must fight back if we are to regain The Narth."

Dai was pleased to hear that. "What about your mother's people?" he said. "Pentwyn belonged to them. There are villages to the north with many men. We can summon them to help us."

Ivor nodded, thinking on the people north of Pentwyn, many of whom were, indeed, distant relatives. Pentwyn belonged to his maternal grandfather, and through his mother had become his. His mother had been born there, in fact, but went to live at The Narth when she married Yestin, Ivor's father. The Narth was where Ivor was born, and he wasn't so apt to surrender it to the English.

But he had to see what was going on there for himself.

"I must speak with The Bryn," he said. "Surely the man knows something. Surely he has been observing this English invasion into my lands. Fud, did you speak with The Bryn at all?"

Fud shook his head. "Nay," he said. "You know he does not like me. The last time I tried to speak to him, he tried to box my ears."

Ivor fought off a grin. "You have insulted him one too many times."

"All I've said is that he's a witch because he makes potions and tells people they will be cured."

"And you do not think that has insulted him?"

Fud didn't have an answer for him. He was a deeply devout man and viewed The Bryn as a sorcerer for the way he peddled his apothecary potions. Weary, he turned away, heading over to his horse and leading the animal off toward the makeshift stables. Ivor watched him go before returning his attention to Dai.

"I am going to Penderyn," he said. "I must speak with The Bryn. Meanwhile, you will send me into the villages to the north and tell them that we require their men. Tell them that Adda ferch Bevan's son, a *Tywysog Elfael*, requires their assistance against an English incursion."

Tywysog Elfael.

Prince of Elfael.

That was what Ivor was, and certainly one of the last of his kind. His mother's people were few these days, but the loyalty toward the smaller ancient kingdom was as strong as it was toward the larger kingdoms, like Gwent and Powys. It wasn't something Ivor usually proclaimed to give weight to his requests, but in this case, he needed to.

He needed help if he was going to fight off this English invasion.

"Right away, Ivor," Dai said. "I will go myself."

"Nay." Ivor stopped him. "If I am going into Penderyn, I need you here to oversee things. Send others you trust and tell them to hurry. We need hundreds of men, at least, but I will take what we can get."

Dai nodded. "I will select the messengers personally," he said. "When will you depart for Penderyn?"

"At dawn."

"Then we have much to do."

There was no time to waste.

CHAPTER NINE

Summer days and summer stars,
And a deep blue sea that glistens like silver.
All at once, the past has turned to shadow,
And the future gleams like diamonds

MADELAINA WAS SINGING that old folk song, having no idea why it had popped into her head. But it had. It was early morning and she was in her garden, as usual, cutting back some mint that had overgrown. Glancing up, she could see the warming rays of the sun as their golden fingers spread out over the garden wall and part of the house. Maybe that was why she sang that song.

Summer days and diamonds.

Everything seemed so bright.

"Here, darling," Celyn said as she came out of the rear of the shop. "I've brought some of those seedlings you've been nurturing inside. Time to get them in the ground."

Madelaina sat back on her heels, looking at what her sister had before deciding where to put them. "That will get bushy," she said. "Those little white flowers will multiply. We'd better put them next to the wall."

As the two of them selected a spot and began to dig, Arthur wandered out and began sniffing around. The big orange cat that slept on Madelaina's pillow also found its way out into the garden, sniffing around for rodents or a quick meal. Celyn picked up a garden implement and began digging holes for the yarrow that Madelaina had so carefully grown. They planted four of the sprouts, chasing off the cat when it came around and tried to dig in their holes. But the last one went in and Madelaina soaked the new plants with water.

"There," she said. "Those should do well here. Now, I'm going to return to those mint plants."

"Cut some of it for Papa," Celyn said, standing up from where she'd been crouched over the new plants. "He needs it for something he's making."

Madelaina nodded, moving back to the mint and catching sight of Arthur as the dog sniffed around in the dirt. He was over by the gate, and the last time he was over there, he'd run out into the alley and found himself a traveler to hump. That had Madelaina remembering the man who had captivated her yesterday.

In truth, she'd thought heavily of him since meeting him.

"Cee," she said, pulling some weed out from underneath the mint, "may I ask you a question?"

Celyn began to harvest the mint she'd told Madelaina to pick. "What is it?"

"A question about men."

"What about them?"

Madelaina could see that Celyn was stripping the leaves, and she shooed her away and took out her knife to cut the stalks instead.

"You said that you never married because you had never found a man that was worthy," she said. "Did you look?"

Celyn frowned. "Of course I looked," she said. "Well… mayhap only a little. But it was enough."

"Enough to tell you that there were no worthy men?"

"Exactly."

"Wasn't there anyone who caught your eye?"

Celyn's frown grew. "I do not want to discuss this," she said, turning for the door. "Bring the mint in when you have cut it."

She went inside, leaving Madelaina wondering why her sister always became so irritated with her when she brought up the subject of the opposite sex. That was usual. Celyn was almost violently opposed to men, not wanting to discuss or even consider the subject, which made it difficult for Madelaina, who really didn't have anyone else to talk to about those sorts of things. Of course, she had a few friends around the village, but they were just girls. Girls with no experience but a great curiosity about the male sex. Celyn was older and wiser, presumably, but she never had it in her to discuss the subject with her sister.

With a sigh, Madelaina cut several stalks of mint and took them into the cottage. They lived at the rear of the structure and on the floor above, but the entire front was The Bryn's apothecary shop, and already this morning he had customers. Madelaina could hear his voice as he tried to convince someone that they needed a potion of crushed daisy petals for gastric problems.

After dropping the mint off on the table in the room they used as a kitchen, she returned to her garden. She began humming that song again—*summer days and summer stars*—as she returned to her chores. Some vines needed tying up, and she was about to do just that when she realized that Arthur was missing. The orange cat had found a patch of sunlight and was sunning himself, but Arthur was nowhere to be found. It was then that she noticed the gate was open. Heading out into the alley, she caught sight of something she didn't think she would be seeing this morning, if ever.

The traveler had returned.

Arthur wasn't humping the man's leg, however. He was sitting politely as the traveler spoke to him calmly and quietly. He was also wagging a finger at the dog, who actually seemed to be listening. But the traveler caught sight of Madelaina as she emerged from the garden, and he smiled.

"Arthur tried to return to his bad habit, but I have told him I will not allow it," he said. "I hope you do not mind that I have scolded your dog."

Madelaina shook her head. "Not at all," she said. "He deserves it."

The man nodded. "He does," he said. "But he is a smart dog. He'll learn not to—"

He was cut off when Arthur spied a female dog and bolted, running after the small white dog, who saw him coming and scampered away. Madelaina tried to call her dog off, but he wouldn't listen. He was off and running.

Frustrated, she sighed heavily.

"He's hopeless," she said. "Thank you for trying to teach him some manners, however. At least you tried."

The man she knew as Trevyn grinned. "Give him to me for a week and he will return to you a changed dog."

She looked at him curiously. "Are you serious?"

"Of course."

"But I thought you had to report to Ivor."

"I did not say this week," he said, winking at her. "It can be any week."

She smiled, feeling rather giddy because he'd winked at her. "Mayhap I shall," she said. "When you return, of course."

He nodded. "Do not forget," he said. "You cannot have your dog running around the village mounting everything that moves. That is simply rude."

She snorted. "It is," she agreed. Her gaze lingered on him a moment, a smile on her lips because she couldn't seem to *not* smile at him. "Are you leaving soon? To find Ivor, I mean."

"Aye," he said. "But I was hoping to speak with your father first, to see if he has anything he wants me to relay to Ivor. Will you introduce us?"

Madelaina nodded eagerly. "Of course," she said, but she cocked her head curiously. "Strange how you've never met him."

Let the lies begin, he thought. "Not strange when you consider my position with Ivor is to spy on the English," he said. "I spend the majority of my time traveling, as you see. I never spend too much time in one place."

Madelaina seemed to accept that explanation. "Your wife must be forgiving."

"I am not married."

He was happy to tell her that. The words came out before she'd even finished her sentence. He wanted her to know that there wasn't anyone special for him, and that just wasn't something he usually did. But there was a spark in her eye that ignited something in him.

No, he wasn't married.

And he decided at that moment that he wasn't too old for a romance.

"I suppose that allows you to travel as you please," Madelaina said, perhaps a bit of flush in her cheeks. "But someday, you may not want to travel so much if you marry."

"You do not think a wife would like it?"

"I am certain she wouldn't," she said. "Unless you take her with you."

He pretended to consider that. "Wise suggestion," he said. "Do you think she would like to travel to London?"

"I am sure of it."

"Paris?"

"Most definitely."

"Where else do you think she'd like to go?"

Madelaina's eyes were sparking again. Every glitter, every twinkle, seemed to shoot straight into his chest, feeding the blaze that she'd already started. He found himself caught up in a gentle flirt he'd not felt the likes of for many years.

"To Ireland," she said. "To Dublin."

He was surprised by her answer. "Hibernia?"

She smiled faintly. "You know it by that name?"

"Do you?"

Madelaina nodded. "My sister has spoken to me of Ireland," she said. "She says we have ancestors on my mother's side from there. I've always wanted to see it."

"Have you traveled on the sea before?"

She shook her head. "I have not," she said. "But I would like the adventure."

He smiled faintly. "You are not content in your little village?"

She shrugged. "I have lived here all my life," she said. "I would like to visit faraway places. I've always wanted to but have never had the opportunity."

His smile grew. "Then mayhap your husband will take you someday."

"I hope so."

There was a pregnant pause between them, one of thoughts and ideas that were far too premature at this early stage in their acquaintance. Kent sensed it. In fact, he very much wanted to answer her with *I'll take you* but caught himself just in time. If the conversation kept going the way it was, he would say just that and he didn't want to. Not now. He had something he had to do first.

But, rest assured, he was going to revisit this conversation at some point.

"I've been to Eire," he said. "I will be happy to tell you about it the next time I come to visit. I think that people who are dreamers appreciate the tales of that ancient land best of all."

"And you think I am a dreamer?"

"I heard you singing that old song when I walked up."

"What song?"

"*Summer days and summer stars,*" he sang softly. "That's an old Welsh song for dreamers."

She smiled. "You know that song?"

"Of course I do," he said. "Remember the last line in it—a*nd the future gleams like diamonds.* Something tells me that your future will gleam like diamonds."

Her brow furrowed. "What makes you say that?"

He shrugged. "Because you are beautiful and intelligent," he said. "You have a mind that goes beyond this village, Madelaina. You dream of things you cannot see. I think you dream of beauty you cannot see, of people and places. Someone like that has a mind that is open to everything the world has to offer because their hearts are pure."

She was staring at him, fascinated by his words. "And… and you think my heart is pure?"

"I think everything about you is pure."

That brought an embarrassed smile to her lips. "No one has ever said such things to me before," she said. "You do not even know me, yet you think well of me."

"I do not need to know you for weeks or months or years to think well of you," he said. "I think well of you now."

That brought more embarrassment to her, but she was also deeply flattered. When he smiled at her, charmed by her reaction, her cheeks grew flamingly hot. She wasn't sure what to say to him because she'd never been in such a position before, so she said the first thing that came to mind.

"Would you like to meet my father now?" she nearly stammered. "Before you say anything more that steals my ability to speak?"

He chuckled. "It will not be the last time I say such things to you, so you had better become accustomed to it," he said. "But aye, I would like to meet your father now. If it is not too much trouble."

Quickly, she nodded, and Kent stepped aside so she could show him the way. Truth be told, he'd follow her anywhere. His first impression of her yesterday, of her beauty and charm, had not been wrong. If anything, he'd underestimated both. Madelaina was a rare jewel, and even though he knew that Bennet was her father, it didn't deter him. Bennet was several years older than he was, and with Madelaina at approximately nineteen or twenty years of age, Kent was only thirteen or fourteen years older than she was. That wasn't too much of an age gap.

Not big enough to matter.

Yesterday, he thought himself too old for a romance, but at this moment, he knew he wasn't. It had been years since he last held a woman in his arms, at least one that mattered. The last woman he'd been fond of was a tutor to the Earl of Cornwall's children. She'd been bright and pretty and he'd thoroughly enjoyed himself with her, but when he wanted to make the relationship permanent, she confided in him that she was destined for the veil and had no intention of deviating. He'd been a little miffed by her choice but moved on with his life. Until this moment, anyway. He knew without a doubt that he was feeling the same attraction to Madelaina that he'd felt with the lovely Lady Anne.

Perhaps even more.

But his attraction to her couldn't interfere with what he was supposed to do. He wanted to meet The Bryn to gather what information he could. Information, unfortunately, that would never make it to Ivor, but it would certainly make it to Torran. Something told him that The Bryn would be a wealth of information.

… if he could only convince the man that he was a spy for Ivor.

That would be the tricky part. He was torn between concentrating on that task, on what he would say to The Bryn, and Madelaina's smiling face. When she moved slightly ahead of him, all hope was lost because he found himself watching her curved backside. He felt like Arthur with those lascivious thoughts, mentally humping Madelaina's leg.

Given what he thought of her, he couldn't help himself.

But he had to force himself to think on his task, of The Bryn, because the moment they entered the front of the cottage, the old man was standing there with a customer. The shop faced out onto the village square with a well in the center of it and mud all around from the innumerable buckets of water drawn from said well. Moss and weeds grew around it.

The interior of the apothecary shop smelled strange. It was a dark shop, with tapers in iron sconces on the wall, but they didn't give off a tremendous amount of light. There were two windows on the front and those were covered by oilcloths. He wasn't exactly sure why it was so dark and mysterious, but he was sure it had something to do with the fact that the man had all sorts of mysterious potions and herbs and probably ingredients that were difficult to find and the sunlight was probably damaging. He remembered his mother, many years ago, mentioned that direct sunlight could be harmful to some medicinal ingredients. She, too, had been a healer, adept in herbs and medicaments.

Perhaps that was why the strange smells didn't bother him.

Unsure how to proceed, he stood by the door as Madelaina walked up to her father and waited patiently until he was finished with a woman who seemed to have sores around her mouth she wanted to get rid of. The Bryn recommended a salve with calendula and took the woman's coin. The exchange had no sooner been made than Madelaina was pulling on The Bryn's sleeve, asking for his attention.

"Papa," she said, pulling him toward Kent. "There is someone who wishes to speak with you."

The Bryn went with her willingly, his gaze falling on Kent immediately. Kent could see that the man had very dark eyes, like he had, and there was an inherent intensity when eyes were that shade.

Probing.

Critical.

"Who are you?" The Bryn asked.

Kent didn't hesitate. "My name is Trevyn d'Einen," he said. "I serve Ivor."

That caused The Bryn to look him over with curiosity and suspicion. "You do?" he said. "Why come to me? I cannot help you."

Kent glanced at the open shop door. "May we speak privately, great lord?"

Great lord was a general title of respect in Wales, much like *my lord* for the English. It was meant to show that Kent was being subservient and humble in The Bryn's presence, something that was surely important if he was to get off to a good start in this association. But he couldn't help but remember what Bennet had told him about The Bryn, how he'd kept his daughter from marrying the man she loved. How he'd told lies about Bennet and ruined the man's stellar career. The truth was that it clouded Kent's opinion of The Bryn somewhat and painted him as a ruthless man, vindictive if necessary. Certainly someone who didn't care if his family members were happy or not.

That caused Kent to proceed with caution.

At first, The Bryn didn't seem to want to comply. He frowned, looking at Madelaina, who nodded firmly before going to shut and bolt the shop door herself. When the chamber was protected from anyone wandering in from the outside, Kent spoke quickly but firmly.

"We have not met, great lord, but I have known Ivor since we were children," he said. "It is my task to watch the English, and the marches in general, and report what I see to Ivor. I have just come to town as of two days ago and saw the English at The Narth. I am told there was a battle and that Ivor has fled north, to Pentwyn."

The Bryn nodded. Then he cocked an eyebrow. "I have never seen you before."

"I know."

The Bryn was expecting more of an explanation. "*Why* have I not seen you before?"

"Because my task, as I said, is to watch the borders," Kent said. "I am a scout for Ivor and it is my duty to remain out of sight. I was on my way to report to him when I saw that the English had taken The Narth."

"If you are a scout, then you should have already known that."

"Not if I am in the north, near Shrewsbury," Kent said steadily. "I came in from the north. I am assuming the English came in from the south, because they certainly did not come in from the north."

It sounded logical, but The Bryn wasn't convinced. "What is happening in the north that is so important?"

"The English have Wrexham again," Kent said. "Shrewsbury is part of the onslaught, as is Wolverhampton."

"Wolverhampton?" The Bryn repeated. "You mean de Wolfe?"

Kent nodded. "The Earl of Wolverhampton now holds Wrexham, and Llewelyn ap Gruffudd is very unhappy about it," he said. "It is critical, as you know, because if the English call for reinforcement of the marches, that means de Lara will clamp down on his section, de Lohr will take the mid-marches, and Gloucester and de Russe will take the southern end. It could mean an entirely new English push into Wales, but now that I come to The Narth to see that it has been taken, I suspect that may already be happening. Ivor must know that he is part of a larger plan."

He'd divulged a good deal of information that wasn't true. The English did hold Wrexham, but that was a battle long over, and the rest of his alleged news was all speculation. He'd meant to give The Bryn the sense that he was being given privileged information, something meant to gain trust. He held his breath while the old man pondered what he'd been told, and Kent could only hope that The Bryn didn't get out of Penderyn much, if at all, so he didn't know for himself about Wrexham. He only knew what he was told.

And he waited.

Finally, The Bryn broke his stance.

"Come with me," he said.

He pulled Kent through another door, into what looked like a comfortable living area. There was a big table and chairs, a big hearth that had multiple cooking implements over it, a bed tucked in next to the hearth, and at least two cushioned chairs from what he could see. Half of the chamber was meant for cooking and food preparation. The Bryn had him sit at the table while he took the chair at the head. Behind them, Madelaina had come into the chamber and softly shut the door. As she stood in the shadows, The Bryn focused on Kent.

"I have heard that there is turmoil in the north," he said. "I had heard about Wrexham, but that was long ago."

Kent nodded. "You know that Wrexham has been a point of contention between the English and Welsh for many years," he said. "In my father's day, William Marshal held Wrexham."

"And de Wolfe holds it now?"

"Him and others."

"And you believe de Russe's sacking of The Narth is related to that?"

Kent shrugged. "It is possible," he said. "But I've not heard of de Lara, Lords of the Trilateral Castles, moving into Wales, nor have I heard of de Lohr. He is the biggest one of all. If he is not moving to claim his stretch of the marches, then there may yet be time. In any case, I must get to Ivor quickly. My purpose in meeting you today was to see if you had any additional information to pass to him."

The Bryn looked at him. Then he sat back in his chair, studying him, clearly contemplating the question. At least, that was what Kent thought.

Until the old man opened his mouth.

"Days ago we had a new English army arrive," he said. "Now, you come to my home giving information and asking for information."

"A coincidence, I assure you."

"What did you say your name was?"

"Trevyn d'Einen," Kent said. "My grandfather's people hold property in the Dovey Valley. He was Baron Carnedd, a title that passed to my great-aunt when my grandfather died. Now the title, and the castle, belong to the English."

The Bryn was frowning. "And you?" he said. "What of your branch of the family?"

Kent sighed sharply, as if miffed by the question. He didn't want to seem too cool or relaxed in the face of an interrogation, fearful all the right answers at the right time would give him away.

"If you must know, my father was a bastard," he said. "I bear the d'Einen name, though it is not my right to do so. By all accounts, my grandfather was a vicious beast of a man who tried to kill the English who had taken over his home, and was murdered for his efforts. My father was born to a girl in Machynlleth, a smithy's daughter, and she never married. I was born of a union between her and a priest. Is my parentage not shameful enough? Should I tell you more to satisfy you?"

Kent had no idea how he came up with that story, because only pieces of it were true. He'd had a great-uncle that he never met, one who died before he was born because he had indeed been murdered when he tried to kill Kent's grandmother. "A vicious beast" was putting it mildly. The man had been pure evil, according to his grandfather. The rest of the story was simply concocted. Kent had always been able to think quickly on his feet, so he hoped his sordid parentage might stop The Bryn's questions. He even hoped it might bring sympathy.

In truth, the tale did bring The Bryn pause. The man stared at him for a few moments before finally shaking his head.

"You have had a troublesome life," he said.

"Not exactly," Kent said, backing down his ire. "But it has been difficult at times. Men of lineage do not wish to associate with me much. Ivor has been one of the only ones. I do everything I can for him, so nay, you've not seen me before. I make it a point not to be around other men. I'm better on my own. And I work very hard for my lord."

Kent was rather impressed with himself for coming up with such a tale. He wasn't a spy by nature, but his training as a knight, and in the politics of England and Wales, served him well. He knew customs; he knew stories. And he knew how to do what was necessary to get what he wanted.

And then there was Madelaina.

She was listening to everything, hearing about his bastard birth from a bastard father. The truth was that he'd be an earl someday and his bloodlines were noble. He served King Henry directly and was a trusted advisor and protector. But he couldn't tell her that. He couldn't tell anyone that.

But, perhaps, someday he could.

"I've no further questions for you, lad," The Bryn finally said. "It seems to me that you mean what you say. When are you leaving for Pentwyn?"

Kent breathed a sigh of relief at what he considered The Bryn's acceptance of his story. "As soon as I can," he said. "I must tell him about Wrexham, but is there anything more to tell him?"

The Bryn grunted, lifting a hand in the direction of the castle. "Tell him new English arrived yesterday," he said. "They fly Henry's flag, which means England's king has now taken over his castle."

"Have you seen any of the English soldiers in the village?"

"Thankfully, I have not. But it is just a matter of time."

"Have you seen any of Ivor's men in the village? I may need to contact them."

The Bryn shook his head. "I've not," he said. "They've all fled north, which they should. So should you. You do not want to be captured by the English. They would like nothing better than to torture you for information."

"I'll stay away from them."

The Bryn nodded and finally stood up. "That's all I can tell you for today," he said. "Do you plan to return here anytime soon?"

Kent couldn't help it; he caught movement out of the corner of his eye and saw Madelaina standing there. He was looking at her when he answered. "Aye," he said. "I'll be back."

Madelaina grinned, a gesture missed by The Bryn because Celyn entered from another chamber. She had her arms full of clothing to be washed, but when she saw the very big, very handsome man at her father's table, she came to a halt. The

Bryn looked at his eldest child, gesturing toward her.

"This is my daughter, Celyn," he said. "Celyn, this is Trevyn d'Einen."

Kent nodded politely to Celyn, who seemed startled to see him. "My lady," he said.

Celyn nodded in return, looking at her father nervously. "I did not know you had guests," she said. "I will prepare refreshment."

"That is not necessary," The Bryn told her. "He is simply passing through our village and your sister has made his acquaintance. We are finished with our conversation now."

With that, he stood up and went back into the shop, leaving Kent and Madelaina and Celyn in awkward silence. Thinking that he should perhaps leave, Kent went to stand up but immediately spied a dark creature next to him. Arthur was looking at him longingly with doggy eyes, and Kent hissed at Madelaina.

"My lady," he whispered loudly, pointing to the dog at his side. "If you please."

Madelaina hadn't even noticed her dog as it entered the chamber and took up position beside Kent. She'd been too busy staring at the traveler. But she shooed the dog away, back out into the garden, and Celyn slipped out after him.

"My apologies," Madelaina said as the dog disappeared. "He seems to like you a great deal for some reason."

Kent stood up. "For some reason?" he said as if incensed. "You mean there is no reason at all to like me?"

Madelaina grinned. "I am sure there is, but how would the dog know?"

Kent tapped his head. "Dogs can sense such things," he said. "They are smart animals."

"Arthur would try to mate with a cart if I let him."

"Well, mayhap there is an exception in Arthur's case."

Madelaina chuckled softly. "I only jest with you," she said. "I am sure there are many good reasons to like you."

Kent felt more pleasure at that statement than he should have. "I hope so," he said softly. "I hope there is something redeemable you see in me."

The smile never left her face. "I do," she said. "I see a man who has done the traveling I wish to do. He has been kind and generous to speak to me. I do hope he will tell me the stories someday, of where he has visited and what he has seen."

"I would be happy to do that anytime."

"Why not tonight?" Madelaina said. "Will you sup with us? It will not be elaborate, but it will be plentiful."

He smiled faintly. "I would like that."

"Then you will come?"

"I will."

"Good," she said, her features alight. "Come when the sun sets. Or you may simply remain here. I have duties to attend to, but you may accompany me if you wish."

God, how he wanted to. He'd never had an invitation that he'd wanted to accept more, but he couldn't. He, too, had duties to attend to—mostly, he needed to return to The Narth and tell Torran what had transpired. Tonight, he could possibly learn more about The Bryn and about Ivor's operations. That was the goal, after all.

But so was sitting in the presence of the glorious creature that was looking at him.

"Alas, though I've never had so happy an offer," he said, "I have things I must attend to as well. I will make sure I return when the night falls."

Madelaina nodded. "We will be glad to have you," she said. "Now, you must leave through the front. Arthur is in the garden and he might latch himself to you if you depart that way."

Kent grinned. "Thank you for the warning," he said, opening the door that led into the shop. "I will see you tonight."

Madelaina followed him to the door. "Until then, Trevyn."

Her eyes were sparking at him again, sparks that were feeding the blaze that was starting to grow. *Such an exquisite creature,* he thought.

He couldn't wait for that evening.

With a lingering smile on her, he quit the shop and headed out into the street. But immediately, he turned into the knight. The spy. His thoughts shifted from the lovely women he'd left behind to what lay ahead for him. In case Madelaina or The Bryn wanted to watch him depart, perhaps seeing which direction he would take or where he would go, he made sure to head south on the main avenue, in the direction of the smithy stalls. Perhaps they would think he had business with them. It seemed logical enough.

At least, he hoped so.

He was building an incredibly fragile trust with them and didn't need to have it damaged by a wrong move, so he continued to the area of the village where the smithies had their forge. It smelled of hot metal and smoke. He lingered, pausing to engage a smithy in a conversation about the types of weapons he could make, all the while aware of his surroundings in case he was being followed. But an hour of speaking to a pair of smithies and observing his surroundings didn't show anything unusual that he could see.

He moved on.

As he was departing the village, heading south so he could

enter the woods, circle around, and come up the road to The Narth, he passed a woman and her daughter as they were heading out of the village. They had a cart that was about half full of flowers, primroses, and daisies, and the woman explained that it was their livelihood but business hadn't been good on this day. It was difficult for some people to pay for flowers, unless they simply wanted the convenience, when they could just as well go out in a field themselves and pick them.

Kent bought as much as he could carry because when he went to have supper with Madelaina that evening, he wasn't going to go empty-handed. He knew she had a big garden, but he hadn't seen flowers and knew women loved flowers. At least, he hoped Madelaina did. After giving the woman his coin, he ducked into the wood and made his way back to The Narth. But if he knew what the future held for him, he might not have been so eager to face it.

An eventful day was about to turn into a catastrophic evening.

CHAPTER TEN

S HE HAD FOLLOWED him.

Actually, Arthur had followed the man known as Trevyn. For some reason, her dog was quite attached to the man's scent, and Madelaina noticed her dog missing shortly after he'd departed. She found the mutt heading south, down the main road, and up ahead she could see Trevyn as he strolled along.

Truthfully, she only wanted to catch her dog and bring him back home, but the more she watched Trevyn, the more enamored she became. She already thought he was the most handsome man she'd ever seen, looking like a god among the villagers of Penderyn, and she simply wanted to watch him from afar. There was no ulterior motive other than to admire him.

And she did.

For about an hour.

Trevyn had stopped in an area where the smithies had their stalls. That area was out of the village center because the smell from the forges was so terrible. No one wanted them any closer than that. They would repair implements brought to them by the farmers, or even wheels or carts. They would also shoe horses and make things that the villagers could use, for example, the shovel she had for her garden. There was nothing interesting about the area where the smithies worked, but Trevyn evidently thought it *was* quite interesting, because he spent an hour there talking to a pair of smithies.

Madelaina didn't want to make a fool out of herself by having him notice that she was watching him, so she stayed out of sight. She had a difficult time keeping Arthur at bay because the dog seemed to want to run to where Trevyn was, so she held fast to him while she spied on Trevyn from behind a tree. It was silly and she knew it, but that didn't stop her from doing it.

She was very much looking forward to supper.

When the hour was up, Trevyn seemed to finish his business with the smithies and then continued south. Up until that point, Madelaina had only been watching him out of sheer admiration. It was nothing more than that. But when he continued to walk south, and she knew very well that there weren't any towns or businesses in that direction, at least for several miles, she began to get curious.

She wondered where he was going.

Perhaps she should have gone home, but she couldn't manage to do it. Inquisitiveness was driving her. There were enough trees and foliage at the southern end of town that she was able to remain hidden as she watched him, so she stayed to the trees, every so often sticking her head out to see where he was. At this time of day, the farmers that came in from the surrounding area were returning home for the night, and she saw him speaking to a woman and her daughter as they pulled a flower cart. Madelaina knew the woman because she came into the village almost every day except church day to sell flowers and plants that grew around her home. Madelaina had even purchased plants from her in the past. She saw very clearly when Trevyn purchased many flowers from the woman.

But that was where it grew strange.

Once the flower woman and her daughter were out of sight, Trevyn went straight into the woods. Madelaina kept waiting for him to come out, but he never did. She waited a half-hour or more for him to make a reappearance, but he never returned, so she made her way down the road to the point where he had disappeared into the woods. She and Arthur ventured into the woods just a few feet, but it was enough for her to see that Trevyn wasn't there.

But Arthur smelled him.

Once she let go of the dog's collar, he began running into the trees. Startled, Madelaina took off after her dog, calling to him and demanding he stop. Of course, Arthur didn't listen and continued to follow the traveler's scent. He followed it through the foliage and onto another road, a smaller path that ran parallel to the village. However, it was also a road that led straight to The Narth.

That was where she stopped.

She had managed to grab Arthur by this time because the dog was determined to keep running until he found the man he was looking for, but the scent seemed to lead up the road to the castle. Confused, and perhaps the least bit concerned, Madelaina quickly headed back into the trees so she wouldn't be seen by anyone at the castle. Her father had told her to stay away from the English, and she would. She didn't want to see them any more than they probably wanted to see her, so she kept her promise. She and Arthur found their way back through the trees and emerged onto the village road. They headed north, back into the village and back to her home. But she was bewildered all the way.

Why *would* the traveler's scent be leading up to The Narth?

Was it possible that he was spying on the castle for Ivor?

That had to be the answer. It was the *only* answer.

… wasn't it?

She wondered.

And she was damn well going to find out.

CHAPTER ELEVEN

"KENT, I DON'T like it," Torran said. "If The Bryn knows ap Yestin so well, at some point, I fear your identity will come into question. You've painted yourself a spy for ap Yestin, but there are too many variables to this. I'm not sure it is a good idea to become so friendly with The Bryn like this."

It would be sundown in about an hour. The flowers Kent had purchased for Madelaina were lying in a trough of water in the bailey until he was ready to depart for the village, but he was receiving some opposition from Torran when he told him of his supper plans.

It was surprising.

"I thought you would agree with this," he said, frowning. "We are trying to discover what we can about ap Yestin's movements. Who better to glean information from than his advisor?"

Torran wasn't particularly moved by the argument. "You are a personal guard to the king of England," he said. "You are not a spy. If you wanted to be a spy, then you should have joined the Executioner Knights."

Kent cocked a dark eyebrow. "My grandfather served under

William Marshal and was an Executioner Knight," he said. "I am a de Poyer. It is in our blood."

But Torran shook his head. "Talking to The Bryn was one thing," he said. "Now you intend to sup with the man and his family? You cannot get too familiar with them or your lies may be more easily discovered. That is what I'm concerned with."

"I understand," Kent said patiently. "But I am already committed to this. Let me sup with the family tonight and find out what I can. I will not do it again."

Torran was going to have to be content with that. It *was* a good opportunity for them to gain some much-needed intelligence, but he was genuinely concerned for Kent's safety.

"I simply do not want you to get in too deep and risk yourself," he said. "Henry will have my head if something happens to you."

Kent gave him a lopsided smile. "Is that all you care about?" he said. "Your head?"

"Aye."

Kent burst into soft laughter. It was just him and Torran in the big entry chamber because everyone else had duties to attend to. Jareth was in the chamber right next to the door, listening to the conversation because the door was open, but he was going over some dispatches that had been left behind when the Welsh fled. He'd been trying to make sense out of them all afternoon, but Kent and Torran's conversation had him distracted.

"To be perfectly honest, we should not even be in this position," he called out to them. "The Treaty of Montgomery that was signed a few years ago by both Henry and Llewelyn ap Gruffudd gives this ap Gruffudd his preferred Welsh lands and gives this territory to the marcher lords. This territory technically belongs to de Lohr and de Clare and de Russe. It may even belong to de Valence of Pembroke. But it does *not* belong to Ivor ap Yestin, no matter what he thinks. The only reason English haven't taken over this place before now is because no one cares about a little village in a little vale on the marches."

Kent and Torran wandered over to the open chamber door. "I am well aware," Kent said. "Do not forget how close Tyr Castle is to this property. Technically, I suppose the de Poyer family has some power over these lands also, but my father has never exercised that. He has a good relationship with the Welsh and considering his primary holding is in the Dovey Valley, dead center in Llewelyn ap Gruffudd's lands—"

Jareth interrupted. "The lands Henry gave to him through the treaty."

"Exactly," Kent said, pointing a finger at him. "Right in the middle of Wales sits an enormous, English-owned castle. Therefore, my father is not going to cause trouble by trying to claim ap Yestin lands. To do so would be to cause unimaginable trouble with his Nether Castle holding."

"Is that why you've not sent word to your father yet?"

Kent nodded, leaning against the doorjamb. "He cannot do anything, nor will he," he said quietly. "My father walks a very fine line with the Welsh. Whatever Henry wants done with The Narth, my father will stay out of it."

Standing next to him, Torran sighed heavily. "I assumed as much," he said. "You did not seem eager to contact him."

"Not for this. Surely Henry must understand that."

Torran stood there for a moment, mulling over the difficult situation the House of de Poyer found themselves in. But that brought him to another concern, one that was increasingly problematic to even consider. Kent had grown up here. He'd already admitted to being a childhood friend of Ivor ap Yestin. Now he was telling them that in the battle for The Narth, the House of de Poyer would not fight. Kent's grandmother was a Welsh noblewoman, his mother was half Welsh, and he had been raised with the Welsh language before he even knew the more popularly spoken language of Henry's court. But even more concerning than all that was the name of Kent's sword.

Insurrection.

Torran couldn't genuinely believe Kent would ever raise a sword against them, but he was coming to wonder if the man's loyalties were not so clear cut. Having Kent side with his old friend, or with the Welsh in general, would be an insurrection, indeed.

Every Guard of Six had a sword with a name. That was something that bound them together, like a secret oath or vow. Each man named his sword something that was important to him. Torran, a former priest, named his sword *Absolution.* Jareth's was *Obliteration.* Aidric's was *Retribution* and Dirk's was *Destruction.* Finally, Britt's was *Annihilation.* All of these titles were fitting for the men who had chosen them, but Kent's was most curious. That had never struck Torran as odd until now. He'd always assumed that Kent had given his sword such a moniker because he would fight insurrection wherever he found it, as a knight sworn to Henry.

But maybe it meant something else.

He wondered.

"Jareth," Torran said after a moment, "why not go with Kent to this supper with The Bryn? You understand Welsh. You can pose as another devotee of ap Yestin's."

Kent looked at him. "I told The Bryn I worked alone," he said. "How will it look if I come to supper with a man and tell him he is also sworn to ap Yestin? I am having a difficult enough time convincing The Bryn to trust me. Jareth will not help things."

"He's probably right," Jareth said. "I will go and hide outside, to keep an eye on the cottage in case Kent needs assistance, but I should not go in."

Torran nodded. "I will be satisfied with that," he said. "Something does not feel right with this, so I would be at ease knowing you were watching Kent's meeting place. At least you will see if anyone is coming or going, and if Kent requires help…"

"I will be there to give it."

Both Torran and Jareth looked at Kent at that point, who simply shrugged. "As long as he remains out of sight," he said. "I do not want anything breaking this fragile trust I have earned so far."

"Understood," Jareth said. "I will keep to the shadows."

"If I need you, I will shout. Keep your ears open."

"I will."

"Good," Torran said, breathing a sigh of relief. "Now, let us speak of what Jareth has been doing all afternoon. Jareth, is there anything in any of the Welsh communications that Kent should be armed with? Anything only a Welshman would know?"

Jareth looked at the missives. It was a small room, smelling of smoke and rot, and it had the odd feature of a very large table in the middle of it. The vellums were neatly arranged now, but it had taken Jareth hours to do so. Like everything else at The Narth, the small solar had been in complete disarray when the English took possession.

He picked up the nearest missive.

"Nothing that seems terribly important," he said. "I—"

He was cut off when the entry door swung open and Treyton appeared. His searching gaze immediately found Torran, and he pointed to the bailey.

"Your comrades have arrived," he said.

Puzzled, Torran and Kent and Jareth went to the door only to see the other half of the Six approaching, three heavily armed knights trudging through the bailey as the veil of night descended. Aidric lifted a long arm to wave at them, and he was flanked by Dirk and Britt.

Torran threw up his hands in confusion.

"What are you three doing here?" he shouted to them. "Henry wanted to keep you with him."

They drew closer, and Aidric shouted in return. "We couldn't be kept away from you," he jested. "Are you not glad to see us?"

"Quickly," Kent said to Torran. "Shut the door."

The three approaching knights laughed and, of course, the door was not shut. They were greeted by their colleagues, practically shoving Treyton out of the way, and he returned to the gatehouse because it was his post. The Guard of Six was together once again, and he was not part of that.

"Tell me," Torran said to them. "Why did Henry release you?"

"Because," Aidric said, hand on his weapon, "if you are going to get in a knife fight with the Welsh, he wanted to send his finest swords. He made that decision the day after you left, and here we are. *Is* there going to be a fight?"

Torran pulled them inside, shutting the door behind them. "Not at this time," he said. "Come in and sit by the fire. I'll tell you what we know, which is different from what Henry told us."

The men began pulling off cloaks and gloves. "I noticed de Russe is still here," Britt said. He was the volatile one of the group, highly intelligent but also highly emotional at times. "You did not send him and his army home?"

Torran waggled his eyebrows. "It is not as simple as that," he said. "De Russe laying siege to The Narth was out of revenge."

"For what?"

"For Welsh from The Narth attacking a de Russe daughter and gravely injuring her," Torran said, looking at the three of them. "I have decided to let them remain for now because this is most definitely their fight. It complicates an already complicated situation."

Britt and Aidric frowned, looking at each other in concern, as Dirk spoke. "Then the son had nothing to do with this?" he said in a deep voice with a slight lisp. The lisp, in fact, was why he was usually so silent in the presence of others. "No foolish actions on his part?"

"None at all," Torran said. "That means they took The Narth to punish the Welsh for making an invalid out of a de Russe daughter. Poor lass was betrothed to a son of Wellesbourne. Treyton seems quite heartbroken over it."

"Then their presence here was vengeance," Aidric said.

"It was."

That settled on the newcomers. That had not been something they expected, much as Torran and Kent and Jareth hadn't expected such news upon their arrival. They'd been expecting a battle with de Russe and had found something quite different but no less concerning. Torran was right—it complicated an already complex situation.

In fact, it made it worse.

"What now, then?" Aidric asked. "Will you inform Henry of the circumstances?"

"I already have," Jareth said. "I sent a missive out this afternoon explaining what we found when we arrived and the fact that we are allowing de Russe to remain until we receive further instructions. But my question is this—if the six of us are here, on the marches, *who* is guarding Henry?"

Aidric waved him off. "A dozen younger knights who are part of the royal household," he said. "You know that group."

"The one led by de Reyne?" Jareth said.

"The same."

"He'll be the next Lord Protector, you know," Jareth said confidently. "Now that Patrick de Wolfe has declined the position."

Torran spoke. "Henry has his Six, but for some reason, he also needs a personal bodyguard," he said. "Patrick de Wolfe would have been an astonishingly good addition as Lord Protector, but as I understand it, he married and wanted to remain in the north with his family. I heard that his wife is the daughter of a Northman king."

"That is one way to make an alliance," Jareth said. "I'm sure that will end all Northman attacks against de Wolfe properties for some time to come. That was very wise of de Wolfe."

"Indeed," Torran said. "But mark my words—Thor de Reyne will be the next Lord Protector. And he has earned it."

The group nodded. They all knew Thor de Reyne, from another powerful family in the north, but this family had ties to Aragon pirates and other powerful undesirables, which made de Reyne a perfect man to be at Henry's side as his personal bodyguard. If Henry needed unsavory support or something more underhanded than what the Six were willing to accomplish, one word to de Reyne and great Aragon mercenaries would do the deed.

It made for interesting dynamics.

"Speaking of earning things," Kent spoke up, "I am preparing to depart to sup with a man who is an advisor to Ivor ap Yestin, the very man this castle was taken from. As much as I would like to remain and sup with all of you, I feel it is more important to glean information from The Bryn."

"The Bryn?" Aidric repeated, looking at Torran and Kent in confusion. "What is that?"

"*Who* is that," Kent clarified, going on the hunt for his cloak. "He is the town apothecary. Jareth was coming to stay to the shadows and watch the cottage to warn me of any approaching danger."

"I'll go," Britt said. When his five comrades looked at him curiously, he simply shrugged. "I, too, grew up on the marches, lest you forget, and I can speak Welsh as well as Kent can. Besides… I'm a better spy than Jareth."

Jareth rolled his eyes. "You are one step above an Executioner Knight," he said. "And I think you are the only one of us that is Blackchurch trained."

"Bennet is Blackchurch trained also," Torran said. "You all know Ben de Bermingham. One of the other knights we brought with us in addition to Orion Payton-Forrester."

"Ah," Dirk said, shaking his head in disgust. "Payton-Forrester. I nearly came to blows with him once. How did he behave on the journey here?"

"Like an arrogant arse," Kent said. "Forget about him. He and Bennet are seeing to the grounds and manning the walls while the rest of us do the real work."

That had Dirk snorting. "He must hate every minute of

that," he said. "Imagine Payton-Forrester commanding the bailey like a common sergeant."

The thought of an arrogant knight being reduced to mundane tasks brought a few grins all around. Kent swung his cloak over his shoulders as Britt also prepared to depart, but Kent turned to Torran as he secured his cloak around his neck.

"Something has occurred to me," he said.

"What is that?" Torran said.

Kent sighed faintly, glancing at Britt. "No one in this group, me included, has ever seen Ivor ap Yestin," he said. "At least, not as an adult. I could identify the child, but not the man. Britt could watch the cottage, but how would he know if Ivor somehow approached and made his way inside? He could not warn me if he does not know the man on sight."

Torran scratched his chin. "True," he said. "The only one who might have seen him is Treyton. Do you want him to go with you?"

"It may be wise."

"Ask him."

Kent did. Heading out of the gatehouse with Britt, he discovered that Treyton had, indeed, seen Ivor ap Yestin and a few of his men when they first arrived at The Narth. He'd seen him a second time when they attempted to negotiate a surrender. Therefore, he knew what the man looked like and was more than happy to act as a lookout.

In short order, Treyton joined the duo heading into the village.

CHAPTER TWELVE

THEY'D BEEN TRAVELING for two days.

Out of the mountainous region where Pentwyn was located, the Welsh had retraced their tracks back to Penderyn. Two days of returning to the vale that was once their home. Once Ivor entered the narrow valley he was so familiar with, the one he'd grown up in, he began to feel both comfort and rage.

Rage that he'd been forced out.

Comfort that he'd come home.

But he wasn't exactly home yet. Ivor and Dai and Fud had come in from the north with ten other men, men who were told to blend in with the villagers and find out what they could about the new English army that had arrived, the one bearing Henry's standard. Since the vast majority of Ivor's men had grown up in this vale, it wasn't a difficult assignment. They knew where to go and what to avoid. They ran home to mothers and fathers and sweethearts. Sweeping in from the north just as the sun dipped below the western horizon, Ivor's men scattered.

But Ivor, Dai, and Fud continued toward the village center.

Ivor was heading for The Bryn's cottage. Astride his sturdy Welsh pony, he dismounted the animal just as they entered the village proper because he didn't want to stand out on horse-back, especially if there were English soldiers in the village. Fud took the horses and disappeared down an alley as Ivor and Dai continued on into the town, trying to stay out of sight. They were just nearing the apothecary shop when they saw it.

Madelaina speaking to a man in the darkness.

That had Ivor ducking into the nearest doorway, concealed by a beam and part of a fence. Dai pressed in behind him, and the two of them watched as Madelaina seemed to be having an animated conversation with the man. At least, *she* was animated. The man was not. And he was a very big man, with incredibly broad shoulders and big arms. Since the village was lit by torchlight and a night watch had already lit several iron lampposts, they could see him well enough to notice that he was dressed in traditional Welsh clothing.

"Who *is* that?" Dai whispered. "Do you know him?"

Ivor shook his head. "I do not," he muttered.

"What do we do?"

Ivor's dark eyes were riveted to the man. "I do not know," he said. Then he began to look around. "Where is The Bryn? And why is he allowing Maddie to speak with this stranger?"

"Mayhap he is not a stranger to them."

That didn't please Ivor, especially when everyone in the village knew that he was sweet on her. Madelaina belonged to him, even if he hadn't asked for her hand yet. *Yet.* He hadn't asked because he hadn't wanted the added burden of a wife at this point in his life, but now he was starting to regret that decision.

"Quickly," he said. "Into The Bryn's garden. We'll enter from the rear of the cottage."

The pair ducked low and scooted across the small alleyway

where they had been hiding. There was a chance the man speaking to Madelaina could see them, but they would have to take that chance. Swiftly, they moved, and ended up in Madelaina's prized garden. Rushing through, they bolted in through the unlocked rear door to find Celyn standing in the kitchen area, surrounded by bowls of food. When she looked up and saw Ivor and Dai, whom she knew, she gasped in surprise.

"Ivor!" she said. "What are you doing here?"

Dai quickly went through to the apothecary's shop, where he could watch Madelaina and her mystery man through the front window, but Ivor went to Celyn.

"Never mind that," he said. "Whom is Maddie speaking with?"

Celyn looked at him as if she had no idea what he was talking about. "Man?" she repeated. But then it occurred to her. "A traveler, I think. He came around yesterday. Trevyn d'Einen is his name. She invited him to sup."

Ivor scowled. "A stranger?" he said. "What does your father have to say about it?"

Celyn sighed sharply and indicated all of the food at the table. "He has said nothing because he is not here," she said. "I have prepared supper and he is off with an old man who pays him a good deal of coin to provide him with potions for his imaginary illnesses."

Ivor raked his fingers through his damp, dark hair. "A stranger," he grumbled. "I should go out there and send him on his way."

Celyn shook her head. "Do not," she said. "You know if you do that, Madelaina will be furious with you. She does not like it when you try to take charge of her."

Ivor was still grumbling. "She is going to have to get used to it."

"Not unless you ask for her hand, Ivor."

He frowned. "I will when I am ready."

"It may be too late by then."

He stopped frowning and looked at her seriously. "Do you think so?"

She shrugged, putting a loaf of bread on the table. "I cannot say," she said. "I have warned her about men. I have warned her about speaking to everyone who talks to her. You know she is friendly and finds interest in people who are not from this vale. She has the heart of a wanderer, Ivor. That is something you cannot contain."

He was listening to her seriously. "But I cannot marry right now," he said. "I have just lost the home I grew up in. My world is in chaos. I cannot marry her and I cannot feed that wandering spirit by taking her out of this vale. My place is here and so is hers."

Celyn looked at him. "Then mayhap you should find a wife who will be content being in your shadow and living in this vale for the rest of her life," she said. "Because that is not Maddie. There is more to her. She deserves more."

"More than being the wife of a prince of Elfael?"

Celyn shrugged. "A prince with no lands," she said. "A warlord who lost his castle to the English. Ivor, I'm simply saying that she may not be right for you. You cannot marry the woman only to make her miserable. That will make you miserable, too, and you will have a miserable life together. Do you not deserve more?"

Before Ivor could answer, Dai was suddenly in their midst. "She is coming," he said, closing the door between the living area and the apothecary shop. "And she is alone."

Ivor immediately focused on the return of Madelaina. "The

stranger has departed?"

"He has headed south, down the road."

"Then I shall get to the bottom of this."

"Careful, Ivor," Celyn said softly. "Tread carefully."

He turned to reply but she was leaving the room, disappearing into the sleeping chambers. Cleary, her move was meant to leave Ivor alone with Madelaina, but Dai was there, so they weren't exactly alone.

But alone enough.

He would never forget the look of surprise on Madelaina's face when she came through the door.

CHAPTER THIRTEEN

"My FATHER COULD not join us for supper," Madelaina said. "Unfortunately, there is a sick man who needs his medicaments, so he is elsewise occupied this evening."

Kent had just arrived at The Bryn's abode, arms full of flowers, only to find Madelaina standing outside, by the front door, as if blocking his way in. There was no sign of the amorous dog, or anyone else for that matter. An intuitive man, he could sense something in her that hadn't been there before.

Hardness.

Something was amiss.

He proceeded carefully.

"Then I do not have to join you," he said. "If it is only you and your sister, I do not wish to make you uncomfortable. You hardly know me, after all. You should not have a strange man seated at your table without your father present."

She arched an eyebrow. "A man who is a bit of a mystery still."

"There's nothing so mysterious about me, I can assure you."

Madelaina didn't take her eyes off him as she spoke. "After you left today, Arthur was quite upset," she said. "He must have felt slighted that you did not bid him farewell, so he tried to follow you."

Kent smiled faintly. "I cannot imagine why I've made such an impression on that dog, but clearly I have."

"Clearly," Madelaina said, but there was almost an accusation in her tone. "I chased him down before he could maul you whilst you spoke with the smithies on the south end of town. I will confess that I find you pleasing to watch, d'Einen. You are unlike anyone I've ever met and you have treated me with kindness and respect, so I hid in the shadows and watched you speak with the smithies simply because I liked to watch you. Is that bold of me?"

His smile grew. "Nay," he said in a low, seductive voice. "Because I would do the same to you if I thought it would not offend you. In case you haven't realized it yet, I find you quite beautiful."

That caused her to lower her gaze out of embarrassment, perhaps even delight that he should say such a thing, but only briefly. "Then you understand my curiosity and attraction," she said. "I had not planned to tell you any of this, but I find that I must."

"I am not troubled by it in the least, but why tell me if you did not want to?"

"Because my dog trailed you to The Narth," she said. "What were you doing at The Narth, Trevyn? Or is that even your name?"

Now, the hammer had been lowered. This was why she'd seemed standoffish. Truthfully, he was shocked she'd followed him that far and he hadn't even been aware of it. He thought he'd been careful about making sure he wasn't followed, but as Torran had so eloquently put it, he wasn't a spy. Now, that was painfully obvious.

He hadn't been careful enough.

Damn...

"You are asking a question, but you have already made up your mind what the answer is," he said steadily. "I do not mind your following me, but I do mind the accusation. You did not have to tell me you watched me because you find me attractive. That is a devious way of trying to throw me off my guard before you make accusations. I will, therefore, take my leave, lady. I will trouble you no more."

He dropped the flowers on the ground and turned away, heading back the way he'd come. But Arthur came out of nowhere and latched on to his leg. He came to a halt, holding up a stern finger to the dog, who immediately released him. By the time he looked up from the mutt, Madelaina was standing in front of him again.

"Will you not even explain this to me?" she said, sounding more pleading and less accusatory. "I want to understand."

He shook his head. "I do not think you do," he said. "You are young, lass. There are lessons still for you to learn in the way you should treat people who have not done you any harm."

He walked around her, leaving her increasingly flustered and frustrated. "Did you go to spy on the English?" she called after him as he walked away. "Is that what you did?"

That gave Kent an idea. He knew that somewhere over by the old livery barn across the street, Britt and Treyton were watching the scene. Oddly, it seemed to him as if there were a lot at stake at the moment. He'd built a budding relationship with Madelaina, one he truly didn't want to end, and he hoped to build one with her father.

He could have made two choices at that moment.

The first choice, and probably the smarter one, was to simply walk away. They would never discover who he truly was and he would no longer be putting himself in danger. The second choice, however, was not the better of the two but it was the choice he wanted to make.

It was the choice to stay.

"If you had asked me politely, I would have told you that," he said as he turned around. "There is a saying, Madelaina—never call a man a liar if you want him to be honest. All you had to do was ask."

"I did ask," she insisted weakly. "I *am* asking. Will you please tell me?"

Gone was the hardness. She was repentant in her manner, which made his turning and leaving all the more impossible. He couldn't look into that lovely face and be angry or offended. The truth was that she was absolutely right to confront him, and it was now he who was doing the manipulating. He hoped he could give her an explanation of his presence at The Narth without outright lying to her. He truly didn't want to lie to her more than he already had.

But he also didn't want this budding relationship to end.

Reaching out, he took her hand.

"It does not matter why I was at The Narth," he said. "The truth is that my business is none of your affair, is it?"

Madelaina shook her head. "Nay," she said quietly, with remorse. "I know you are trying to do good for Ivor."

"I am trying to do good for what I believe in," he murmured, bringing her hand to his lips and kissing it gently. "I am a warrior above all."

His kiss to her fingers had done something to her. She looked as if she'd just ingested lightning. Her eyes were wide and her body seemed to be twitching. *Trembling*. She looked at her hand in his, stunned, before her gaze returned to his face.

"Why… why did you do that?" she managed to stammer.

"If you do not like it, I will not do it again."

"I like it."

He chuckled at her swift answer. "Good," he said. "Because I would probably do it again even if you did not want me to."

"Are hands the only thing you kiss?"

His eyebrows lifted at the rather intimate question. "Nay," he said. "But we are standing out in the street. I will not kiss anything else on your person for all the world to see."

She suddenly broke into a giddy grin and began to giggle. "I do not know why I asked that," she said. "Was it too terribly bold?"

"Horrifically bold."

"Does that mean you think less of me?"

"I think more of you."

"Will you kiss my hand again sometime?"

"I will," he said. "When the moment is right."

"When will that be?"

He chuckled again. "When you least expect it."

She smiled because he was. "Very well," she said. "I look forward to it. Now, will you forget my prying into your affairs and sup with my sister and me?"

Kent's gaze moved to the front door of the apothecary shop for a moment. He wanted to sup with The Bryn to try to establish some trust with the man and was disappointed that he wouldn't be in attendance. But he was even more disappointed because he was about to decline Madelaina's invitation. They were already on brittle ground with her questioning him about The Narth, and truthfully, he didn't think it would be a good idea for him to sup with two unmarried women without a chaperone. There were a variety of reasons why it wasn't a good idea, as much as he would have liked to. Perhaps when Madelaina explained to her father that he had declined to sup with her and her sister alone, it might show The Bryn that he was an honorable and trustworthy man.

That was the hope, anyway.

"As much as I would like to, I do not believe I should," he said. "Without your father present, it would not be proper for me to do so. I am sorry. Please know how disappointed I am, but I believe it is for the best."

Madelaina's face fell. "Of course," she said. "You are correct. How foolish of me not to realize that."

"You are not foolish," he said. "Far from it. But if I were an untoward man, I would gladly take sup with you and your sister and give no regard for your reputation or what your father might think. This way… I am an honorable man and I would prove it. But I look forward to supping with you and your family in the future."

Madelaina was fighting back her disappointment but nodded, forcing a smile. "It will be very soon," she said. "If you are able, please come by tomorrow. I am certain my father will also want to express his regret for not being able to sup with you."

He nodded. "I will," he said. "But now, you must go back inside. I can feel a chill in the air."

Madelaina started to walk backward toward her father's shop, but she came to a halt. "Where do you sleep at night?" she asked. "What I mean is… do you have a roof over your head? Or do you sleep in the trees? Because I am certain my father would let you use our small stable to sleep in. You should have some shelter."

He smiled. "You are kind to worry over me," he said. "But you needn't worry. I do have shelter."

He didn't elaborate and she didn't press. He could tell that it was difficult for her not to keep on with the questions. It did his heart good to realize that, because when one was interested in someone, one wanted to know all about them. Even whether or not they had shelter for the night. As he watched Madelaina turn for the shop, he softly called to her.

"Wait," he said.

She paused, turning to him curiously only to see that he was nearly upon her. Reaching out, he took her hand again and brought it to his lips for a lingering kiss. A hot-breath, steamy kiss against her tender flesh that seemed to convey the interest he was feeling for her.

Madelaina's knees nearly buckled.

"I told you I would do it again when you least expected it," he murmured, a twinkle in his eye. "Now, go inside. I will see you on the morrow."

Madelaina nodded rather dumbly, turning for the door once more and cradling the hand he'd kissed. She swore she could still feel his heated lips against her skin. Lifting the latch on the door, she disappeared inside. But not before he heard the faint strains of a song in her soft, gentle voice—

All at once, the past has turned to shadow,
And the future gleams like diamonds

Kent grinned at the words, things they'd spoken off. Strange how that little song had come to mean something to him when it never had before. He waited until she'd gone inside before turning away and heading south again. He'd been caught once being followed, by Madelaina no less, and he wasn't going to take that chance again. Britt and Treyton were over in the livery and he didn't want to be seen with them in case prying eyes were watching—villagers or even Madelaina—so he continued south, out of sight of the village center, before he dared slip into the darkened woods.

This time, he made doubly sure he wasn't followed.

But he was.

CHAPTER FOURTEEN

MADELAINA WALKED RIGHT into a tribunal.

"Who was that man?"

The demand came from Ivor, standing in her father's darkened apothecary shop. Madelaina gasped at the sight of him, shocked, and quickly shut the door.

"What are you doing here?" she said. "Quickly—come away from the window. *Hurry!*"

She hurried them back into the living quarters, but he ignored her haste. "Answer me," he said. "Who was the man you were speaking with? Your sister said he was a traveler."

Madelaina's surprise at seeing Ivor now turned to the shock of his question. "Did you not see him closely?" she asked. "He is—"

Ivor cut her off. "I could see a big man but little more than that," he said. "Celyn says his name is d'Einen. Trevor or Trevyn or something like it. I do not remember. *What* were you speaking of?"

That brought Madelaina great confusion. Ivor was asking who Trevyn d'Einen was? A name he could not even remember? But if he knew the man, why didn't he recognize the name?

"Trevyn d'Einen," she clarified. "Ivor, he is—"

Ivor didn't let her finish a second time. "You are not answering my question," he said angrily. "Who is this stranger? What does he want from you?"

Stranger.

Ivor called Trevyn, a man who allegedly spied for him, a stranger.

No name recognition.

Nothing.

That threw Madelaina into a world of bewilderment. She didn't understand any of it. But a few moments of puzzlement gave way to the realization that Ivor didn't know whom she had been talking to. Not only did he not recognize the name, but he said he'd gotten a glimpse of a big man and made no mention or recognizing the features. He didn't know him.

That could only mean one thing.

Trevyn, as he called himself, had been lying.

Realization hit her like a hammer. Her first reaction was to blurt out Trevyn's lies and tell Ivor what had happened, but she stopped herself just in time. She didn't want to see Trevyn hurt, which was exactly what Ivor would do—go after him and hurt him.

But then the speculation came.

Trevyn seemed to know an awful lot about Ivor. He knew about the politics and he knew the region. He knew everything. That could only mean one thing—that Trevyn was an English spy. Trailing him to The Narth had been her biggest clue, but, fool that she was, she'd let him convince her otherwise. He was part of the English contingent, an Englishman who spoke perfect Welsh. When she'd asked him what his business was at The Narth, he'd never given her a straight answer because he knew if he did, his lies would unravel.

He *had* to be a spy.

God, she felt stupid.

But she also felt strangely protective.

"He… he is a cousin to a smithy in town," she said, lying as she went because she had to think of something quickly. "He came to town yesterday looking for something to ease a burn. His skin. Something for his skin, I think. I introduced him to my father because of it."

She stammered through that explanation, praying that Ivor would believe her. She didn't even believe it because, to her, she sounded like she was struggling her way through an excuse that hardly made any sense. She held her breath as Ivor mulled over her explanation.

"Then why did he come back?" he demanded. "What were you speaking of out there?"

She turned to look at the door as if she could see the street beyond and, consequently, Trevyn. "The salve my father gave him did not work well," she said. "He came back to ask if there was something else."

"Then you should have let him speak to your father," he said. "The Bryn should know better than to allow his daughter to speak with strangers."

"My father did not like the look of him," she said, suddenly fearful that Ivor might ask The Bryn about this salve-needing cousin of the smithies. "You know my father thinks the smithies are a band of outlaws who charge people too much for their services. The fact that this man is a cousin to them has caused my father to think poorly of him. If you do not wish to see me in a world of trouble, you will not tell my father that he came back tonight. Promise me."

Ivor waved her off. "You worry too much."

"*Promise me.*"

"I promise," he said irritably. "But where *is* your father?"

"He is tending Old Adda."

Ivor rolled his eyes. "Old Adda has been dying for the past ten years," he said. But he sighed heavily—apparently close to believing what she had told him, because his anger seemed to ease. "You should not have spoken to him alone, you know."

Madelaina nodded quickly. "I know," she said. "But you know that Celyn does not speak to men at all, and most especially not strangers, so there was no one else. And you… When in the world did you get back to the village? You know there is a new army of English at The Narth. They arrived two days ago."

She was trying to turn the subject away from her and away from Trevyn. Much to her relief, Ivor was easily manipulated this night. He was weary and perhaps not mentally able to do more verbal battle with her than he already had. He yawned and plopped himself down in the nearest chair.

"I heard about the arrival of Henry's army," he said. "Fud has been in town. He saw them."

Madelaina moved toward him anxiously. "Then you should not be here," she said. "They've not come to town yet, but it is only a matter of time. You must return to Pentwyn."

He eyed her. "I was thinking you could come with me."

The mood between them abruptly changed. It went from his anger and her pleading to his hopeful tone and her outrage with his rather improper question.

She scowled at him.

"I will *not* come with you," she said. "What a terrible thing to ask, Ivor. Me? Return with you to a fortress full of men? You must think very little of me to ask such a thing."

He was on his feet again, now apologetic. "I did not mean it the way it sounded," he said. "I meant… I meant as my wife."

Madelaina's eyes widened. "Your *wife*?" she said, incredulous. "Ivor, I will *not* have this conversation with you. And in front of Dai! What are you thinking?"

A faint knock on the shop door caught her attention as Ivor sank into his chair, sorry he'd even brought the subject up. As he hung his head, turning to the food that was on the table, Madelaina opened the door to the shop and walked through it, going to the front door. It was dark outside, so she couldn't really see who it was, but she assumed it was her father, returning from Old Adda's bedside, so she unbolted the door and opened it.

"I'm afraid I have something that belongs to you."

The man she knew as Trevyn was standing in the doorway, his eyes glittering at her and a smile lurking on his lips as he pointed to the black dog at his side. Grasping the mutt by the neck, he pushed into the apothecary shop, pulling the dog with him.

"I was down to the smithy stalls when I realized he was following me," he said. "Would you mind tying him up so he will not follow me? I would hate for him to become lost or injured. It is dark out tonight."

Madelaina didn't even know what to say at the sight of him. She was stunned, actually. Stunned speechless. All she could think of was Ivor in the room next door and this man… this *spy*… standing in front of her.

"I… I can keep him with me," she managed to stammer. "I did not realize he was gone."

Trevyn grinned, looking damn sexy in the dim light. "He

has a special talent for finding me," he said. "I must smell good. Do I smell good?"

"I would not know."

The words didn't come from Madelaina, but from someone else standing in the doorway to the living quarters. Both Madelaina and her visitor turned to see Ivor as he came out into the apothecary shop, his dark gaze riveted to Trevyn.

In fact, Trevyn seemed quite surprised to see him.

"My apologies," he said to Madelaina. "I did not know you had a guest. I should not have entered, but I wanted to make sure the dog was remanded to your custody."

"You were not interrupting," Madelaina said. She was caught in a horrifically tense situation so she did the only thing she could do. She made introductions, as if nothing was amiss.

"Trevyn, this is Ivor ap Yestin," she said. "Ivor, this is Trevyn. D'Einen is the last name, I believe. He is a cousin to one of the smithies, though quite honestly, I do not know which one. I never asked."

Trevyn had a look on his face that suggested he was bewildered, quite briefly, but immediately he realized the gravity of the situation. To his credit, he didn't falter in words or action.

"The smithy named Jonas," he said, throwing his thumb in the direction of the road heading south. "He is a cousin on my mother's side."

Ivor's face was like stone. "How is your burn?"

Madelaina spoke to Trevyn. "I told him you came here for salve for your burn," she said. "And you came back again because you needed something else. I am sorry I could not be of much help tonight. You must return tomorrow and ask my father, as I told you."

Things were happening very quickly, and the situation

could deteriorate in the blink of an eye, but Trevyn didn't appear nervous or edgy in the least. If anything, he seemed to relax, because he smiled weakly at Ivor.

"I am not a smithy by trade," he said, rubbing a spot on his palm, perhaps a spot that had been burned. "I am a man who raises and sells horses, but I should have known better than to touch a hot hammer. My mother used to put butter on burns to ease them, but I thought The Bryn would have something else. I am sorry I came so late. I truly did not mean to interrupt anything."

Ivor was looking him over quite closely. "Where are you from?"

"Dovey Valley."

Ivor's eyebrows lifted slightly. "Then you are far from home."

"I was seeing a man about a horse down in Chepstow. I am on my way home now."

"Did you buy the horse?"

Trevyn shook his head. "I did not," he said. Then he tilted his head in the direction of The Narth. "But I am certain the English have all manner of good horses. I should just steal one of theirs."

Ivor stared at him a moment before the corners of his mouth twitched. "You are a brave man."

"Or a stupid one."

Suddenly, Dai was in their midst. He went straight for Trevyn, shoving the top of a short blade into his back and ordering him to raise his arms. Trevyn did, without hesitation, and Dai searched him for a weapon. All he came up with was a small dagger and a purse with some coin.

"He's not armed," Dai said to Ivor. "Put your arms down, man."

Trevyn complied, but he seemed distinctly displeased with what had just happened. "You could have asked me if I was carrying a weapon," he said to Dai. "I would have told you."

Dai sheathed his short sword. "We can never be too careful, big man," he said. "Ivor is a prince and I protect him."

Trevyn had been friendly with Ivor, but he was distinctly less friendly with Dai. "Then he should leave the village, because The Narth is crawling with English," he said. "It is not safe for him here."

"What do you know about the English at The Narth?" Ivor asked.

Trevyn tore his gaze away from Dai. "Only what I've seen and heard," he said. "And I've heard about you, too."

Ivor nodded faintly. "Then you know what happened here not long ago."

"I know."

"Who is your allegiance to?"

"Llewelyn."

"Have you been to battle with him?"

"If he calls for men, I answer if I can."

"You have the look of a warrior."

"Mayhap in my youth I was passionate enough," Trevyn said. "But these days are devoted to horses. Better money in it."

Madelaina, who had been watching the exchange with great trepidation, thought she needed to move the men along. She wasn't sure when her father would be home and didn't want him walking in on this little scene. So far, Ivor only thought Trevyn was a customer of her father's potions, but any further conversation might change that opinion.

She had to get Trevyn out of there.

"Ivor," she said, "there is food waiting for you and Dai, so do not let Celyn's efforts go to waste. Go eat. Trevyn, we will bid you a good evening. Thank you for bringing Arthur back to me."

Trevyn took his cue.

"Thank you for your assistance," he told her as he headed for the door, pausing before he opened it to look at Ivor. "It has been an honor to meet you, great lord. You stand for the strength of Wales. You live with dignity. I shall not forget this day when I met a prince of our people."

With that, he was through the door and out into the night. Madelaina quickly closed the door and bolted it, still holding on to her dog as she herded Ivor and Dai back into the kitchen, where the cooling food was waiting for them.

God, what a night, she thought. She'd never been so shaken in her entire life. But she was also thinking something else.

Trevyn, who are *you?*

CHAPTER FIFTEEN

K ENT MADE IT back to The Narth in record time. He tore through the gatehouse, through the bailey, and into the keep. The great room was empty, but the small chamber off the entry was not.

Jareth was there.

"He's here!" Kent said as he burst in. "Ivor is in the village!"

Jareth had been hunched over a Welsh dispatch, trying to decipher the writing, but Kent's shouting revelation had him on his feet.

"Did you hear rumor or did you see him?" he asked.

Kent was winded from having run so fast, so far. "I saw him," he said, trying to catch his breath. "I spoke to him. He did not recognize me."

Jareth could see that the encounter had Kent rattled. "When did you last see the man?" he asked. "How old were you?"

Kent took a deep breath, trying to still his excitement because that wasn't usual with him. He was, on the whole, quite unflappable.

But the sight of Ivor had him going.

"I'd seen six summers," he said. "We were very young.

Truth be told, if someone hadn't introduced us, I would not have known him on sight."

"I would have," Treyton said, pushing in through the open door. "I'd know that bastard anywhere. Did you see him?"

Kent turned to Treyton and Britt, just entering the keep. "Aye," he said. "I saw him in the apothecary shop. You did not see him enter?"

Treyton shook his head. "Nay," he said. "We did not see anyone enter but you, but we also didn't have a good vantage point of the rear of the establishment."

"Then he must have come in that way," Kent said. "However er he entered, he was in the shop."

"Then we capture him," Treyton said firmly. "We swarm the apothecary's shop and we take him alive. I will punish him in place of the men he refused to turn over to me."

Kent could see how distressed Treyton was. The man finally had justice for his sister within his grasp and wanted to take it with both hands.

Take *Ivor* with both hands.

Truthfully, Kent wasn't entirely sure how he felt about that. Perhaps there was part of him that hoped Ivor had been smart enough to stay in his mountain fortress, away from the English who wanted his hide, but that was not to be. His return had put him in legitimate danger because de Russe was here for vengeance for his sister and emotions were feeding his decisions and opinions.

He wanted what he'd come for.

But Kent wasn't so sure.

"We must find Torran," he said after a moment. "This is a delicate situation, Treyton. You'll have to let someone without the emotional investment you have make this decision."

Treyton's eyes narrowed but he didn't say anything.

He didn't have to.

His expression said it all.

Treyton had just spent the past couple of hours watching the village center of Penderyn and, more specifically, watching the apothecary shop where Kent was conducting business. His task had been to watch the comings and goings and listen to conversations if he could, but it had been late enough that there were no comings, or goings, or even conversations that he could hear. People were in for the night, having their supper and going to bed. He never saw Ivor ap Yestin enter the apothecary shop, but now that he knew where the man was, he wasn't going to let this go. These men who personally served Henry wanted to debate the subject of Ivor and decide what to do about it.

But he didn't.

There was no debate.

He knew what he had to do.

In a huff, Treyton turned and left the keep, leaving Kent and Jareth and Britt. They watched the man go, knowing he was unhappy with the fact that he had no say in the issue of Ivor ap Yestin, at least nothing superseding Torran's commands, but they let him go. He was young and emotional and truly felt the needs of his family should be more important than anything else. Not that anyone really disagreed with him, but there was a larger political picture to consider.

"Where is Torran?" Kent finally asked.

Jareth pointed upward. "His chamber," he said. "I do not think the man has properly slept since we left London, so he said that he was going to lie down before supper."

"We need to wake him," Kent said. "He'll want to know."

No one could disagree.

The three of them headed to the sleeping quarter above.

☙

"HE'S IN TOWN."

Treyton wasted no time in gathering the gatehouse men to him, all of the de Russe men because Torran had put them in charge of the gatehouse. That meant Treyton had a crowd of men who had been part of the siege of The Narth, men who would like nothing better than to capture the man who had escaped them.

Treyton's grim announcement had their attention.

"Are you certain, my lord?" someone asked.

Treyton nodded firmly. "I am," he said. "And we must act now. If we cut off the head of the viper, he will no longer strike. That means we will capture ap Yestin and avenge my sister once and for all."

His men nodded eagerly and Treyton's rage was fed. Validated. They wanted what he wanted. He was back in the heat of battle, laying siege to The Narth and determined to get to the bastards who had harmed his sweet sister. Talia, a delicate lady with lovely manners who was very much in love with her Wellesbourne betrothed.

Michael Wellesbourne was an excellent knight and a decent fellow, though Treyton had heard, more than once, that he had a fondness for a baker's daughter in the village near his home. Treyton had even asked him about it, and Michael had assured him that it was a rumor dredged up by the baker and his wife, offended that they couldn't pawn their spinster daughter off on the local lord's son.

Treyton had taken him at his word.

Every man had their troubles. Treyton had been around long enough to know that and the rumors didn't affect his respect for the man. The marriage between his sister and the House of Wellesbourne would be yet another marriage between the two families, cementing what was already a strong familial alliance. Treyton had vowed to Michael that he would find and punish the Welsh for what they did to Talia, and although Michael wanted to join him, he preferred to spend his time at Talia's bedside should she awaken.

Treyton could understand that.

Therefore, he was determined to punish those responsible for his sister's ambush, and every de Russe man there knew it. Torran de Serreaux had put Treyton and his men in charge of the gatehouse, so here they were, ready to slip off into town on foot because the village was just that close. And the lure of Ivor was just that great. Gathering horses would attract attention and there were plenty of Henry's men around that would see it, so they were prepared to close the distance on foot.

"We are ready, my lord," the man closest to him said. "What will you have us do?"

Treyton looked around. He had about five hundred men with him total, but only a third of those men were at the gatehouse tonight. Everyone else was sleeping or simply off duty. Rather than summon the entire group, he was willing to work with what he had. He couldn't take all of them lest Henry's men grow suspicious.

"He is at the apothecary's shop," he said. "He seems to be alone. Who was with me when we raided the village after my sister was injured?"

Several hands went up, including the man who had asked the question. Treyton pointed to that man.

"Gather everyone who was on the raid," he said. "Enough to total fifty men. The rest we will leave here at the gatehouse because I do not want Henry's men trying to stop us. The gatehouse is our domain, and if they believe it is still properly manned, we will not draw their attention. Do you understand?"

The man, named Rufus, nodded. "Aye, my lord," he said. "I will form the group bound for the village right away."

As the man dashed off, Treyton hissed at the other men to spread out and act normally. He knew that at least two of the Guard of Six were around. He'd seen them prowling the bailey, getting to know the place, but the problem was that he had no idea where those two had gone. He did, however, know that de Bermingham and Payton-Forrester were overseeing the kitchens and hall and other domestic duties, so they wouldn't be anywhere near the gatehouse. He was going to have to hope that the two rogue Guard of Six men were out of sight of the gatehouse when he made his move.

And he intended to make it immediately.

The longer the wait, the more antsy he became. There was no telling how long Ivor would actually remain at the apothecary's shop, so Treyton didn't want to delay. He wanted to get to the man before he vanished again. As he stood there and twitched anxiously, Rufus informed him that the men were ready to go.

And go they went.

But not unnoticed.

☓

HE DIDN'T WANT to be in the kitchens anymore.

Orion was on the western portion of the wall, away from the kitchen and smoke and that slovenly cook who kept tasting everything he cooked with the same spoon and then belching loudly enough to strip the mortar off stone. He farted, too, driving Orion out of the kitchens when Bennet was brave enough to stay. He didn't trust the cook, he said, so he was going to watch every move the man made to ensure Henry's troops wouldn't be poisoned.

That had been about an hour ago. Orion had been watching the road that ran adjacent to Penderyn, but there hadn't been much activity on it. He could see the village from his position, the silver skeins of smoke trailing up from cooking fires as the night deepened and a hush settled over the land. His position also afforded him the ability to see part of the road leading up to the gatehouse, so he saw distinctly when Kent returned and two more men after him, one of whom was Treyton de Russe. He didn't know who the second man was, but he would find out.

It seemed that Kent and Treyton were having all the fun.

Orion didn't like being kept out of the chain of command and was positive he'd never forgive de Serreaux for assigning him to domestic duties. He even toyed with making a formal complaint to Henry about it, but that probably wouldn't be the best move. The Guard of Six could do no wrong in the eyes of the king, and even Orion knew that. Still, the urge to complain was strong, but it was something he was going to have to forget. He may have been petty, but he wasn't vindictive.

He would just have to suffer.

"I've not been up here yet. The view is remarkable."

Orion turned around to see Bennet coming up behind him. "It is," he agreed. "It is peaceful, too. It is difficult to believe there was a siege here not long ago."

Bennet noted part of the wall that had been knocked out by

a projectile. "There is damage, but I've seen worse," he said. "I agree with you, however. The place is surprisingly unmarked."

Orion simply nodded, knowing that Bennet had not come up here to make idle conversation. He'd come to the wall for a purpose, and Orion was willing to acknowledge that.

"I apologize for abandoning you in the kitchens," he said.

"Nay, you do not."

"Nay, I do not," Orion agreed, hanging his head. "If that man farted one more time, I was either going to push him into the hearth or suffocate, so truly, I left to save my life and his."

Bennet snorted. "How noble of you."

"I am a noble man."

Bennet sighed, leaning on the wall next to Orion. "You keep telling me that," he said. "So far, all I've seen is a complainer and a man prone to think he is better than everyone else. But I am certain that noble man is buried underneath all of that bluster. Hopefully I will see him before I am dead, or my time spent with you will have been wasted."

Orion burst into soft laughter. "Do you not like me just a little?"

"Not even a little."

Orion's laughter grew. "Cheppy, how can you say such things to me?" he said, but it wasn't really a question. More like another complaint. "I suppose I shall have to like you enough for the both of us."

Bennet grunted. "Monty, when you say things like that, it makes me want to push you over this wall."

The hated nicknames were introduced once again. The last time that happened, the mood between them had gone cold. The potential was there for the situation to repeat because they had not addressed that little skirmish since it happened. They'd spent the afternoon together, for the most part, and no mention of it had come up.

But it did now.

Now, neither one of them could ignore it.

"You know why the name you have selected for me does not please me?" Orion said as he continued to gaze out over the darkened landscape. "I had no choice in serving de Montfort. I hated every minute of it. I did not agree with his ambition, but because I was sworn to serve his wife, I was given no choice. Had I been given a choice, I would have fought for Henry and Edward. Hearing you call me by that man's name reminds me of a failure I could not control. No man likes to be reminded of that."

Bennet was looking over the landscape, too. He didn't say anything for a moment, mulling over Orion's honesty. He was surprised by it, frankly, because he hadn't thought the man had it in him. Orion always came across as a superficial arse, not given to anything deeper than what was on the surface, but that was evidently not true.

Perhaps his honesty earned the same thing from Bennet.

Perhaps it was time.

"Thank you for telling me," he said quietly. "You already know that I was the commander of Chepstow about twenty years ago, but what you do not know is how it ended. I was about your age, mayhap younger, and I fell in love with a woman who became pregnant with my child. I wanted to marry her, but her father refused us. In order to preserve his daughter's reputation, he told the world that I had seduced and raped her. In order for me to protect her, I did not fight back. I let the world believe what he told them. I left Chepstow in shame and I never married. I cannot marry someone else when I still love her. Therefore, calling me 'Cheppy' as you have does not bring back the fondest memories. It only reminds me of pain."

By that time, Orion was looking at him. That hint of deep feeling he'd shown with his confession was now quite obvious as Bennet confessed his own sins. Shockingly, there was a good deal of feeling in his expression.

"Forgive me, Bennet," he murmured. "I did not mean to hurt you. I will not say it again."

Bennet met his gaze. "Actually," he said slowly, "I do not mind if you do now because you have asked forgiveness. You have shown great compassion. That tells me that your heart is, indeed, noble. And a noble man should not have to serve anyone against his will. I am sorry you had to."

Orion smiled faintly. "Call me Monty if you wish," he said. "Because you are the first man I've ever told my story to who truly believed me."

"No one else has?"

"If they did, they still judge me for it."

"I do not judge you," Bennet said. "In fact, I hold you in great esteem because in spite of your feelings toward de Montfort, you still kept your vow of service. It takes a man of great honor to put his convictions aside in order to fulfill his oath."

Orion smiled weakly. "That is not something I've heard," he said. "Thank you for saying that. I am grateful."

Bennet smiled in return, but his reply was cut off when he caught sight of something over Orion's left shoulder. Orion instinctively turned around to see what had the man's attention, only to witness dozens of men pouring out of the gatehouse under the cover of darkness. One of them stood aside, pausing, directing the others to rush toward the village in different groups—and in the torchlight of the gatehouse, they could see who it was.

A big knight bearing long, dark hair.

"Is that de Russe?" Orion hissed. "What in the hell is he doing?"

Bennet moved closer to Orion, seeing what he was seeing. "I do not know," he said with concern. "But whatever it is, it cannot be good."

Together, they watched de Russe as he instructed groups of men, all of them on foot, all of them rushing into the line of trees that separated the road from the village to the southwest.

Armed men.

"Is… is he directing his men to *storm* the village?" Orion said in disbelief.

Bennet grabbed him by the arm. "Come," he said. "We must see what is happening. And where is de Serreaux? We must make sur he is aware of this."

Orion was already on the move. "Find him," he said. "I will see what de Russe is up to."

They were moving down the tower turret, taking the narrow stairs quickly and emerging into the bailey. Their attention was on the gatehouse, where there still seemed to be quite a few de Russe soldiers, standing about as if nothing was amiss. Orion started to move toward the gatehouse but Bennet stopped him.

"Wait," he said, grasping the man's arm. "If something is going on, it will be you against two dozen de Russe soldiers, so do not go alone."

Out of the corner of his eye, Bennet caught sight of a pair of Henry's soldiers, men coming from the direction of the hall. Bennet whistled loudly between his teeth, motioning the men toward him.

They came on the run.

"Where are Henry's knights?" Bennet asked calmly but quickly.

The men pointed back toward the hall where the soldiers supped. "Three of them are in the hall with Sir Stefan," the soldier with a red beard said. "I don't know where the others are, my lord."

"Find them," Bennet said, his voice smooth and deep in command. "Tell them that de Russe is sending his armed soldiers into the village and the Six must come immediately. From what we saw, about three or four dozen de Russe soldiers went toward the village, so tell Sir Torran immediately. *Go.*"

The soldiers fled as Bennet returned his focus to the gate-house. "Now you may go see what de Russe is up to," he told Orion. "But I am going with you."

Orion put his hand on the hilt of his magnificent broad-sword, a weapon that he was never separated from because it was so expensive. "Then let us find out," he said ominously.

They did.

CHAPTER SIXTEEN

I T HAD BEEN a quiet evening until that point.

That horrible, cataclysmic point.

That was when everything seemed to explode.

Doors, windows, and walls. Pieces of wood and stone were flying everywhere. Seated at the table in her father's kitchen over the remains of a good meal, Madelaina screamed with terror when armed men burst into the cottage. A section of a door hit her in the back, nearly knocking her silly. But she caught the flash of a blade, and the first thing she did was dive under the table to protect herself.

But Ivor and Dai didn't.

They were armed.

It was surprising how tough two Welshmen were against two dozen or more English soldiers. Madelaina held on to the table leg as the table itself was buffeted around and, eventually, someone broke it. They crashed through the top of it, nearly squashing her, but she managed to scream and escape, darting into the door that led to the bedchambers. Celyn was right there, however, and she smashed into her sister before demanding they close and lock the door.

Terrified, they had the door shut and bolted, listening to the battle in the kitchen.

"What is happening?" Celyn asked, weeping.

Madelaina shook her head. "English soldiers," she said, her voice quivering. "They must have come down from The Narth. But why…?"

She suddenly came to a stop. *Why* did they come down at this particular time?

Why, indeed.

Could it be because Trevyn, whom she knew to have lied about being a scout for Ivor, had run there and told them?

The only answer she could come up with was… aye. He had.

"Oh, God," she breathed, closing her eyes in realization. "*I* did this. I think I did this."

Celyn had no idea what she was talking about and, given the noise on the other side of the door, didn't much care. Madelaina could be dramatic at times, and that was all she attributed the comment to.

Until the bolted door suddenly collapsed as several men crashed through it.

Screaming, the women were pushed further back into the sleeping chamber where The Bryn slept, with a secondary chamber next to it where the women slept. The truth was that they didn't have anywhere to go at this point except the second chamber with a door that didn't bolt, so Madelaina picked up a broken piece of door, grabbed her sister, and backed up against the wall. If anyone came close, she was going to brain them.

But she never had the chance. At this point, the fighting had ground to a halt because Ivor had been knocked unconscious when he came crashing through the door with four or five soldiers on top of him. Madelaina and Celyn watched the soldiers haul the man up, dragging him back into the kitchen, and Madelaina followed. Celyn was right behind her, trying to get her to come away, but Madelaina wouldn't. She watched the soldiers lay him on the kitchen floor next to Dai, who had blood all over him.

Madelaina gasped.

"What did you do to him?" she said angrily, in their language, as she rushed to Dai's side. "Where is the blood coming from?"

A big knight with shoulder-length dark hair was standing a few feet away, watching her. "Who are you, lass?" he asked.

Madelaina found the source of the blood, a big puncture wound near Dai's liver. "My name is Madelaina," she said, quickly looking to her sister back in the doorway. "Get me something to stop the blood. Hurry!"

Celyn disappeared. Madelaina put her hand over the wound, trying to stanch the flow of blood, as the big knight came around to Ivor's side, looking down at her.

"This man is Ivor ap Yestin," he said, pointing to Dai. "Who is that?"

She'd started to answer when there was suddenly another big fight out in her garden. She couldn't have known that it was the men Ivor had brought with him to Penderyn, men who had been fanned out in the village before word got around that a crisis was happening at the apothecary shop. So they came running, in a group, straight into a horde of armed soldiers. Somewhere, Arthur was barking, which sent Madelaina into a panic.

"Please," she begged the big knight. "Please do not hurt my dog. He will not bite, but he barks."

The man's dark eyes lingered on her for a moment before he shouted orders out to the men fighting in the garden, telling them to leave the dog unharmed. There was more fighting and grunting and barking until someone came flying in through the rear window and hit the floor hard. Meanwhile, Celyn rushed out into a room full of strange men, bearing rags and other things. She was terrified of men in general, so for her to come forward to help was a testament to her truly kind and helpful nature. She sat down next to her sister and began to help her as the fighting dragged to a halt.

"More dead Welshmen out there," said an English soldier who came in through the garden door. "What do you want me to do with them?"

The knight looked up from the women tending the injured man. "How many?" he asked.

"At least seven," the soldier said. "We managed to capture two, but the remainder ran."

"Put the dead on the street," the knight said. "Let the villagers see what happens when they hide men who nearly killed my sister."

As the soldier ducked out, Madelaina's head came up, and she looked at the knight. "They are not rubbish, you know," she said, her voice quivering. "They were brave men, like you."

The knight cocked a dark eyebrow. "They are not like me."

"They love their country, like you," she said. "They are defending it, as you defend yours. That makes them more like you than you think. They do not deserve to be left on the street."

His eyes narrowed. "For what they did to my sister, they deserve worse."

"What happened to your sister?"

He regarded her for a moment. "My sister is about your age," he said. "She was traveling home and was attacked by men that we tracked back to this village. Back to The Narth. Ap Yestin would not turn those men over to us to face justice, so we sacked the castle. We had good reason for what we did, not that I am obliged to explain it to you."

By this time, Celyn was trying to shush her sister, but Madelaina ignored her. "I am sorry for your sister," she said. "Will she recover?"

"The physic does not think so."

Madelaina was genuinely distressed to hear that. She looked around, at Dai and at Ivor, who was starting to come around, and then back to the knight.

"I know these men, great lord," she said earnestly. "You do not know me, but my name is Madelaina. My father is the town apothecary. We are simple people and the men at The Narth are not killers. They hardly venture out at all."

The knight shrugged. "Be that as it may, *someone* went out," he said. "They beat my sister and stole her valuables. We found her rings here in the village—they had been given to the merchants to sell."

"Merchants? In Penderyn?"

"Aye," the knight said, but he was evidently finished speaking with her because he turned to the man beside him. "Take the bodies of the dead over to the church. I may not leave them in the street, but the message is still clear. Woe to those who protect the men who harmed my sister."

With that, he turned away, directing his men, telling them to clear out of the shop and take the prisoners back to The Narth. That meant that Ivor was yanked off the floor, still only half conscious, and two men pushed Madelaina and Celyn out of the way so they could take Dai. But their actions came to a halt when two more knights entered the small space, weapons drawn.

"*What* did you do, de Russe?" a knight with blond hair and pale blue eyes asked angrily, looking at the busted-out chamber. "What happened here?"

Treyton held his ground. "What does it look like?" he said. "I've captured Ivor ap Yestin and he will face justice for what his men did. Stay out of this, Orion. This is none of your affair."

"Stop." The older knight next to Orion held out his hand to prevent anyone from moving another inch. His intense gaze was on Treyton. "You have made a complicated situation worse."

"You will stay out of it, too, de Bermingham," Treyton said. "This does not concern you."

"I beg to differ," Bennet said. "What do you think is going to happen when you take ap Yestin back to England with you, or wherever you decide to put the man on trial? Do you think the Welsh princes, especially Llewelyn, are going to sit by and do nothing?"

Treyton's jaw twitched. "I am taking the men who assaulted my sister."

"You are taking a Welsh warlord to face justice, not the men who actually harmed your sister," Bennet said strongly, which wasn't like him. He was usually consummately cool in any situation. "Think about what you're doing, man. You are starting a war on the marches that may sweep everyone and everything. This situation is bigger than you and your need for vengeance."

Treyton took a long, deep breath. "Get out of my way."

Bennet didn't move. "Fight me and you'll have Henry down

around you," he said. "If you think you are man enough to start a war with your own king, then by all means, start the war. But you'll leave your share of blood on the ground, I assure you."

He meant it. Bennet was a big man with a big sword, but de Russe was also a big man with a big sword. But he was young and reckless, which put the odds in Bennet's favor. As the two men sized each other up and Treyton tried to figure out how to respond, Orion pushed his way between them and shoved back one of the men holding Ivor by the face. When the man tried to fight back, Orion slapped him.

After that, the fight was on.

Once again, Madelaina and Celyn were caught in the middle of something brutal and dangerous. Madelaina shrieked and grabbed her sister, yanking the woman over to the wall to get her out of the battle zone. She tried to escape, but there were men grabbing her, restraining her, and above it all, she could hear the knight called de Russe telling his men to take everyone prisoner.

Even the women.

She screamed, and Celyn screamed, but Celyn also fainted. She slithered to the ground as Madelaina tried to beat the English soldiers off her. It seemed like a losing battle, and she was genuinely terrified that she was going to end up a prisoner of the English.

But then something strange happened.

The older knight, called de Bermingham, was suddenly there, dispatching the English soldiers that were grabbing at Celyn. His sword made quick work of them and, abruptly, he scooped Celyn into his arms and grabbed at Madelaina, telling her to take hold of his tunic and follow him. For lack of a better reaction, because he seemed to want to help, Madelaina did as ordered and he slipped out into her garden, which had been torn up by the English soldiers. The knight continued out into the alleyway, rushing away from the fight and away from those who were trying to take the women captive. He ran into someone else's garden, down between two houses, and ended up on another small road.

Then he came to a halt.

"Where is the nearest inn?" he asked Madelaina. "One that has rooms to let."

Madelaina was bordering on frightened, confused tears. Sniffling, she pointed toward the east. "Th-that way," she stammered. "The Moth and the Flame. Why?"

"Because you are going to hide there."

Madelaina didn't argue. The man was obviously trying to help her. He seemed determined to. Leaving the fight behind them, they rushed down the road to the tavern with the moth burned into a board over the doorway. The knight kicked the door open and entered the half-empty common room. But his sharp action of busting through the door brought everyone to a startled pause.

He spoke to the first serving woman he came across.

"You," he said. "Where is the innkeeper?"

The woman pointed to the rear. "There," she said nervously. "Kitchens!"

The knight continued on his quest, heading toward the rear and nearly plowing into a man wearing a big leather apron as he emerged from the kitchen.

"Are you the innkeeper?" the knight asked.

The man nodded. "I am," he said, slicking back what hair he had on his head, which wasn't much. "What do ye want?"

"A chamber for these women," the knight said. "One that is

clean. And bring them regular meals for as long as they stay."

The man scratched his head. "I've only got two rooms," he said. "The big room is empty, but it'll cost ye."

"How much?"

"Two shillings a day."

"I'll pay you for five days," the knight said. "Meals included?"

"Aye."

"Where is the room?"

The man pointed to the very rear of the inn. "Back there," he said. "Do they want food now?"

The knight looked at Madelaina, who shook her head. "Nay," he said. "Just sleep for tonight."

The innkeeper motioned him on, and the knight took the women down the corridor, to the last door. Assuming that was the chamber, because the innkeeper wasn't really specific, he had Madelaina open the door.

In they went.

It was dark and cold inside. There was a rather large bed shoved against the wall and the knight gently laid Celyn down upon it. As Madelaina went to her sister to see how she was faring, the knight turned for the door. He had a comrade back at the apothecary shop who found himself in a fight and intended to quickly return, but on second thought, he couldn't just leave the women like this. They were cold and frightened. He turned to look at them, compassion in his expression.

Nay, he couldn't just leave.

Hunting around, he found kindling and a flint and started a fire in the hearth. As he blew on the sparks to grow the blaze, Madelaina watched him from her perch next to her sister's head.

"Why did you do this?" she asked. "Do not misunderstand me—I am grateful. But I do not understand why you did it."

His focus remained on the fire. "Because you were about to be taken prisoner," he said. "I do not think you want to become a prisoner of the English."

"*You* are English."

"But I am not seeking vengeance like the other knight was."

"Is he from The Narth?"

"Aye."

"Are you?"

"I am."

"What is your name?"

"Bennet de Bermingham, my lady."

Madelaina fell silent, looking to her sister now that some light was beginning to fill the chamber. Celyn was starting to stir, and Madelaina put a gentle hand on her forehead as the woman's eyes rolled open. She blinked, staring at the ceiling, before her eyes moved to Madelaina.

"What happened?" she asked hoarsely. "Where am I?"

"At The Moth and the Flame," Madelaina said quietly. "This kind knight brought us here to escape the English, who wished to take us prisoner. Do you remember?"

Celyn looked at her as if she had no idea what her sister was talking about, but then her eyes began to widen.

"My God," she breathed. "I thought I saw… I saw…"

"Who?"

Celyn swallowed hard, her expression seemingly one of hesitation. "Someone I used to know long ago," she finally said. "It does not matter. We must go home."

"We cannot," Madelaina said. "They wanted to take us prisoner along with Ivor and Dai. As I told you, this very kind knight brought us here to hide. We must stay here until the English return to The Narth."

"What about The Bryn?"

Madelaina shook her head. "I do not know," she said. "He will probably be with Old Adda all night. Hopefully, anyway. I can go to Adda's cottage and tell him not to come home yet."

Over near the hearth, the knight stood up. Celyn caught the movement out of the corner of her eye and turned to look at him about the same time he turned to look at her. It took Celyn all of a split second to realize who her sister's "kind knight" was.

"Sweet Jesus," she breathed, propping herself up on her elbows. "It… it really *is* you. I did not dream it."

Bennet came away from the hearth, his gaze riveted to her. "Nay," he murmured. "You did not dream it."

The sound of his voice had Celyn bursting into quiet tears. Her hand covered her mouth. "You are here," she wept softly. "You are truly here. How… why? I do not understand why you are here."

Bennet was fairly emotional himself, unusual for the normally composed man. "I am with Henry's contingent," he said hoarsely. "Believe me, it is purely by chance. But when I saw de Russe leave The Narth and head toward the village with armed men, I went after him. The fact that he ended up in your home… I did not know it was your home until I saw you there."

Celyn sat up all the way, swinging her legs over the side of the bed. She was still weeping softly. "It is so good to see you," she said. "Not a day has gone by that I have not thought of you and hoped you were well."

He took a few steps closer to the bed, his gaze never leaving her face. "I am well," he said. "Are you?"

Celyn nodded, suddenly catching sight of Madelaina sitting

next to her. Madelaina was looking at her sister with great bewilderment, and seeing her expression brought more tears. Celyn took the young woman's hand, holding it tightly as she returned her attention to Bennet.

"This is Madelaina," she sobbed. "I see you in her. I have always wanted to tell you that."

Bennet's gaze left Celyn, drifting over to Madelaina, who clearly had no idea what anyone was talking about.

"You never told her?" he said.

Celyn shook her head, looking at Madelaina and seeing the increasing puzzlement in the woman's features. "Nay," she said to her sister. "There was no reason to tell you the truth."

Madelaina frowned. "Tell me what truth?" she said. "*What* is happening here? Celyn, do you know this knight?"

Celyn was looking at Bennet when she answered. "Aye," she murmured. "I do."

"*How* do you know him?"

Celyn simply wept. She couldn't even speak. Watching the situation unfold, Bennet took another timid step forward. He could get a good look at Madelaina now, who was positively exquisite. Such a beautiful girl. And he could also get a good look at Celyn, who had only grown lovelier over the years, as far as he was concerned.

As lovely as she had been twenty years ago.

"I do not think you have a choice but to tell her now," he said to Celyn. "Unfortunately, I cannot stay. I left my colleague back in your cottage in the midst of a fight, so I must go back and help him. But I will return, I swear it."

Celyn wiped at her face, nodding. "Of course you must help him," she said. "And… thank you for helping us as well. I do not know what would have become of us had you not acted swiftly."

Bennet was clearly torn about leaving, but Orion was in danger and he had to get back to him. But he took a moment to look at the woman who should have been his wife and the daughter they had created together out of love.

He could have stayed there forever.

"Do not leave this chamber," he said, forcing himself to turn for the door. "I will return, but do not leave."

Neither woman said anything. Madelaina was looking at Celyn, who had her face buried in a hand, weeping quietly. They heard the door close softly but didn't bother looking over to see if the knight was truly gone. Right now, it was a pivotal moment between them. Madelaina could feel the weighty mood as she gazed at Celyn.

"Tell me what he was talking about, Celyn," she said. "What haven't you told me?"

Celyn took a deep breath and wiped the tears on her face, lifting her eyes to look at Madelaina. She forced a smile, reaching up to touch the young woman on the cheek.

"There was never any reason to tell you," she murmured. "The Bryn made the decision as to how things should be, and, fool that I am, I let him. I let him ruin my life. And I've let you live a lie because that is what he wanted."

"What lie?"

Celyn sighed faintly. "Long ago, when I was about your age, I met a man and fell in love," she said. "You know I do not speak of my younger years, Maddie. That is because it is too difficult for me to do so. I loved him so very much. We wanted to marry. But The Bryn forbade us."

Madelaina's brow furrowed as she tried to put the pieces of

the puzzle together. "Why did he do that?"

"Because my love was English."

Madelaina's eyebrows lifted in surprise. "Saesneg?"

Celyn nodded. "He was the commander at Chepstow Castle," she said. "We were in Chepstow because The Bryn and Mother wished to visit a man who sold ingredients from all over the world. He was a merchant from Calais. I met my love that day because he was in town to buy a sword. We took one look at each other, and I swear to you that I heard angels sing. There was an instant attraction, and after two days, I knew I loved him. We were mad for one another. You've often asked me why I have never wed and I've never given you an answer. Now, I will tell you—I've never wed because I've never stopped loving my knight. The Bryn may have stopped our wedding, but he could not kill what was in my heart."

Madelaina was listening with growing suspicion. The man that was just in this chamber—the English knight—seemed to know what Celyn knew. His words were providing Madelaina with clues.

You never told her?

Realization dawned.

"It was him," she said, gesturing toward the chamber door. "That knight. It was *him*."

Celyn nodded, tears popping into her eyes again. "Aye," she whispered tightly. "It was him. He is your father, Maddie."

Madelaina's features twisted with confusion. "*Him?*" she said, aghast. "He… he and our mother were…?"

Celyn shook her head quickly. "Nay, not that," she said. "The woman you've always believed to be your mother is, in fact, your grandmother. And The Bryn is your grandfather, not your father. I am not your sister, but your mother."

Madelaina's eyes widened and she stumbled off the bed, staring at Celyn in horror. "*You* are my mother?" she gasped. "But… but that's not possible!"

Celyn nodded. "It is and I am," she said, watching Madelaina struggle against an emotional breakdown. "I became pregnant and we planned to marry, but The Bryn discovered our plans and stopped us. He petitioned the Earl of Pembroke, because Chepstow was part of his properties, and had Bennet sent away by telling him a lie—he told the earl that Bennet had raped me, which was absolutely not true. But the earl believed The Bryn and Bennet was sent away in shame, his career in ruins. When people in the village realized I was with child, The Bryn told all of them that an English knight had raped me, so I was forgiven. The knight was not. When you were born, we felt it best to raise you as my sister, not my daughter, for your sake. Even though many in the village knew of the pregnancy, they managed to keep it a secret. You never heard that you were my daughter, did you?"

Madelaina's eyes were like saucers, her hand over her mouth in shock. "Once," she breathed. "When I was very young. A boy teased me about it, but that was the only time. And I remember that his mother severely punished him. I… I never thought any more about it. Mayhap I should have."

Celyn watched her anxiously. "The people who knew of my pregnancy kept it secret for fear of The Bryn, I'm sure," she said. "He is an apothecary and could easily poison their food or their water. So they believed. But The Bryn used to be a warrior, long ago, before he fell in love with Mother, who was also English. Did you know that?"

Madelaina wasn't sure what she knew. Her mind was so muddled that she could hardly think. "Mother said she was born in Pembrokeshire," she said.

"To an English family," Celyn said. "Her father served William Marshal."

More revelations. Madelaina's hand came away from her mouth and she sank onto a stool, dazed.

"All of this does not seem possible," she said. "I… I am at a loss for words. I do not know what to say."

Celyn stood up and went to her. "Do not say anything," she said, putting her hand on Madelaina's head. "And you do not even have to address me as your mother. We may continue as we've always been, but you are old enough to know now. Old enough to understand that your real father, Bennet de Bermingham, is a son of the Earl of Louth. He was born in Ireland and he trained at the Blackchurch Guild. He is a fine man and a fine knight and what The Bryn did to him wasn't right, but he did it to spare me and to spare you. You are born of Irish nobility and Welsh royalty, Maddie. That is something to be proud of."

Madelaina looked at her. "That is what you think?" she said. "That I am proud to be Welsh and Irish? I do not care about that in the least. I feel as if my entire life has been a lie. You must let me come to terms with it before you go around telling me how proud I should be of my lineage."

With that, she turned away from Celyn, unable and unwilling to look at her for the moment. There were a great many things rolling around in her head, not the least of which was the events of the evening. So much had happened, so much out of her control, and she was struggling with it. A man she didn't know was evidently her father, and the woman she believed to be her sister was her mother.

It was overwhelming.

Feeling sick and disoriented, she pulled the little stool over to the hearth and sat there, staring into the flames and pondering the very sharp turn her life had just taken. She could have called Celyn a liar, but she knew the woman didn't lie. But in this case, she'd certainly kept the truth from her. More than that, nothing she'd known was the same, nor would it be ever again. To top everything off, the man she knew as Trevyn wasn't Trevyn at all, but someone who had flattered her and been kind to her, enough so that she'd let her guard down for him. Perhaps that had been a mistake.

Nothing was as she thought any longer.

God help her, the entire world was on its end.

Putting her face in her hands, Madelaina wept softly.

CHAPTER SEVENTEEN

"MY MOTHER HITS harder than you do!"

Orion emphasized that statement with a boot to the face and the de Russe soldier went flying backward, into a wall. But there were more to take his place, and after swinging every chair, every pot, every cooking implement and even a few pitchers, Orion had run out of ammunition and resorted to kicking and punching. He had big hands and big fists, and his strikes could be devastating, but the truth was that he was simply overwhelmed with all of the de Russe soldiers. They'd been unable to remove Ivor or the wounded Welshman because Orion was giving them such a bad time, but little by little, they were wearing him down. No one wanted to draw a weapon because it would be English upon English if that was the case, and not one man in that chamber wanted to go that far.

Not even Treyton.

He was furious at Orion, who was preventing him from moving his prisoner. He wasn't exactly defending the man; he was simply creating chaos. He served Torran, and subsequently Henry, and because Torran hadn't been part of this raid to capture Ivor, Orion was putting up quite a fight.

But it didn't last for long.

Treyton was preparing to make a final move to get Orion out of the way so that he could remove Ivor when more armed men suddenly appeared. They came rushing in through the apothecary shop as well as through the rear garden, and suddenly, Treyton and his men were being swarmed. Because he saw swords, Treyton unsheathed his own weapon and soon his men were following suit. There were flashes of blades all over the dim chamber, and somewhere in the middle of it they could hear someone shouting.

"De Russe!" It was Torran. "Put the weapons away or I will have my men disarm you and your men and throw the lot of you in the vault. Do you understand me?"

Treyton had opened his mouth to reply when Bennet suddenly came crashing in through the rear of the cottage, shoving men aside and throwing punches until he got to Orion. One look at Orion's bloodied mouth and Bennet shoved his fist into the face of the nearest de Russe soldier in a blow that sent the man down to the ground, unconscious. He fell over Ivor, who had come around by this point, and Ivor groaned as the soldier's head hit him in his soft belly. Bennet was about to throw another punch when Orion threw his arms around the man from behind, trapping his arms and preventing him from fighting.

"Nay, Cheppy," he said, grinning with bloodied teeth. "No need to kill anyone. I'm quite all right, though I appreciate your sense of timing. I knew you'd come back for me."

Bennet was furious, struggling to calm down as Torran stepped into the chamber with Kent directly behind him. Kent saw Ivor and another man on the ground, with a limp de Russe soldier on top of him, and he yanked the soldier off and tossed the man aside. Ivor labored to sit up with Kent standing guard as Torran faced off against Treyton.

"You stupid fool," Torran growled. "You had no authority to come in here and do this."

Treyton flared. "I have every right," he said hotly. "Ivor ap Yestin is responsible for my sister's fate and I have every right to bring the man to justice."

"I told you to wait for Henry's answer," Torran said, his jaw twitching angrily. "You are creating more problems by acting so rashly."

Treyton was so enraged that he was quivering. "I do not care if I am creating problems," he said. "But I will tell you this—my father and his army can get here much sooner than any message, or reinforcements, from Henry. Mayhap we will act without the king's permission, but I say now that I do not care and neither does my father. We will punish those responsible for Talia's assault. You are a knight, de Serreaux, sworn to uphold the oath of chivalry. That means protecting the weak. Why would you stand in our way after this ghastly attack on my sister?"

Torran was trying to keep his temper in check. He'd just run all the way from The Narth to prevent Treyton from making a very big mistake, in his opinion, but Treyton didn't seem to appreciate the delicate situation they were in. He hadn't from the start. Crooking a finger at Treyton, Torran pulled him out of the chamber and into the apothecary's shop, but Treyton would go no further. He wouldn't go out on the street where they could talk in private.

Torran was forced to address the matter within earshot of others.

"Listen to me and listen well," he said to Treyton, his voice low and steely. "No one is trying to prevent you from seeking justice. Your sister deserves it. But you also must realize that making an example of a prince of Wales, and a revered warlord, will have catastrophic consequences."

"That does not matter to me."

"Then Clearwell will be the target of every Welsh warlord with a thirst for English blood," Torran said. "They will be seeking revenge against *you*. Is that what you want?"

Treyton understood very well what Torran was suggesting, but his sense of vengeance clouded everything else. Frustrated, he began to fidget.

"If that had happened to your sister, what would *you* want?" he demanded.

Torran sighed sharply. "I would want exactly what you want," he said. "But not this way. You must let Henry have a say in this."

Treyton was grinding his jaw stubbornly. "I will not," he said. "Punishing ap Yestin is our right."

He wasn't going to budge. Torran could see that. But if he could at least stall the man, maybe that would be time enough for Henry to respond. Better yet, if he could get Gaspard de Russe to weigh in on the situation and perhaps rein in his reckless son, that might be the best option they had.

In any case, he had to force everyone to calm down.

"It is your right," Torran said as evenly as he could. "No one is trying to take that away from you. But you must at least send a message to your father about this. More than you, he has a right to make this decision because it was *his* daughter who was injured. Will you not even send word to your father before you end a man's life for something he did not do?"

That brought Treyton pause. The first flickers of uncertainty appeared in his eyes. "I want ap Yestin as my prisoner," he said.

Torran nodded. "He shall be," he assured him. "Take him back to The Narth and put him in the vault. But let your father make the final decision on ap Yestin's fate, because if the man is executed, it will light the marches up for years to come. You do not want the death of men in battle to be on your conscience for a decision you made in anger."

That statement nearly took all of Treyton's drive out of him, mostly because Torran was right. He was acting recklessly, but not without cause. Not without a reason.

He had to make Torran understand that.

As Torran and Treyton hashed out Ivor's fate, Kent was still standing where Torran had left him, right in the middle of The Bryn's large kitchen with two dozen de Russe soldiers standing around and about the same number of Henry's troops crowding in. In particular, he was standing over Ivor in case any de Russe soldiers decided to harass the man.

There was chaos going on, or had gone on, and Kent was baffled at Treyton's move to capture Ivor without any authority to do so. He looked down at Ivor, who was bent over the man next to him, the one that was clearly wounded. There were bloodied rags on the man's belly. Perhaps Kent should have been concerned about Ivor and the wounded man, but he was more concerned by the fact that the cottage was torn apart and he hadn't yet seen Madelaina. It was possible she was in another chamber, safe from the madness.

He could only hope that that was the case.

"De Bermingham," he said, calling over to Bennet. "Where is the family that lives here?"

Bennet had pulled himself out of Orion's grasp and been

endeavoring to forcibly calm himself. Hearing Kent's question, he simply shook his head. He didn't want to shout out their location for the de Russe soldiers to hear, not when he was trying to hide the women from them, so he motioned Kent over. Kent moved around Ivor and the wounded Welshman, coming into close proximity to Bennet and Orion.

"What is it?" he said to Bennet. "Where are they?"

Bennet kept his voice down. "De Russe wanted to take them prisoner as well, so I've hidden them," he said. "They're up the street at that inn where Stefan was infested with vermin. It was the only place close enough at short notice, but I suggest we move them to The Narth for their own safety."

Before Kent could answer, Stefan appeared in the rear garden along with Britt, Aidric, and Dirk. Jareth had been left behind in command of The Narth, but the rest of the Six had come running to head off Treyton. As Stefan headed in Kent's direction, Britt took a swing at a de Russe soldier who had inadvertently bumped into him. Given the volatility of the situation, it wasn't surprising, but Kent grabbed Stefan by the arm.

"These soldiers need to be cleared out of here," he said loudly into Stefan's good ear. "Torran and de Russe are discussing the situation, but the soldiers need to be cleared out for everyone's safety. They have no reason to be here and, frankly, I don't want them around ap Yestin."

Stefan nodded. "We'll clear them out," he said, turning to Aidric and Dirk. "Move the soldiers out. Kent wants them removed."

Britt was still wrestling with one of the soldiers and Stefan found himself breaking up the fight as Aidric and Dirk began shouting orders, moving the soldiers out through the trampled garden. Stefan and Britt joined in, and soon enough, the four of them were steadily moving the soldiers out. The chamber was clearing. Even Orion got in on it because he loved yelling at men and pushing them around. Bennet started to follow the group to lend a hand, but Kent stopped him.

"Are the women unharmed?" he asked.

Bennet nodded. "Frightened, but unharmed," he said. "It was a mess when we got here, Kent. De Russe and his men had all but destroyed the cottage and the women were in great peril."

"Where is The Bryn?"

"He went to tend a sick man and has yet to return."

Kent eyed him a moment. "Give your last contact with the man those years ago, I believe that is a blessing."

Bennet nodded reluctantly, on a subject he didn't want to discuss. "Aye," he finally said. "I suppose so."

Kent's gaze lingered on the man. "Are you well?" he asked quietly. "Seeing Madelaina's mother must have been a shock. If you wish to talk about it, I will listen."

Bennet looked at him in surprise. But only for a brief moment. "I've gone for twenty years without anyone lending an ear or sympathy to my situation," he said, smiling weakly. "It is strange for me to hear you say such things."

"I will not say it again if it unsettles you."

Bennet shook his head. "It does not," he said. "Oddly, it gives me a sense of value. As if what I feel and think is worth something."

Kent put his hand on the man's shoulder. "You have value to me, if that matters."

"More than you know."

Without much more to say, at least in the middle of this

situation, Kent looked around at the ravaged chamber, which had, in fact, been quite heavily damaged by de Russe's antics, and all he could think of was Madelaina in the middle of it. Strange how a man who was unused to thinking about a woman should suddenly take to it so easily. His thoughts shifted from Bennet's feelings to Madelaina's safety.

"Where is that inn?" he asked. "Which direction?"

Bennet motioned to him. "Come with me," he said. "I will take you."

Kent started to move, but not before he paused in front of Orion, who was standing by the garden door as if to ensure the de Russe soldiers wouldn't try to enter again.

"Guard those Welshman with your life," he said, pointing to Ivor and the wounded man. "Do not let them leave and do not let anyone but Torran take them."

Orion nodded sharply. "Aye, my lord."

With that, Kent followed Bennet out of the mashed garden and into the alley beyond. He was about to follow the man east, toward the road, when something caught his eye.

A sad dog face.

Arthur was cowering in a corner of the garden, frightened by all of the activity and violence, and Kent whistled softly to the dog, calling him. With hardly any prompting at all, Arthur came out of his corner and trotted over to Kent, who patted the dog on the head, trying to give him some comfort. Since they were off to find the dog's mistress, Kent encouraged the dog to follow him and, quite easily, Arthur did.

The main avenue seemed quiet at this hour, probably because the villagers were too frightened to leave their homes after the ruckus de Russe caused. There was virtually no one out at all and shutters were closed over cottage windows. The mood all around was dark and fearful as they moved swiftly up the avenue, heading for a dwelling up the road with pinpricks of light emitting from the windows. The only source of warmth and illumination, drawing them to it like moths to flame.

When they finally reached the inn, Bennet shoved the door open and Kent followed, bringing the dog with him. They didn't stop in the smoky, smelly common room, but instead headed to the rear of the establishment. Bennet came to the very last door by the exit out into the livery yard and paused, rapping on the panel softly.

A shaky voice answered.

"Who is it?"

"'Tis me, my lady," Bennet said. "Please open the door."

After a moment, they could hear the bolt being thrown. Slowly, the door inched open and Madelaina's face appeared. Since it was dark in the corridor, she could only really see Bennet, and she opened the door wide to admit him. As he stepped in, Kent came up behind him and into the light.

Startled, Madelaina stepped back, her eyes wide on him. A hand flew to her mouth, and a moment later, she simply turned her back on him.

She didn't want to see him.

Kent, of course, knew why. They hadn't spoken since she'd lied to Ivor about who Kent was. He knew that she was fully aware that he'd lied to her about his identity. He was fully aware that she probably hated him for it.

He found that he was fairly desperate to explain himself.

"My lady," he said softly, pulling Arthur into the chamber. "I brought you something."

The dog came in, wagging his tail, bumping into Madelaina, who put her hand down to pet her beloved dog.

"I am grateful," she whispered tightly.

Kent merely nodded, tearing his focus away from her to see that Bennet was standing over Celyn as the woman sat on the bed, gazing up at him. He didn't know if the two of them had been given a chance to speak in private, but he suspected not. Perhaps it was time to give them that privacy—for certain, he needed some with Madelaina.

"My lady?" he said to her. "Will you come with me, please? I have a need to speak with you."

Madelaina simply shook her head, petting her dog as she faced the hearth. With a faint sigh, Kent came up behind her, as close as he could get without touching her, and whispered into the back of her head.

"Please, Madelaina," he murmured. "I beg you."

She didn't say anything. She just stood there. But suddenly, she moved around him, giving him a wide berth, and left the chamber. Kent quickly followed, with Arthur trailing behind them both, and he followed her out into the livery yard.

When they were gone and it was just Bennet and Celyn in the chamber, Bennet paused for several long moments before looking at Celyn. She was sitting on the bed, her head lowered, looking at her hands.

Bennet had never felt so much angst in his life.

Angst for a moment he'd never thought would come. Angst for a life he wanted so badly, one that had been brutally ripped away from him, leaving a shell of a man behind. The last time he was alone with Celyn, they were planning their elopement, so he found himself having flashbacks of The Bryn breaking in through the door with an ax in his hand, threatening Bennet as Celyn threw herself between the two and tried to defend him.

He closed his eyes tightly to the memory.

"I think she likes him," Celyn murmured softly.

Bennet's eyes opened and he looked at her lowered head. "Who?"

"Maddie," she said. "I think she likes the man who came with you."

"Kent?"

Celyn looked up at him. "I thought his name was Trevyn?"

Bennet shook his head. "I fear that is what he is about to explain to Madelaina," he said. "He told her that was his name when he met her, but it is not."

Her brow furrowed. "I do not understand," she said. "I briefly met him, only once, but I've not spoken to my sister about him since. My comment was because in our brief introduction, I could see the way Maddie looked at him. That is why I said I believe she likes him."

Bennet nodded, but only in that he understood what she meant. Not that he agreed with her statement. Frankly, he was more concerned with her. The more he realized that they were actually alone and The Bryn wouldn't be crashing in through the door, the more eager he was to speak with her.

"Tell me what happened tonight," he said. "How did that chaos get started?"

Celyn shrugged her shoulders as if she really didn't know. "I prepared supper as I usually do," she said. "Maddie had invited Trevyn to dine with us, and Papa was amenable, but I do not usually sup at the same table as men I do not know. I never have. All this to say I was not in the kitchen when the English arrived. I was in my chamber, sewing, and I heard the noise. When I came out of my chamber, Madelaina came rushing out of the kitchen and ran into me. We were trying to leave but got caught up in the fighting. We were simply trying to protect ourselves when you came."

"Then you did not know that Ivor was a guest at your father's table?"

She shook her head. "I thought it was Maddie's traveler," she said. "What happened tonight? I do not understand."

Bennet sat down on the bed, a foot or so away from her. "What do you know about the English being at The Narth?"

She cocked her head thoughtfully. "I know that they came a short time ago and Ivor ap Yestin fled to the north."

"Do you know *why* they came?"

"Nay. Why?"

"Because the daughter of an English warlord was assaulted not far from here as she traveled," Bennet said. "Her father traced the perpetrators to this village. Evidently, they found the woman's jewelry here, being sold by merchants. They assumed those from The Narth were responsible, so they sacked the castle."

Celyn was looking at him in surprise. "Is that why?" she said, shaking her head in disbelief. "Truthfully, I do not pay much attention to news in the village or rumors. Maddie is the more sociable. She and my father seem to know everything."

His focus lingered on her for a moment. "I am glad I found you when I did," he said. "I am glad I was able to bring you to safety."

Celyn nodded, but the weight of the conversation was growing heavy. They'd discussed the situation, Bennet had explained it, and now the conversation was transitioning into an obvious direction.

The two of them.

"I could not believe it when I saw you," Celyn finally said. "I have been dreaming of this moment for over twenty years,

Bennet. What would I say to you if I ever saw you again? Somehow, I thought it would be in a more peaceful setting. Not in the middle of a battle."

He smiled weakly. "Not ideal circumstances, to be sure," he said. "But I am still grateful for them. Grateful that de Russe sacked The Narth. Grateful that it brought me to you again, if only briefly."

Celyn returned his smile. "There is so much I want to ask you but I do not even know where to start," she said. "The last time I saw you was as The Bryn was taking me away. Then I sent the missive to you in secret after Madelaina was born. You did not reply, of course, but I hoped you had received it."

"I received it," he murmured.

The smile didn't leave her face as she studied him, acquainting herself with lines in his face that perhaps weren't there before. He looked older, and more mature, but he was still the handsome man she'd fallen in love with. It didn't seem possible that so many years had passed, because it was almost as if they'd never been apart. She could still feel the same comfort with him, the same sense of safety and adoration. He was the same Bennet she'd fallen in love with, now here before her.

It was a precious moment.

"After you left here, you returned to Chepstow," she said.

He nodded. "I did."

"But The Bryn had you removed."

"He did."

"Where did you go?"

He sighed faintly, thinking on the past twenty years and the life he'd led. "Back to Ireland," he said. "I went back for a while and then returned to serve at Richmond Castle, about as far away as one can get from Wales. I served in the royal corps, serving the king, until I was sent to Henry's household about six months ago."

"You spent the past twenty years at Richmond?"

"I spent about fifteen years there. The rest was in other places."

Celyn nodded in understanding, but there was one question she wanted to ask him that she wasn't sure she really wanted the answer to. Still, she was compelled to ask.

She had to know.

"Did you marry, Bennet?" she asked softly.

He shook his head. "Nay," he said. "Did you?"

"Nay."

"Why not?"

"Because it would not be fair for any man to live in your shadow," she said. "I have only loved one man. There is no room for anyone else."

Bennet's expression filled with understanding, with sympathy, and perhaps even a little joy. "That is exactly how I feel," he said. "I did not realize you would still feel the same way."

Her expression softened. "Of course I do."

He puffed his cheeks out in a gesture that suggested relief. "I am glad," he said. "You will never know how glad. And to see you again... This moment will give me the strength to carry on."

The warmth faded from Celyn's eyes. "Bennet... do you think... do you think we will ever be together again?" she said. "Or is that an impossible dream? Are we to simply remain accustomed to our lives as they are, without one another?"

He shook his head slowly. "I do not know," he said honestly. "I'm sure your father still feels the same way about a marriage between us. The man ruined my life, Celyn. I let him do it because I would rather have me ruined than you ruined. I do not have any fond feelings for him and, truthfully, I am not entirely sure how I would react if I asked him for your hand and he denied me again. I might have to kill him, and we could not build a marriage together that was based on a murder."

She looked at him, a little shocked, before forcing a smile. "I should not have asked you such a question," she said. "We have only just seen each other today, after so many years apart. Forgive me for asking. It was foolish."

Reaching out, Bennet impulsively clasped his big hand over hers, their flesh touching for the first time in twenty years. The shock of it brought Celyn to tears.

"It was not foolish," Bennet said, watching her features crumple. "It is a natural question. I never married, nor did you. We wanted to marry each other, but that was not to be twenty years ago. I think… I think that if we were to try again, I would not ask your father. We would simply do it, and there is nothing he could do about it once the deed was finished. Alas, I have thought about that very thing for years. I have relived the day your father separated us over and over in my mind. I have often chastised myself for not being braver in the face of his refusal. I've spent twenty years with his lies hanging over my head, Celyn. Twenty years of being relegated to a lower-level knight because of a lie an old man told. What he did to me was not fair. But what he did to you was worse."

Celyn looked up at him, wiping at her cheeks with her free hand. "What did he do to me?"

"Destroyed your dreams."

Celyn had calmed a little by now, sniffling away the last of her tears, but she was looking at his big hand as it covered hers. "Madelaina is my dream," she murmured. "I could not have you, but I could have a piece of you in her. You did not even have that."

He nodded, giving her hand a gentle squeeze. "She seems like a well-mannered young woman," he said. "You have raised her well."

Celyn smiled up at him at the mention of their daughter. "She is wise beyond her years," she said. "She reminds me of you in that way. You were always so wise and calm. She has those traits, too."

"I hope I have the opportunity to come to know her."

"I hope you do, too."

"Bennet?"

"Aye?"

"Will you sit here and hold my hand? May we simply enjoy that for the moment?"

He smiled faintly. "I would like that," he said. "Unfortunately, I cannot remain too long. There is much happening at The Narth with the capture of Ivor, and I must return. I do not want them to come looking for me and, subsequently, find you. You must stay out of sight until this issue with Ivor is settled."

Celyn understood.

In the dim light, in the silence of the night, they simply sat on the bed, holding hands, feeling the warmth and adoration between them that had never died. Love like that wasn't meant to.

It was meant to last forever.

CHAPTER EIGHTEEN

T HE LIVERY YARD was empty, fortunately.

After leaving Bennet and Celyn, that was where Kent and Madelaina found themselves for their moment of privacy. The yard was dark and cold and quiet with the only light coming from a lamp in the stable for the stable servant. One side of the stable was open, exposing the animals inside, and they could see the servant moving around by the weak light, bedding the creatures down for the night. When they moved to the middle of the yard, away from everything and everyone, Madelaina came to a halt and whirled on him.

"You lied to me," she said. "I asked you what you were doing at The Narth and you lied to me. You *are* English!"

He'd expected the accusation and was fully prepared to defend himself. "I am," he said. "And I will explain everything if you will listen. Believe me, Madelaina, if I'd had another choice, I would have told you the truth from the start. But I did not have that choice."

"Why not?" she demanded. "Why did you not have the choice of truth?"

He could see how upset she was, but at least she was willing to talk. That was something. "The day we met, I was simply getting a sense of the village," he said evenly. "Then your silly dog found me. You came to my aid and I thought it would be our one and only meeting. But after speaking to you for all of two minutes, I knew I wanted to see you again. Not because you freely spoke of your family and the village, but because you are beautiful and charming and bright. You know how it is at dawn, with the sun rising? The very second before the sun bursts free of the horizon, everything is dark and cold. But the moment the sun breaks, the world becomes bright and new again. That is how I felt when I met you—cold and dark, but the moment you started to speak, I felt bright and new again."

His flattery had her wavering a little. "Then why the lies?"

He shrugged. "Would you have spoken to me if you knew I was an English knight?" he said. "I do not think so. We had such an easy conversation, the likes of which I have rarely had in my lifetime, and you called me a traveler. Do you remember? I wasn't a traveler, but you gave me the idea. I saw a way to keep speaking with you. To keep seeing the sun come into my world. So I became a traveler."

It was logical, but she was still hurt and defensive. "Is Trevyn really your name?"

He shook his head. "Nay," he said. "It is the name of my father's grandfather. He was Welsh. My father is half Welsh, but my grandmother, his mother and Trevyn's daughter, is also full Welsh. She taught me the Welsh language before I learned anything else."

"You speak it perfectly."

"I know," he said. "My name is Kent de Poyer. I am the heir to the Talgarth earldom, which includes Nether Castle and the Honour of Tyr, which contains Tyr Castle. My father is

Caledon de Poyer, Earl of Talgarth. I serve King Henry as one of his personal guard."

She looked at him with less anger and more curiosity. "Kent," she repeated softly. "Is that not a land in England?"

He smiled faintly. "It is," he said. "Known as Cantia by the Romans, the county of Kent is an old and beautiful land."

"You were born there?"

"Nay," he said. "I was born in Wales, at Nether Castle."

"Then you are Welsh-born."

"Aye, I was born in the country."

"Then you did not lie about that."

His smile faded. "Nay," he said. "Other than my name and not being truthful with my vocation, and mayhap a few things I told your father, I've tried very much not to lie to you. I find liars abhorrent, but in this case, it was necessary. I hope, with time, you will forgive me, Madelaina."

She shrugged, unwilling to commit to forgiveness just yet. "What about Ivor?" she said. "You clearly do not know him, because he did not know you."

He lifted his eyebrows, conceding that fact, at least as she saw it. "I *do* know him," he said. "But Ivor does not recognize me. When we were lads, very young, we were the best of friends. I've not seen him since I was six years of age. Thirty years is a very long time. You must understand that there was a part of me, although I was doing Henry's work, that wants to protect Ivor. I saved his life, once, when we were children. There is part of me that still wants to save him."

Madelaina lingered over that. By this time, the anger was out of her expression and manner, but she was still confused, still hurt. "Will you save him?" she said. "The English have him now."

Kent nodded. "I know," he said. "And I will do everything I can to save him, but you can help me."

"How?" she asked. "What can I do?"

Reaching out, Kent took her hand. He was willing to take the chance that she would let him hold it, hoping she would, and he was thrilled when she didn't pull away. Gently, he held her small hand between his two big ones.

"The entire reason for this trouble is because an English girl was assaulted by Welsh who were traced back to The Narth and to this village," he said. "The knight who captured Ivor is that girl's brother. He is bent on vengeance. If you could help me find those who committed this terrible crime, there would be no reason for Ivor to be imprisoned."

Madelaina nodded seriously. "I know of this event," she said. "The knight who broke into my home told me."

"That is her brother, Treyton," Kent said. "Do you know anything about this assault? Have you heard anything at all?"

Madelaina shook her head. "Nay," she said. "That is the truth. The first we heard about it was when the English came, raided the village, and then laid siege to The Narth. Honestly, Ivor and his men are not like that. They do not attack unsuspecting women."

"You know the character of these men?"

She nodded. "I've grown up with many of them," she said. "They are not evil. They do not beat their wives or steal. But they are dedicated to the freedom of Wales and to Ivor. If they are attacked, they will fight back."

He considered that. "That contradicts what de Russe has told us," he said. "What of his sister's jewelry being sold in the village? How did they get it?"

Madelaina shook her head. "I do not know," she said honestly. "But there must be an explanation."

He didn't have much to say to that because he couldn't think of an alternative. Facts were facts. But this wasn't the moment he wanted to get into an argument with her, not when things between them were so fragile. But that thought took him to his next point with her.

His intentions.

He honestly didn't know he had any until this moment. But looking at her, feeling her hand in his, he felt so strongly about her that the impact of it shocked him. The woman he'd thought he felt something for those years ago couldn't compare to his attraction to Madelaina. Perhaps he simply hadn't been ready for a romance that would lead to marriage until this very moment.

Looking at her, he couldn't imagine a lifetime of not having her by his side.

"Every situation has its truth," he said after a moment. "There is a beginning, and an end, and someone is responsible for that. It is possible that someone in Ivor's command perpetrated this assault. It is equally possible that someone else did and they are trying to make Ivor and his men look guilty. However, given the circumstances and the clues, all signs point to someone in this village. Mayhap you can discover the truth that will exonerate Ivor. In any case, I would like your help. And I would like something else."

She cocked her head. "What else?"

"To court you."

That brought substantial shock. Madelaina looked at him with a mixture of disbelief, delight, and terror. Her hands flew to her mouth and she began to back away from him.

"I… I do not know what to say," she said.

"You do not have to say anything. Simply think about it."

She stared at him for several long moments, each one causing him more anxiety than the previous. When she finally did speak, it was quietly and hesitantly.

"Is this truly the place to speak on such things?"

"Is there a better time?" Kent said. "We are being honest with one another. I cannot think of a better time to tell you what is on my mind."

She sighed, averting her gaze and staring at her feet. He could see that she was thinking on what he'd said because she was puckering, and unpuckering, her lips. Then she looked at him once more.

"I would be lying if I said I was not interested or that you do not draw feelings out of me that I did not know existed," she said. "But that was when you were Trevyn. I thought you were one of us. I thought you were a simple man who might possibly consider settling down with the daughter of an apothecary."

Kent sighed with regret. "Please do not tell me I have ruined things because I did my duty as I saw it," he said. "I wish things could have been different, but they were not. That does not mean I am not an honorable man who would do his best to make a good husband."

As she looked at him, her eyes began to well. "I do not know," she whispered tightly. "Any trust we were building is gone. You lied to me."

"I told you why."

"What if what you are telling me now is a lie, too?"

"You mean what if I am not Kent de Poyer, but someone else?"

She nodded, quickly dashing away a tear. "I do not know if I should trust you."

Those words were like a shot to the heart. He didn't want to hear it, but he understood why. After a moment, he shook his head. "I do not know what more I can say," he said. "I *am* Kent de Poyer, son of the Earl of Talgarth. I serve Henry, England's king. I am a knight of the highest order. I am a man of my word, and when I told you I was someone else, it was to protect me as well as to protect you. If you cannot believe me, then there is nothing more to say, but just know… know I would have been true to you for the rest of your life, Madelaina ferch Bryn. You would have had all of me, forever. If that is worth fighting for, then all you need to do is tell me you will think on it. Just a word will do. Please give me that hope."

Madelaina tried to speak up but the words wouldn't come. She didn't know what to do or what to say, confused and overwhelmed and full of conflicting emotions. When she didn't speak up right away, Kent realized she probably wouldn't. Or couldn't. In any case, the more the seconds ticked away, the more his heart was slowly being crushed under the weight of his disappointment.

Little by little, it was turning to dust.

To spare the remainder of his dignity, he turned away, leaving Madelaina standing in the livery yard with tears streaming down her cheeks. But he only made it as far as the door before coming to a halt. He just couldn't seem to make himself walk through that door and away from her forever.

"Madelaina, my dearest," he said, feeling pain in the very words he was speaking. "Do you truly have no hope to give me?"

Madelaina couldn't take the agony or the pressure. She broke down into sobs. "I want there to be," she wept. "But you must understand that so much has happened today. My home was destroyed by English soldiers and then I discovered that the woman I believed to be my sister is, in fact, my mother. The man I believed to be my father is my grandfather and everything I believed my life to be is a lie. And then there's you… I do not need more lies today. All I can go on is your word, but everything you've told me was a lie and now you tell me that your name is Kent and that you are an earl's son. You are expecting too much from me today. Everyone is expecting too much from me today and I cannot give anything more."

She wept angrily, wiping at her tears furiously. She was deeply unsettled and rightly so. Therefore, Kent did the only thing he could do. He returned to her and took her by the hand.

"Come with me," he said gently. "Come along. That's a good girl."

She started to walk, but not really. She was too busy weeping. At least she wasn't trying to pull away. But, seeing what trouble she was having, Kent bent over and scooped her into his arms, holding her tightly as he went back into the inn. He carried her into the common room, over to a small alcove by the hearth. There was an old man sitting there but Kent kicked him out, setting Madelaina down gently on the bench before quietly issuing orders to a serving wench who came to see what the trouble was. The woman went on the run for food and drink as Kent sat down next to Madelaina.

She tried to scoot away from him this time, but he put his arm around her shoulders and held her against his torso. She was stiff and resistant, but only for a few seconds. Very quickly, he could feel her relax. As if she were melting into him. The serving wench brought a pitcher of wine and two cups, and he chased the woman away before pouring Madelaina a full measure.

He held the cup to her lips.

"Drink," he said softly. "It will do you good."

Madelaina sniffled and sobbed, but she took the cup and downed about half of it in two or three big swallows. Kent had to chuckle because that was a lot of wine, very quickly, for a rather petite lady. She coughed as she finished the last swallow and set the cup down.

"That's terrible," she said, wiping her mouth with the back of her hand.

Kent peered at the contents of the cup and took a drink, discovering that it was, indeed, terrible. It was nearly vinegar. The serving wench quickly returned with a bowl of something steaming, wooden spoons, bread, and butter, but Kent grabbed her before she could run off again.

"This wine is shite," he said. "Take it away and bring us something better. The best you have. I shall pay your price, so do not be concerned that I cannot or will not."

As the wench scurried off again, Kent took his arm away from Madelaina long enough to break up the brown bread and hand her a hunk, but she declined.

"I am not hungry," she said. "But I thank you just the same."

"You do not mind if I eat, do you?" he asked.

She shook her head.

As Kent dived into a mutton stew that wasn't bad at all, Madelaina simply sat there in silence. The wench returned a third time with more wine and Kent tasted it before he approved. It was better, something the innkeeper evidently kept for himself, but he let Kent have some because he was willing to pay well for it. Kent poured Madelaina a full cup once again, and this time, she nearly drained it in the first few swallows.

Kent watched her closely.

"It seems to me that you've learned new things about your-self today that you've found shocking," he said. "Did Celyn tell you everything with regards to your birth?"

Madelaina was looking at her wine cup. "She told me enough."

Kent took a bite of bread before continuing. "Bennet told me what happened also," he said. "He is your father."

"That is what Celyn said."

"What bothers you so?"

She took a deep, steadying breath as she thought on his question. "I suppose because she did not tell me this sooner," she said. "I do not think it is fair."

"Why would you think that if she did it to protect you?"

She looked at him then. "Is that what you think? That she was protecting me?" She looked back to her cup, shaking her head. "I think it was selfish."

Kent shrugged, perhaps not completely agreeing with her. "That is difficult to know, since you were not in the same situation," he said. "I agree that you have the right to be unsettled by this, even upset by it, but I do not think you have the right to judge your parents for the situation. In Celyn's case, she was forced into silence by The Bryn. Think about how much she must have suffered all of these years, knowing what she knew and unable to tell you. Do you not think that was a difficult burden for her?"

"Then she should have relieved herself of this burden and told me," Madelaina said. "She had no right to keep it from me."

Kent could hear the hurt in her voice. "Let me ask you something," he said. "If The Bryn told you to do something, would you do it?"

She nodded. "Of course I would."

"And if he told you not to do something, would you still do it?"

She faltered. "It depends on what it was."

"Does it?"

She knew what he was driving at and looked away. "She still should have told me."

Kent turned back to his food. "You're young," he said. "You do not understand that sometimes, the best thing to do is to bury something extremely painful. Your mother loved Bennet very much, from what I was told, and he loved her in return. When they were denied a marriage, by your grandfather, it surely must have torn your mother's heart out. Can you imagine her pain? Not being able to be with the man she loved? Bearing his child and being forced to live a lie by calling her daughter a sister? I think Celyn suffered very much. And I think you should show some compassion. Not everything is clear all the time, Madelaina. Sometimes choices in life are the most muddled thing imaginable. Like a woman who must pretend her child is not her own. And a man who is doing his sworn duty and being forced to lie about it. It does not make us bad people. It makes us noble in the truest sense."

Madelaina hung her head. "It is so difficult to comprehend."

"I know," he said. "You and I spoke once about traveling and seeing the world. You've lived your entire life in this village, surrounded by people you know and trust, and everything is peaceful and comfortable to you. But life is not always comfortable and peaceful. The measure of your character is how you respond to things that invade that peace and comfort. Will you become angry and run? That is a weak person's response. Or will you understand that life is about change and we must all rise to the challenge? You'll be the better for it."

He was right. His voice had been low and soothing, filling her ears, her mind, like warm honey. She was calmer now than she had been earlier and it was easier for her to digest what he was telling her. If she were honest with herself, she was glad that he had not walked out on her after the discussion in the livery yard. She was glad that he'd brought her inside and was trying to comfort her on what was inarguably one of the most difficult days of her life.

Will you rise to the challenge?

He was also right about the fact that she had lived a relatively easy life. That was the kind way of putting it. The unkind way of putting it would be to say that she'd lived a spoiled life or a naïve life. Even though she had seen twenty years, in many ways, she was still young because she'd never had a chance to get out and see the world, to see people and understand the world at large. She spent all her time in that little village and that beautiful vale in Wales.

She had been protected by it.

Now, she was facing some difficult truths. She still couldn't believe that Celyn was her mother and not her sister, and perhaps she would never fully accept that, but she was going to have to try. Just as she was going to have to try to understand that her father was not the man she had known and loved all these years. Her real father was a stranger.

Could she rise to this challenge?

Madelaina wasn't sure. But she didn't want to be weak, as Kent had suggested. She'd never viewed herself as a weak person. In fact, she'd always considered herself strong and reasonable, but at this moment, she wasn't acting strong or reasonable. She was acting like a fool.

And then there was Kent.

Could she ever trust him again? That was a very good question. Since the moment they met, he had been kind and considerate and wise and even sweet. She knew she could get used to his holding her hand, and kissing her hand, and when he put his big arm around her shoulders, she wasn't hard-pressed to admit that she had never felt more safe or protected in her entire life. That wasn't a feeling she'd ever had before, and it was something she knew she could come to crave.

Did she want him to leave her? She had to think about that, because part of her was fearful to trust him again, but the larger part of her wanted to trust him. He was a knight, serving the English king, no less, which meant he was no ordinary warrior. He was a man of training, and of great skill, and clearly a man to be trusted. If the King of England trusted him, then perhaps she should be willing to as well.

Nay, she didn't want him to leave her.

But she was struggling with the concept of trust.

"If Celyn had told me everything a month or even a year ago and I was still wallowing in distress, then you would have every reason to tell me that I am being weak," she said after a lengthy pause. "But she only just told me. I have the right to be upset about this at this time."

"I would agree with that."

"I told you that you were expecting too much from me today."

"Understood, my lady."

"As for you," she said. Then she paused and looked at him. "As for you, I want you to swear something to me."

"What is that?"

"That you will never lie to me again, ever."

"Upon my oath as a knight, I swear it."

She looked deep into his eyes. "Because if you do, I will never trust you again."

Her words had impact. He believed her implicitly. "Understood," he murmured. "Does that mean you will let me court you?"

She sighed heavily. "Mayhap," she said. "But if I do, I will do something different that Celyn did not. I will give you permission to court me no matter what The Bryn says."

Kent waggled his eyebrows. "He was successful in preventing Celyn and Bennet from marrying," he said. "He may not be keen on letting another English knight court a daughter. Or granddaughter in this case."

Madelaina shrugged. "In the spirit of total truth, he has been expecting me to marry Ivor," she said. "In fact, Ivor proposed marriage to me this very night, but I refused him."

That statement surprised Kent because it was the first time he'd heard about Ivor having interest in Madelaina. Considering the relationship Ivor had with The Bryn, however, it wasn't surprising. Surely Ivor had noticed pretty, smart Madelaina. The man would have had to be blind not to.

Kent began to get a sick feeling in the pit of his stomach.

"My lady, if Ivor has already declared for you, I will not usurp his claim," he said. "You did not tell me that you were spoken for."

"That is because I am not," Madelaina said. "Ivor has never staked a claim, but he has shown romantic tendencies from time to time. I can tell you that they were not reciprocated."

"You are certain?"

"This is not a moment for me to lie to you, Kent. I am certain."

Kent. It was the first time she'd used his real name, and it sounded like music to his ears. He wanted to grow old hearing her sweet voice in his ear, whispering his name. But the mention of Ivor also brought up a very real issue—that Ivor was now a prisoner and Kent needed to get back to The Narth to see what had become of him. As much as he wanted to remain with Madelaina, he couldn't.

"Very well," he said. "Since we are trying to reestablish trust tonight, I will take you at your word. But you reminded me that I must get back to The Narth. That is where Ivor was taken."

"They will not hurt him, will they?"

Kent shook his head. "Not if I have anything to say about it," he said. "And I have a lot to say, believe me. Let me take you back to your chamber and make sure you are safe before I leave."

Madelaina nodded, immediately standing up from the bench. Kent stood up beside her, pausing a moment to take her hands and bring them to his lips for a tender kiss. He watched a faint mottle come to Madelaina's cheeks as she smiled shyly at him.

He grinned.

"I told you I would do that when you least expected it," he said.

"Every single time?" she asked. "Must every kiss be unexpected?"

He gazed at her a moment before dropping her hand and grasping her by the upper arms. He was taller than her by more than a foot, so she craned her neck back to look at him just as he deposited the sweetest of kisses on her lips.

"Was that one unexpected?" he murmured.

Madelaina could hardly catch her breath. The kiss had made her head buzz, as if she'd been struck by lightning.

"Aye," she said, swallowing. "Unexpected. But not unwelcome."

"Good," he said. "As the song goes, the future, for us, gleams like diamonds."

"Do you truly think so?"

"I do."

She sighed. "I hope so," she said sincerely. "I truly do."

He eyed her. "You are still unsure about me."

"I think it is simply going to take time."

That was as good as he could hope for at this point. He let go of her arms, grasping the wine pitcher and cups with one hand while taking Madelaina with the other. The common room of the inn was only half full, quiet with uninteresting people, as he took her back to the large chamber she was sharing with Celyn. The closer they drew to the door, however, the slower Madelaina moved.

"Must we remain here tonight?" she asked. "I would like to return home."

Kent shook his head. "Nay," he said. "Bennet said that de Russe wanted to take you prisoner, too, so you will remain here. It will be safer."

Before she could argue, Kent caught sight of Arthur out in the livery yard and whistled to the dog, who came running. He knocked on the chamber door, which was swiftly opened by Bennet, who stood back and admitted Madelaina and the dog. Before Kent could say a word to Bennet about returning to The Narth, Madelaina came to a stop and turned to the older knight.

"Celyn told me about you," she said, taking a moment to

study the man. "I suppose I should introduce myself, but that seems so peculiar under these circumstances."

Bennet smiled faintly at her. "It does seem strange," he agreed. "May I tell you something?"

"You may."

"I have a sister, and you look like her. I can see her in your eyes."

"I do not look like my mother?"

His smile grew. "You do, indeed," he said. "You are beautiful like your mother but with shades of my sister. And you were named for my mother, who was a strong and bright woman. I do not know if you were told that, so I should like to be the one to tell you. You do your grandmother proud, Madelaina, and I am grateful."

Some of the awkwardness drifted out of the encounter as Madelaina returned his smile. It was hesitant, and even awkward, but the gesture meant something. "I did not know that," she said. "Mayhap sometime you will tell me about her."

"I would like that very much."

Without much more to say, because she was still a bit unbalanced by the newness of her birth revelation, Madelaina went over to where Celyn was, sitting beside her on the bed. Both Bennet and Kent were watching her, but Kent finally tore his gaze away and looked to Bennet.

"We must go," he said quietly. "There is much happening at The Narth and Torran may require our assistance."

Bennet nodded. "I am ready," he said, but he cast Celyn a final glance. "Stay here tonight, my lady. Do not leave and do not open the door for anyone but me or Kent. Is that clear?"

Both Celyn and Madelaina nodded. It was enough for the knights, who quit the chamber and headed out of the rear exit, making their way to the street that would take them back to the apothecary's shop. Noting the cottage was quiet and dark, they changed direction and headed back to The Narth with all due haste.

Something told Kent that an already-eventful night was about to become even more eventful still.

It was just a hunch he had.

CHAPTER NINETEEN

"**I**'VE HEARD SOMETHING."

The words were quietly uttered in Treyton's ear. He and his men were heading back to The Narth on foot and it was Rufus, the seasoned soldier, who had Treyton's ear. In the middle of their pack was Ivor, his hands bound and a gang of weapon-wielding soldiers crowded in around him. Treyton was at the front of the group as they trudged up the dark, muddy road with Rufus walking beside him.

"What have you heard?" Treyton asked, not looking at the man.

Rufus kept his voice quiet. "I've heard that one of the Six is a friend of ap Yestin's," he muttered. "Do you wonder why they protect the man so rabidly? It is because one of them is a friend."

That news came as a distinct surprise to Treyton. "A friend?" he said. "A Welsh prince is a friend to one of Henry's guards?"

"An old friend, I'm told."

Treyton looked over his shoulder, back into the pack of men following him. Far back behind them were the Guard of

Six, making sure the de Russe men didn't kill Ivor in their quest for revenge. Treyton was viewing them as his enemy now, certainly not men he felt any camaraderie with, considering they were preventing him from doing as he wished with Ivor.

The bonds of allies were beginning to fracture.

"I *knew* something was amiss," Treyton hissed, facing forward. "There is a traitor among them. Mayhap that is why they came in the first place. Not at Henry's command, but to interfere in de Russe affairs. Mayhap they intend to side with ap Yestin in order to prevent me from doing what is my right to do."

"Anything is possible, my lord," Rufus said. "It makes their presence here… concerning."

"I would agree with that," Treyton said. "Which one of them is it?"

Rufus shook his head. "That was not made clear to me, but think about who has grown up on the marches in this area," he said. "You are well aware that Kent de Poyer's father has property just over the hills. If ap Yestin grew up at The Narth, and de Poyer spent his childhood at Tyr Castle, I think we have our answer."

Treyton was looking at him with some anger. "It *has* to be de Poyer," he said. "I do not think it could be anyone else. And it is also well known that Kent's grandmother is full Welsh, so he grew up with the Welsh. Cousins *and* comrades."

"Comrades like ap Yestin."

"Exactly," Treyton said. "I am, therefore, not going to let de Poyer's muddled loyalties stop me from doing what needs to be done. De Serreaux has tried to convince me that should any harm come to ap Yestin, it will result in a war along the marches that will threaten thousands."

"Mayhap he lied to cover this relationship with ap Yestin."

Treyton nodded. "And now he has been discovered," he said with some satisfaction. "You will tell de Serreaux that I want to speak with him when we return to The Narth. And put Ivor in the vault under guard."

"Aye, my lord."

As Rufus went about carrying out Treyton's commands, The Narth loomed ahead. There were dozens of soldiers crowding around the gatehouse, watching the returning troops and wondering what had happened in the village. There was a definite separation between de Russe troops and Henry's troops as they came through the gatehouse, and surrounded by a gaggle of de Russe soldiers was a dark-haired man in traditional Welsh clothing with his wrists bound. That man was taken down into the vault beneath the gatehouse, but it was with an escort of de Russe men, along with Orion and Stefan to ensure Ivor didn't have an "accident" and fall down the stairs. Torran had sent them along because he didn't trust the de Russe men not to do just that.

The mistrust, between everyone, was getting worse.

It culminated in a physical confrontation between Treyton and Jareth. As Treyton came up the steps to the keep, Jareth was standing in the doorway watching the activity in the bailey below. Without a word, Treyton tried to push past him, into the keep, but Jareth made a rather large blockade. Angry that his way inside was being blocked, Treyton tried to shove Jareth out of the way with his shoulder. Jareth may have been the diplomat of the group, and the academic, but he was also a highly skilled knight and quite powerful. When Treyton tried to ram him, he shoved back and ended up pushing Treyton halfway down the stone stairs. When Treyton caught himself, he roared with anger and charged back up the steps, but Jareth balled his fists.

"Try that again and I'll do more than push back," he growled threateningly. "If you behave like my enemy, I will treat you like one, so be aware."

Treyton came to a halt just out of Jareth's range. "Get out of my way," he snarled.

"Nay."

Infuriated, Treyton did what he shouldn't have done—he charged forward to dislodge Jareth and was the recipient of a booted foot to the face. Down he went, tumbling down the stairs until he came to the bottom. Dazed, and with a bloody scrape that went the width of his forehead, he was trying to pick himself up when Torran, Britt, Dirk, and Aidric walked up.

"What happened?" Torran asked as he looked up at Jareth. "What did he do?"

Jareth was quite displeased with Treyton's behavior. "He tried to ram into me to get into the keep," he said. "The man didn't say a word—he came up the stairs and threw his shoulder into me when he reached the door. He tried it again and I kicked him in the head. And now you see where he has landed."

Torran looked down at Treyton. In fact, the four knights all looked down at Treyton as the man struggled to stand up and shake off the bells in his head. No one moved to help him.

"De Russe," Torran said with disgust in his tone, "I do not know what ails you, but if you do not cure it, I am sending you and your army home on the morrow. What on earth possessed you to ram Jareth?"

Treyton was on his feet now, facing off against Torran. "I have a better question for you," he said furiously. "Where do *your* loyalties lie, de Serreaux?"

Torran had no idea what the man meant. "The same place

your loyalties lie," he said. "To God and country."

"What about de Poyer?"

"Same."

"Are you telling me that they do not lie with his friend, ap Yestin?" Treyton nearly shouted. "It all makes sense to me now, why you have been advising me against doing anything rash when it comes to Ivor ap Yestin. It is because de Poyer is his friend. The man's loyalties are torn!"

Britt reached out a fist, fast as lightning, and punched Treyton in the jaw. As the man toppled sideways, Aidric and Dirk pulled Britt back, away from a fight. Torran even put himself between the pair so Treyton wouldn't come back at him.

He pointed up the stairs.

"Get into that keep," he said threateningly. "Get up there and behave yourself. You and I have things to discuss."

Rubbing the right side of his face, Treyton cast Torran a baleful expression before heading up the stairs. This time, Jareth gave the man plenty of room to get by him as he followed him into the keep. Torran, Dirk, Aidric, and finally Britt followed.

A difficult night was about to get worse.

CHAPTER TWENTY

T HEY'D RUN THE entire way.

Kent and Bennet reached The Narth just as the gates were closing for the night. There was a good deal of activity all around, with the de Russe men manning the gatehouse once again. Kent stopped the first sergeant he came across and asked where the prisoner had been taken.

The man pointed down to the ground.

The vault.

Leaving Bennet to head toward the keep, Kent made his way down the narrow, slick stairs that led into the vault. There was only one cell, in fact, and there was no door on it, so four soldiers stood at the base of the stairs to prevent Ivor from trying to leave. He ordered the soldiers to go back up the stairs and guard the entry, which they reluctantly did. No one disobeyed a knight, most especially not one of Henry's guard, so the soldiers made their way back up the stairs as Kent moved toward the lone cell.

Ivor was sitting in a pile of dirty straw, his knees drawn up and his head in his hands. It was dark in the cell because the only sources of light were two feeble torches jammed into iron sconces near the stairs. It also smelled horrifically, as if animals had been living down there. Kent noticed that Ivor's wrists were bound, something he intended to remedy, but first he had to establish some trust.

There was only one way he could think to do it.

"Hen Gastell," he said quietly.

Ivor stirred. His head remained in his hands, his knees still drawn up, but gradually, he lifted his head, his features twisted in confusion.

"What did you say?" he asked.

Kent crouched down a few feet away from him. "Hen Gastell," he said. "Do those words mean anything to you?"

Ivor wasn't in the mood for riddles. He simply put his face back in his hands. Kent could see that he wasn't going to get any answer out of the man.

Not that he blamed him.

It had been a hell of a night.

"Do you remember an English lad who saved you from drowning in the river?" Kent said. "A young lad who told you not to cross the water, but you did it anyway and fell in?"

Ivor didn't move for a moment. Then his head came up slowly, his face no longer contorted in confusion. But there was surprise. Kent could see that he had the man's attention, so he continued.

"*Summer days and summer stars, and a deep blue sea that glistens like silver,*" he sang softly. "We used to sing that song as we played at the Hen Gastell until I went off to foster. Do you remember now?"

Ivor looked at him, eyes wide. "Kent?"

"It has been a long time, Ivor."

When Ivor realized who it was, he began to get emotional.

"My God," he breathed. "Is it really you?"

Kent pulled a small dagger out from his waistband and leaned forward, cutting the bindings around Ivor's wrists. "It is me," he said. "I was introduced to you at The Bryn's cottage as Trevyn d'Einen. You did not recognize me and, honestly, had you not been introduced as Ivor ap Yestin, I would not have recognized you, either. We've both grown considerably in the last thirty years."

As soon as Kent cut the bindings, Ivor grabbed the man's hand, looking at him in amazement. "Kent," he gasped. "Nay, I would not have recognized you, but now that I look in your eyes, I can see that boy. It really *is* you!"

Kent smiled. "Aye, it really is," he said. "Ivor, I am sorry this happened. Please know I had no part in it. A knight named de Russe blames you for the attack on his sister. Did you know that?"

Ivor didn't let go of his hand, but he nodded. "Aye," he said. "The same knight who sacked The Narth. He came to me with that story about his sister and insisted I was responsible for her attack or was protecting the men who were."

"Are you? And were you?"

Ivor didn't hesitate. "Nay," he said. "I know nothing about it in spite of the evidence de Russe supposedly has. It was not me or my men, Kent. I swear that upon all that is holy."

"I believe you," Kent said. "Something about this situation just doesn't seem right, but de Russe is convinced the Welsh perpetrated the attack."

"So he has told me."

"He intends to punish you for it," Kent said. "He intends to make an example out of you."

Ivor sighed heavily and let go of Kent's hand. "Then he

punishes an innocent man," he said. "Do you know where the man who was with me is? His name is Dai. He was wounded in the skirmish."

Kent shook his head. "I do not know," he said. "But I shall find out."

Ivor had to be satisfied with that for now. He was a little overwhelmed at seeing his old friend, who had grown into an enormous man of great power. Clearly a man who had seen, and experienced, much in life, and there was an inherent curiosity about that. Ivor would have been absolutely overjoyed to discuss old times if this had been any other situation, but somehow, it didn't seem right. Still, he couldn't help himself.

He wanted to know.

"You have my thanks," he said sincerely. "Tell me, lad, how have your parents been? Your father? I heard that he is the Earl of Talgarth now. Is he still angry with me for dragging you out to play at the old castle those years ago?"

Kent grinned. "Probably," he said. "My father can hold a grudge longer than anyone. But he is well, as is my mother. Thank you for asking."

"That is good to hear."

"And you? You have been well all these years?"

Ivor nodded, leaning his head back against the cell wall. "I have," he said. He gestured to Kent, in full protection, and smiled. "I suspect I've not had your adventures, but it has been a good life."

"I am glad to hear that."

"Have you married?"

Kent shook his head. "Nay," he said. "But… there is a special woman for me. I've simply not asked her to be my wife yet. And you?"

Kent asked the question knowing full well what the answer was, but he wanted to hear it for himself. He wanted to see if Madelaina's take on the attraction between her and Ivor was as casual as she made it sound or if they were madly in love and she hadn't been truthful.

He was curious about Ivor's answer.

"I've not married," Ivor said, shrugging as he averted his gaze. "No time. It seems I'm married to Wales, to protect her against the Saesneg as a husband would protect a wife. But I've clearly done a very poor job if I am in here."

"This was not your fault," Kent said. "But you should have remained at Pentwyn. It is safer for you there."

Ivor looked at him. "You know of Pentwyn?"

Kent nodded. "It seems to be common knowledge in the village, and you know that servants are willing to talk for the right price," he said. "Why did you come back?"

"To see what the English had done to my castle," Ivor said. Then he looked at the man, his shoulders, his arms, and finally his hands. He pointed to them. "Did you truly burn your hand, Kent?"

It took Kent a moment to realize what he was talking about. Ivor was referring to the excuse Madelaina had given him about Kent's presence at her home. Kent didn't hesitate to hold up his hands so that Ivor could see that they were perfectly fine.

"Nay," he said quietly, shaking his head. "I was at the apothecary's shop to sup with The Bryn and his daughter, but she must have thought I was in danger with you there. She lied about my identity and the situation, but I am certain she did it to protect me."

"Why would she do that?"

"Because she did not want any violence, I suppose."

Ivor considered that, possibly accepting it. For now. "Why *were* you there?" he asked.

The way he asked it tipped Kent off that it was more than just a normal inquiry. It was a territorial inquiry because, in Ivor's mind, Madelaina was his territory.

Kent was careful in his answer.

"I was there to gather information on you," Kent said. "We were told that The Bryn was one of your advisors."

"That is all?"

"What more would there be?"

"A pretty lass, mayhap?"

"She is very pretty," Kent agreed. "But I was there for information at that time. Nothing more."

Ivor seemed to accept the information because he really didn't have a reason to doubt him at this point. "'Tis your duty, I suppose," he said. "Did de Russe ask you to find me?"

"Nay," Kent said. "I do not serve de Russe. I serve the king as one of his personal guard."

That seemed to impress Ivor, steering him away from the rather touchy subject of Madelaina. "Truly?" he said. "One of the king's men? You were destined for great things, my friend. I am proud to hear that."

Kent nodded his thanks, vaguely, but his manner seemed to be growing edgy. "Ivor, I do not mean to be rude, but there is much at stake here for you," he said. "You are in a dangerous situation."

Ivor sighed faintly, looking around the dingy cell. "I realize that," he said. "Did you come to help me escape?"

That was a good question. Kent believed in Ivor's innocence, but allowing the man to escape from custody was a tricky matter. He stood up, hands on his hips as he gazed down at the

Welsh prisoner.

"Let me see what de Russe intends," he said. "The problem is that there are about one hundred de Russe men in the gatehouse, all of whom will see if I remove you from the vault, so you must be patient. I swore to you once that I would never take up a sword against you, and I meant it. But preventing a man from punishing his prisoner is something that could haunt me for the rest of my career, so let me discover what de Russe's intentions are and plan from there."

Ivor nodded, though he seemed disappointed. "I understand," he said. "And I swore to you once that I would never take up arms against you, either. But I did not make that vow to any other English fool."

Kent cocked an eyebrow. "Ivor, if you attempt to escape, they will kill you," he said flatly. "For now, you must remain here and remain compliant. Will you do that for me, please? I cannot help you if you are dead."

Ivor wasn't pleased with the situation, but he understood. With a nod, he settled back into the dirty straw.

"This is not an ideal situation, but I will say that I am glad to see you, Kent," he said. "I hope we have the opportunity to speak again, and on things other than de Russe's vendetta."

Kent smiled weakly. "I hope so, too," he said. "I thought about you over the years and wondered how you fared."

Ivor snorted sarcastically. "I have fared so well that I am now in my own dungeon," he said, slapping at the straw. "There is some irony in that."

"Indeed," Kent said. Then he held up a hand to the man, a gesture that suggested he simply sit there for now. "Be patient. I will return."

Ivor nodded, but Kent could see the hope in the man's eyes.

Hope that an old friend might actually help him.

    But Kent wasn't so sure he could.

    God help him, he just wasn't.

CHAPTER TWENTY-ONE

"SHOUTING AT ME is not going to help the situation," Torran said. "*You* are the one who acted rashly, de Russe. Not me. You do not seem to care if the marches descend into a hellscape of fire and death, but I can assure you that Henry will. He will hear about your reckless behavior."

Treyton was facing off against a chamber full of Henry's men—Aidric, Jareth, Dirk, Britt, Orion, Stefan, and Bennet were backing up Torran during this explosive exchange. Treyton had no one but himself in support and knew he was close to being removed from The Narth and sent home in disgrace, but the one thing that was keeping that from happening was the fact that Ivor was in the vault—his prisoner—and if he left, he would take Ivor with him. That was his legal right, considering he'd captured the man.

And it was clear that Torran didn't want Ivor taken from The Narth.

That realization fed Treyton's rage.

"I am not shouting at you," he said, though it was done loudly in spite of his protest. "The point is this—any magistrate in the country will legally side with me in this matter. Ivor ap

Yestin is my prisoner and you cannot take that from me."

"No one is trying to take that from you," Torran said evenly. "But you are thinking with vengeance in your heart and not a sense of the welfare of others."

"I do not care about others!" Treyton burst out. "I care about my sister and justice!"

"Do you not have the patience to actually find those responsible?" Torran said. "Or do you simply want to arbitrarily punish a man you think *may* have men under his command who have committed this heinous crime?"

Treyton was backed into a corner. Literally. They were in the large, two-storied entry chamber, the one with the big hearth and tables, and he was standing with his back to the hearth. If he went any further, he would end up in it.

"I do not like the fact that you are treating me as if I've done something wrong," he said. He slapped himself in the chest. "*I* have not done anything wrong. I am doing something that any of you would do if your sister had been attacked and beaten so badly that she cannot walk any longer. If you looked at your sister with her broken fingers where they stole her rings, or an eye that was so badly broken that she will never look the same again, you would have the same sense of vengeance in your heart that I have. If you did not, then you are not worthy of being a man."

Torran sighed, saddened at yet more detail of Talia de Russe's injuries. "Treyton, no one is treating you as if you have done something wrong," he said. "We would all like to see justice served for your sister. But there are two problems we are facing—the first problem is that you have a Welsh warlord, a prince of Elfael, in your custody, and you know how volatile that is. The Welsh do not take kindly to their princes being treated poorly, especially for crimes they did not personally commit. The second problem is what I just mentioned—Ivor ap Yestin did not order the attack on your sister, nor did he participate in it. You would be punishing an innocent man, which makes this situation so very much worse."

Treyton had his arms folded across his chest angrily. "He will not tell me who committed this attack, so he gives me no choice."

"You have a choice, Treyton. But you are too stupid or too stubborn to realize it."

Torran hadn't spoken those words. Everyone turned to see Kent entering the keep, his gaze fixed on Treyton, who had once been someone he had shared a peaceful acquaintance, if not an actual friendship, with.

But not anymore.

As Kent walked up on the group, he made his way straight to Treyton.

"The man didn't hurt your sister," he said in an icy tone. "He did not order his men to do it. Why can you not take him at his word?"

Treyton scowled. "Did you not hear what I told you when you first arrived?" he said. "Merchants in the village were selling my sister's rings."

"Did you ask them where they got them?"

"Where else would they get them?" Treyton said hotly. "The Narth overlooks the village, Kent. There were five hundred Welshmen in the fortress when we sacked it. Where else would those jewels have come from?"

"Then you did not ask them."

"They would not tell us!" Treyton snapped. "Why do you think we sacked the castle?"

Kent cocked an eyebrow. "Do you really want to know?" he said. "I think you sacked it in revenge for the merchants being unable, or unwilling, to tell you where they got the rings. I think you sacked it on a whim, before you thoroughly investigated the situation. I think you did it because you were angry and nothing more. You're so determined to find the men responsible for Talia's injuries that you're willing to destroy innocent men simply because you can."

Treyton was red in the face by the time Kent was finished. "I did not want to believe what I heard about you, but it seems that I should have," he growled. "You speak like a fool."

Kent rolled his eyes. "God's Bones, Treyton," he said sarcastically. "By all means, tell me what you heard about me. Let us all hear what you've heard."

"That Ivor ap Yestin is an old friend of yours," Treyton said. "I've also heard that every member of the Guard of Six has named his weapon. Yours is named *Insurrection*. Is that what will happen now? You will stage an insurrection and side against your own countrymen in protecting a murderer because you are a traitorous bastard?"

Kent leaned in Treyton's direction, preparing to take a swing at the man, but Torran stopped him. Orion and Stefan, however, had no such restraint. They charged forward and would have made it to Treyton had Bennet and Britt and Aidric not stopped them. Orion took a swipe at Treyton and made contact, nearly toppling the man back into the hearth before Bennet managed to drag him away. Britt and Aidric were pushing back Stefan, who was seemingly furious.

"What did he say?" Stefan demanded. "If Orion thinks it is bad enough to charge, then I stand with him. What did that bastard say?"

"He called Kent a traitor," Orion shouted over to him. "He needs to be taught a lesson."

"Then let's get him!"

The pair charged again, but too many hands were holding them back. Meanwhile, Treyton had moved away from the hearth so he wouldn't end up in it. Chaos threatened to descend and Torran knew he had to do something.

He motioned to Jareth.

"Go to the vault," he said. "Take Dirk with you. Bring ap Yestin up here. Let us get to the truth of this once and for all."

Jareth and Dirk bolted, heading swiftly out of the keep. Kent managed to pull himself away from Torran, struggling to cool his temper as he headed over to Orion and Stefan.

"Orion," he said, slapping the man lightly on the cheek. "I've been called worse, lad. *You've* probably been called worse, too. Look at how concerned Bennet is about you. He's an old man and you are going to give him heart failure with your behavior, so shut your mouth and sit down. Please."

Orion wasn't happy with the command, but he obeyed. He stopped struggling and found a seat with Bennet as his minder, and the man wasn't going to let Orion get into any trouble on his watch. The two had formed a strong bond, and that was clear. The group stood in silence, spreading out over the chamber as they endeavored to cool their tempers. Kent made it over to one of the tables, perching on the end of it, watching Treyton like a hawk.

The mood in the hall was heavy and dark.

Kent could feel it but didn't care. He wasn't surprised that Treyton had heard about his relationship with Ivor, because others knew. Men talked and men overheard. He could see why Torran hadn't wanted him to tell Treyton of his association with Ivor on the day they arrived because, clearly, Treyton thought the worst, just as Torran suspected he would. But he knew now and Kent wasn't going to deny it. Those few years of his youth when he and Ivor were friends were important to him. Those were years when he learned to be tolerant of people who had different backgrounds than he did. He found interest in those who were different.

He wasn't going to let Treyton trivialize that.

"Now you see why I did not want you to tell him that you knew Ivor," Torran said quietly, walking up beside him. "Vengeance can make a man twist things around. He's not thinking clearly."

"You're wrong," Kent said, his focus on Treyton. "He is, indeed, thinking clearly. He wants to blame everyone for his sister's injuries and, soon enough, is going to blame me also."

"He has no reason to."

"Mark my words."

Torran didn't have much to say to that. He hoped Kent wasn't right, but then again, there was no telling. But he knew one thing.

The situation was going to get ugly.

They proceeded to wait in silence for several long minutes until Jareth and Dirk reappeared with Ivor between them. There were some de Russe soldiers on the stairs to the keep, having followed the two royal knights, trying to get their hands on Ivor because they knew who he was. They'd been told that the prisoner was responsible for Talia's injuries, and there was some talk of throwing him from the wall, but several of Henry's soldiers intervened and the sounds of a brawl wafted in through the open entry door.

Torran motioned to Jareth and Dirk.

"Quickly," he said. "Bring him in and bolt that door."

Dirk went to throw the bolt and seal the keep as Jareth took Ivor to the table that Kent was sitting on. Ivor sat, looking at the men around him without much emotion, but when it came to Treyton, he was wary.

Torran looked at Treyton but pointed to Ivor.

"There he is," Torran said. "Ask him your questions. Get the answers you seek."

Treyton's face was set in a permanent frown as he moved in Ivor's direction. He was keenly aware that Kent was seated only a few feet away from his prisoner, which thoroughly irritated him. *Birds of a feather,* he thought.

The first thing he did was point at Kent.

"Do you know this man?" Treyton asked.

Ivor looked at Kent before nodding. "I do."

"*How* do you know him?"

"We were friends, as children."

"Do you know his brothers?" Treyton asked. "He has several."

"Henry, Clarke, Edward, and Owen," Kent said, eyeing Treyton with hostility. "What is your point?"

Treyton cocked an eyebrow. "Your friend can speak for himself."

"Then ask him some relevant questions and stop being an idiot."

That only inflamed Treyton. He looked at Ivor, moving closer. "Henry, Clarke, Edward, and Owen," he repeated, almost mockingly. "Do you know them?"

Ivor shook his head. "I know *of* them," he said. "I know that one of them is the garrison commander at Tyr Castle, but I do not know which one."

"You've never had any contact with them?"

"Nay."

"What are you driving at, Treyton?" Torran interrupted.

Treyton looked at Torran, at Kent, and shook his head in disgust. "I'm simply putting the pieces of this puzzle together," he said. "I am allowed to interrogate my own prisoner, and if you interfere, I'll go to the local magistrate."

Torran snorted rudely. "And do what?" he said. "Honestly, Treyton, you've gone from bad to worse with your irrational thinking. Do you know who the local magistrate is? Rex de Lohr, the Earl of Cheltenham. He is allied with Henry and with de Poyer, so if you think to cause problems, I would not try. You'll only look ridiculous."

Treyton shook his head, clearly furious, as he looked between Torran and Kent. "You have been trying to discourage me from seeking justice for my sister since you arrived," he said. "Frankly, I did not know why you even came to The Narth, but I am starting to."

Kent looked at Torran. "This should be good," he muttered before turning his attention to Treyton. "Go ahead and tell us this great revelation."

Treyton wasn't amused by Kent's attitude. "I think you brought Henry's troops here to keep me from discovering the truth," he said. "And that is exactly what I am going to tell my father when he arrives."

"What truth?"

Treyton pointed to Ivor. "His family and the de Poyer family are allied," he said. "That made me realize that the de Poyer family must be involved in this."

Kent frowned. "Are you mad?" he said. "No one is involved in anything."

"I do not think that's true," Treyton said. "Ivor would not turn over the men responsible for my sister's attack because I suspect they are at Tyr Castle, being hidden from me by Ivor's great friends, the de Poyer family."

Kent hadn't been expecting that bit of foolishness, and he rolled his eyes, looking at Torran to see that the man thought Treyton's fantasy to be fairly foolish as well. Kent wiped a weary hand over his face.

"You are creating situations that are simply not true," he said. "Treyton, no one is hiding these men, least of all my brother, Henry, who is the garrison commander at Tyr. Henry is an honorable man who would never do such a thing even if Ivor managed to ask him, which he did not."

Treyton wasn't convinced. "I am going to have my father petition Henry for an impartial magistrate to interrogate your brother," he said. "I sent word to my father the day you arrived, you know. You told me to, and I did. He will be here soon and will know about this situation."

"And what is that?"

Treyton grunted, a disagreeable sound. "That there is something amiss because Henry's men seem to be allying with the Welsh and not an English warlord who is loyal to the Crown," he said. "My father will know everything because it means that this… this *corruption* goes deeper than just Ivor ap Yestin. I think de Poyer is involved in this and you do not want me to discover that."

Kent simply looked at Torran. He was the leader of the Six, and although Kent wanted to throttle Treyton, he wasn't going to act on a whim. He would wait to see how Torran wanted to handle this, because the truth was that the House of de Russe could cause trouble for the Earl of Talgarth and his holdings.

Nothing that could be proven, of course, because it was all just a fantasy, but word could get around. It wouldn't reflect well on Caledon or his sons that Gaspard and Treyton de Russe were calling them traitors because they helped cover up a beating of a young woman.

"De Russe, you are a madman," Ivor spoke up. "Understand me—I am sorry for what happened to your sister, but neither me nor my men had anything to do with it. I do not even know where this attack happened because you've never made that clear. The only thing you've done is make demands for criminals who do not exist, and rather than actually try to find them, you have grown lazy and complacent and seek to place the blame where it does not belong. That does not serve justice for your sister."

Treyton exploded. "You will not speak of my sister," he boomed. "You will keep her from your mind, you murderous bastard. She had everything in the world to live for and now… now she cannot walk and we do not know if she will ever speak again. Her face is misshapen from where she was beaten. Her fingers were broken as your men yanked her rings off. And you wonder why I want to discover who did this? I will discover them and I will punish them!"

He moved toward Ivor, causing the man to leap up from his seat to put some distance between them. "I am not the only one seeing your irrational behavior," he said, dodging behind the table. "And I am not denying involvement because I am afraid of you. I am denying involvement because it is the truth!"

Treyton launched himself at Ivor, which predictably brought the wrath of Kent. Ivor was smaller than Kent, and faster, and managed to dodge out of the way as Kent and Treyton collided. With flying fists and grunts, the fight was on.

As the two of them grappled across the table, a great pounding could be heard. Someone was hammering on the entry door, the one Dirk had bolted, and the reverberation could be heard all throughout the hall. Someone wanted very much to get in the door, but Torran wasn't in any hurry to answer it. But the pounding didn't stop, and as Kent and Treyton ended up on the floor, with Kent smashing the man's face into the stone, Torran grew irritated with the continuous pounding and motioned to Bennet, Orion, and Stefan.

"See who it is," he said. "If it is a de Russe soldier, throw him over the side of the stairs. Aidric, Dirk—you will be the second line of defense in case they try to break in."

As the knights moved to the entry door, preparing to toss whoever was pounding on the door off the staircase and into the bailey below, Torran and Jareth and Britt were watching Kent pound the senses out of Treyton. Treyton was a big man, but Kent was too much for him. Over near the hearth, Ivor had picked up an iron fire poker and was preparing to use it on Treyton should the man come near him.

"Are you not going to stop this?" Ivor asked, indicating the fight. "They will kill one another!"

Torran watched as Treyton managed to throw up a fist and clip Kent in the chin. "It will be over soon enough," he said. "I think this has been a long time in coming, so let them fight it out. It will cool their blood."

"*Torran!*"

At the sound of his name, Torran turned toward the entry door to see an older man in well-used protection entering the keep. There were a couple of other men with him, but they were held back by the knights at the door. Only the older man had been allowed through. As he drew nearer, Torran could see the de Russe dragon on the tunic he wore. Approaching the area near the hearth, the older man saw the fight and scowled.

"Treyton!" he boomed. "What is the meaning of this?"

The man's voice was loud and Treyton immediately stopped wrestling with Kent. His head popped up from where Kent had him pinned on the ground.

"Papa?" Treyton said in surprise. "My God… *Papa!*"

Kent's attention was diverted enough by the new arrival that Treyton was able to shove him over and get out from underneath him. He was on his feet, bloodied and beaten, as he approached his father.

Gaspard de Russe looked at his son in outrage.

"*What* are you doing?" he demanded. Then he started pointing to the men around him, whom he did not recognize. "Are these Henry's guard?"

"Aye."

"Why on earth are they beating you?"

"He made the first move, my lord," Kent said, unwilling to be made out to be the aggressor in this situation. "I was responding to his aggression."

Gaspard looked at his son, deeply displeased. "Damnation, lad," he muttered. "Not again."

Treyton was without defense and he knew it. There were nine witnesses to attest to the fact that he'd moved first, so he did the only thing he could do.

He pleaded.

"Papa," he said, desperately needing his father's sympathy. "It is not as it seems. I—"

Gaspard cut him off with a wave of his hand. "I do not wish to hear your excuses," he said. He looked off to his left, where Torran and a few others were standing. "Well? Who are you?"

Torran answered. "I am Torran de Serreaux," he said. "I command Henry's Guard of Six. We've not met, my lord, but Henry speaks highly of you."

Gaspard eyed the man. "My son told me that you had come," he said. "I'd just arrived home when I received my son's missive, so I hurried back. He told me *why* you came."

Torran nodded. "I have Henry's missive addressed to you that will explain everything," he said. "I will fetch it."

Gaspard held up a hand. "That is not necessary," he said. "When you hear what I have to say, you will understand why."

"What's amiss, Papa?" Treyton said. Then his eyes widened. "Oh, God… Did something happen to Talia?"

Gaspard nodded. "She regained her wits," he said, sounding relieved. "Just as I reached home. I was able to speak with her for the first time since the attack and discover just what really happened."

That was good news as far as Treyton was concerned. "Then this is a fortuitous moment, because Ivor ap Yestin is my prisoner," he said, pointing to the man over near the hearth with the iron poker in his hand. "Unfortunately, Henry's men do not seem to want me to punish him for the crime. De Poyer in particular seems to be complicit with the man and has protected him."

"Complicit?" Gaspard repeated, confused. His gaze moved from his bloodied son to the man he'd been fighting. "Is that what this is about? You want to punish a man for your sister's attack?"

"Of course I do."

Gaspard was beginning to grasp the situation and what his son had been up to. He nodded in understanding. "I see," he said, but his gaze moved to Kent. "You're de Poyer?"

Kent nodded. "I am, my lord."

Gaspard looked him over. "I've not seen you since you were a lad," he said. "You look like your father."

"Thank you, my lord."

"Papa," Treyton said, interjecting himself into the conversation. "Did you not hear me? We now have the man who is responsible for Talia's assault."

Gaspard shook his head. "He is not responsible."

That brought surprise from everyone listening. "What do you mean by that?" Torran said. "Have you discovered something, my lord?"

Gaspard nodded. "Indeed I have," he said. "Treyton, I've come to fetch you because we are abandoning The Narth."

Treyton's eyes widened. "We are?" he said, shocked. "But… *why*?"

"Because we are going to punish the true assailant."

"Who is that?"

Gaspard looked at his son. "According to your sister, it was her own betrothed who committed this heinous crime," he said. "Talia recognized some of the men as being friends of Michael Wellesbourne. It seems that he would rather marry that baker's daughter, so he tried to stage the murder of your sister and make it look like a robbery. With Talia out of the way and the Welsh to blame, he can marry whomever he wishes."

Treyton's jaw dropped. "And you are certain of this?"

Gaspard nodded. "That is what your sister told me," he said. "She evidently heard the men speaking of it when they thought she was unconscious. We are, therefore, going to take our army to Wellesbourne Castle and make sure they know that we will not tolerate an assault on our women. Michael has a good deal to answer for."

It was stunning news, but it explained so much. Kent hadn't been the only person who said that something about the attack on Talia de Russe seemed odd. Others had said it, and if they hadn't said it, they thought it. Now, they were discovering the truth. The Welsh were vindicated.

But no one was more stunned than Ivor.

The man was standing with his mouth hanging open, looking between Treyton and Gaspard in horror. "Then all of this… the sacking of my home… was a mistake?" he said incredulously. "God's Bones, man… Do you not get your facts straight before you go about ruining people's lives?"

Gaspard looked at Ivor with the poker still in his hand. "We were meant to ruin you," he said, more subdued. "We were meant to go off on a wild chase while the real culprit remained unchallenged. It seems that was the plan, because the men who took Talia's rings, the Wellesbourne men, deliberately took their haul to Penderyn and sold it to a merchant for very little money. Given that it was a good bargain, the merchant took it. It seems they selected Penderyn purely at random, or at least there is no connection that me or my advisors can see. But I will find out for certain."

"And that's how the merchant got her jewelry," Ivor muttered in realization.

"That's how," Gaspard said. His gaze lingered on Ivor a moment, apologetically. "I hope you understand that our assault on The Narth was only to seek justice for my daughter. That is all I am interested in. It is not because I hate you or your kin. It was simply to punish who we believed to be the culprits in this situation."

Ivor sighed heavily and tossed the iron rod aside. "I suppose I can understand that," he said. "But you killed my men and thrashed my home. I've done nothing, yet you upended my life."

Gaspard nodded. "I will accept that," he said. "And I will make amends. I will help you rebuild whatever needs rebuilding. I hope you can accept that as an apology on our part. We were misled and, consequently, you received punishment you did not deserve."

Ivor simply stood there, dazed and upset. Kent and Torran glanced at each other, silent words passing between them, before Kent looked at Ivor.

"He is trying to be fair, Ivor," Kent said quietly. "He is admitting his mistake and offering to help you."

Ivor nodded. "I know," he said. "And I am appreciative. I was just thinking about the vows you and I made when we were lads. You swore never to fight me and I swore never to fight the English from Nether or Tyr. Do you remember?"

Kent smiled faintly. "I do," he said. "You told me that if other English were to fight you, then you would have to fight them to defend yourself."

"I kept that vow. I only defended myself."

"You did."

"What do you mean?" Gaspard said, moving closer to Ivor and looking between him and Kent. "You two have known each other a long time?"

Kent nodded. "We met as boys," he said. "We would play at an old castle on the marches. We made pacts, as boys sometimes do. Treyton was concerned that our friendship as children had turned into some kind of alliance and that I was trying to protect Ivor from de Russe justice. If Ivor was guilty, I would not have stood in your way, but he was innocent and Treyton did not seem to think so. Something about this entire situation seemed odd from the start, but your son did not want to acknowledge that. He was singularly focused on the Welsh as the guilty party."

Gaspard looked with displeasure at Treyton, who shrugged weakly. "I could only base my decision on the evidence," he said. "It was all we had to go on. And Talia deserves justice."

Gaspard understood and didn't disagree, but he'd hoped his son would have been more fair in his judgment. He turned to Ivor. "I can only apologize for the fact that we were misled," he said. "But it was deliberate. If you and your men wish to join me in punishing Wellesbourne, I would welcome you."

That seemed to perk Ivor up a great deal. His eyes widened at the offer and he looked at Kent to see the man's reaction. Kent smiled weakly, nodding his head in support. In fact, all of Henry's men seemed to be in approval of Gaspard's offer, and Ivor stood straight, no longer feeling hunted, and brushed the ash from the fire poker off his hands.

"I would be honored to join you, great lord," he said to Gaspard. "And then you can help me repair the damage to The Narth."

"Agreed," Gaspard said. Then he looked at his son and crooked a finger. "You. With me. Now."

With that, he turned on his heel and headed toward the entry of the keep with Treyton following, head hung. The father was about to have words with his son over his behavior at The Narth, and those words would not be pleasant ones. Everyone watched the pair filter out, and once they were gone the relief in the chamber was palpable. Both Torran and Ivor converged on Kent, who was wiping the blood away from his nose and checking to see if he had any broken teeth.

"Well?" Torran said, mirth in his eyes. "Will you survive?"

Kent moved his jaw around. "Probably," he said. "But thank God for Gaspard's appearance. I fear we would have been in a dire situation without him."

Torran chuckled. "You speak the truth," he said. "In fact, I should follow them and see what Gaspard plans to do."

"Other than berate his idiotic son?"

Torran shrugged. "Treyton is a loyal brother and I commend him for it," he said. "Few men would protect a sister so rabidly. But he is also a stubborn arse and deserves whatever scolding his father gives him."

With that, he headed for the door, taking Jareth with him. The other men were filtering back into the small solar near the entry door, leaving Kent and Ivor standing near the hearth. Kent pointed to the poker on the floor.

"Were you really going to use that?" he asked.

Ivor scratched his chin, grinning. "I was thinking on it," he said, but quickly sobered as he looked at Kent. "Once again, you have saved me. I do not know what I've done in my life that I should be rewarded with a friend as loyal as you, but know that I am grateful. That is twice I owe you for my very life, and I shall endeavor to repay the debt, however I can."

As Kent listened to his words, a thought occurred to him. It would more than likely be a difficult request for Ivor, but in this case, Kent was going to be selfish. The more he thought on it, the more hope, and excitement, he felt.

"Do you mean that?" he said. "Because if you truly feel indebted to me, there is something you can do that would save my life in another way."

Ivor looked at him curiously. "Save your life?" he said. "How?"

"You can give me happiness to last a lifetime."

Ivor was *extremely* curious now. "Anything," he said. "What can I do for you?"

Kent told him.

CHAPTER TWENTY-TWO

Penderyn

T HE BRYN WAS extremely unhappy.

"How can you ask me such a thing, Ivor?" he said. "From you. Of all people—from *you*!"

Ivor sat across from the man at his shattered kitchen table, the one that had been in the midst of the fight the previous night. Ivor had arrived at The Bryn's home at dawn just as the man was returning from tending Old Adda and stood with him as The Bryn was overcome with horror at the condition of his home. Fortunately, Ivor was there to explain everything, including the fact that Celyn and Madelaina were safe, and as soon as The Bryn regained his composure, the two of them moved inside and began to assess the damage.

Until Ivor brought up the subject of Madelaina and a certain English knight.

Then everything came to a halt.

At first, The Bryn had been greatly confused on the subject matter, until Ivor realized that the man only knew Kent as Trevyn d'Einen. Madelaina had used that same ruse when she introduced Kent to her father. Ivor was forced to explain the situation and that d'Einen was, in fact, an English knight named Kent de Poyer.

A man who very much wanted to marry Madelaina.

That was when The Bryn exploded.

"I realize it is not expected," Ivor said. "And I fully realize you were expecting that I would marry Madelaina one day. But let us be truthful with one another—Madelaina does not love me. And although I am very fond of her, I do not love her either. But I know someone who does."

The Bryn waved him off angrily. "I do not wish to discuss this now," he said. "Look around you, Ivor—my home is in ruins. May I, at least, restore my home before you bring up such a tactless subject?"

Ivor could see his point, but he didn't agree with it. "Why wait?" he said. "We can speak of it as we are fixing your table or restoring your door. I am afraid this is not a subject that you can ignore."

"Why not?"

"Do you want Madelaina to end up as Celyn did those years ago?"

That shook The Bryn. It also told him that something serious had been going on behind his back, something he'd been entirely unaware of. Madelaina was an adult woman, and he didn't pay much attention to her daily activities because he trusted her, and also because they weren't usually scandalous in nature. She spent most of her time in the herb garden or working in his shop. But perhaps he should have suspected something was afoot when she introduced him to the big, handsome Trevyn d'Einen.

Who wasn't Trevyn d'Einen, after all.

He didn't want to discuss any of this right now, but perhaps he should. Nay, he didn't want Madelaina to end up as Celyn did, those years ago.

Mayhap he needed to listen to Ivor.

"Damnation," he muttered. "Is that what this has come to? Another Saesneg?"

"You married a Saesneg," Ivor reminded him quietly. "You gave up your family for her. You started a new life for her. Why do you not let your daughters have the same love that you had? You have already failed Celyn. Do not fail Madelaina."

The harsh words nearly doused all of The Bryn's resistance. The old man sat there, frowning, avoiding making eye contact with Ivor. He was hotly opposed to what Ivor was suggesting, but on the other hand, he had been in the same situation, once. But this was different.

... wasn't it?

The Bryn was a man who controlled the village, and, in many ways, he'd advised and controlled Ivor through that advice. He could give counsel but he couldn't take it well, mostly because it pointed out his shortcomings.

No man liked to be reminded of his failures.

"Celyn's circumstance was different," he muttered. "She was young. *Too* young."

"She was old enough to love."

"She was also old enough to conceive a child, but that does not make her old enough to fathom the consequence of what she did," The Bryn fired back, but it was without force. Reliving the decision he made for his daughter, something he'd secretly agonized over throughout the years, was not something that made him feel good about what he'd done. "Do you not understand? I did not want her to suffer as I had suffered. I wanted her to marry a Welshman and live with the approval of her people. I lived without the approval of mine, and it was difficult."

Ivor could see that he was struggling. "So you denied her love in exchange for respect."

The Bryn was resolute. "She did not suffer the same fate as I did."

Ivor peered at him curiously. "How did you suffer?" he said. "It is true that your people disowned you, but you at least had the love of a good woman. Celyn had the respect of her people, but that is a cold comfort when one is lying in bed at night, alone and sad. All I am saying is that you must not make the same mistake again. Kent de Poyer is a good man, better than any man you can hope for. He is my friend and will treat Madelaina with love and respect. She will want for nothing. And someday, she will be a countess. A lady revered by her subjects. Do not let prejudices stop you from making the right decision for Madelaina, I beg you."

The Bryn was clearly wavering but was too stubborn to admit it. He sighed heavily, perhaps with regret, but perhaps also with resignation.

Old age had softened him.

"You plead strongly for this Saesneg," he muttered. "You are also pleading for the woman you hoped to marry."

Ivor smiled wryly. "Life is full of surprises," he said. "It is as I told you. Maddie does not love me, and although I am fond of her, I think Kent would make her happier. In fact, I know he would."

The Bryn pondered that for a moment. "A countess, you say?"

"A countess married to a man who serves Henry directly," Ivor said. "There is no finer man for her, I promise."

The Bryn grunted. "So you've said," he said. "But I will ask Madelaina. I want to hear what she thinks about all of this. And you promise me that my women are safe?"

Ivor nodded. "That was the first thing I told you when I arrived," he said. "Do you know who took them to safety?"

The Bryn shook his head. "You?"

Ivor frowned. "I was a prisoner," he said. "The person that took them to safety was Bennet de Bermingham."

The Bryn stared at him for a moment as that name sank in. *It couldn't be!* Slowly, he closed his eyes and turned away.

"God," he muttered. "Not that man. Not him."

"He serves with Kent," Ivor said steadily. "He saved Celyn and Madelaina from harm. And he wishes to speak to you."

The Bryn looked at him sharply, seeing the smile playing on his lips, and stormed up from the table.

"Stop toying with me," he said. "You know I do not wish to see him and you know why."

"I know," Ivor said. "It was explained to me last night. After Gaspard de Russe took his son away, Kent spoke to me about Madelaina and then summoned Bennet, who told me what happened with Celyn. He told me the entire story. Truly, Bryn, I must say that I was surprised to hear what happened. While I understand why you did it, to protect Celyn, it all could have been avoided if you'd just let them be married. Instead, Bennet has lived the last twenty years with your lies defining his career and not even having the woman he loved as comfort. I think you owe the man."

"I do not owe anyone!"

"Don't you?"

The Bryn turned to Ivor, preparing to berate him, but he couldn't muster the conviction to do it. He knew what he'd done those years ago. He was well aware that he'd ruined a man's career. Though it had been necessary, deep down, he wasn't proud of it.

"You do not understand," he said. "Celyn, pregnant and without a husband, would have condemned her for the rest of her life. I had to do something. I had to *say* something."

"I know," Ivor said. "Strangely enough, Bennet does not seem to harbor any ill will. He does not wish to scold you for what happened those years ago. But he does want to ask you a question."

"What is it?"

"If he can marry Celyn."

The Bryn didn't react for a moment. He simply stared at Ivor. Then he put both hands on his face in a gesture of both disbelief and surrender.

"God," he muttered. "Say it is not so."

"It is," Ivor said quietly. "Please let your children be happy. You have that power. It is not fair to them that you were able to marry your forbidden love and they cannot. You are not protecting them, you know. You are condemning them to a lifetime of unhappiness when excellent men, devoted men, are ready and willing to be their husbands."

The Bryn dropped his hands from his face, looking at Ivor. "And you?" he said. "If you do not marry Madelaina, then who?"

Ivor grinned. "That is also dependent on you," he said. "It seems that Bennet has a lovely sister, much sought after. If I can convince you to allow him to marry Celyn, then Bennet shall introduce me to his sister."

He waggled his eyebrows happily, and The Bryn gave up. He could see where this was all leading and he knew what he had to do. No more resistance, no more stubborn refusals and tantrums. It was finally time to let all that go.

Ivor was right—he had to let them be happy.

"Such a day already," he moaned. "You are expecting me to make these important decisions immediately."

"I am expecting you to give this your attention," Ivor said. "The cottage can wait. Think of Celyn and Madelaina's happiness now."

The Bryn signed heavily. "If I do, will you leave me alone?"

"I will."

"Very well," he said. "Where are these men, that I may speak with them? And without you around. You have the tongue of a viper, convincing me to do things as if I have no will of my own."

Ivor laughed softly. "You indeed have a will," he said. "As long as you are doing the right thing."

The Bryn scowled at him. "Where are they?"

Ivor pointed toward the garden, and The Bryn turned to see four people standing out there—Madelaina and the man she'd introduced as Trevyn, and Celyn and Bennet. He even saw Arthur as the dog nosed around in the garden. He hadn't noticed them before because his back had been to the garden. He marched over to the broken garden door and yanked it open, pushing it aside when one of the hinges snapped.

"God's Bones," he muttered, shoving the door enough to prop it up before facing those in his garden. His focus was on the men. "You two will help me repair this place, since it was your comrades who did this. Then we will speak on your wishes, which Ivor has explained to me."

"And?" Madelaina said, her face full of hope. "What will your answer be?"

The Bryn frowned at her. "That is between me and the Englishman."

Madelaina, who had been full of forgiveness that morning when Kent came for her at the inn, wasn't willing to wait for her grandfather's answer. She took Kent's hand, holding it tightly, as she faced the old man.

"Please," she begged softly. "What will your answer be?"

The Bryn sighed sharply. "If I tell you, will you come inside and clean this cottage regardless of my answer?"

The hope faded from Madelaina's eyes a little. She was fearful of what he was going to say. "Aye," she said honestly. "I will do what needs to be done."

The Bryn could see how his question had upset her, but to her credit, she was facing it bravely. He crooked a finger at her and she went to him. Reaching out, he pulled her into a fatherly embrace, gazing down at her sweet face.

"Of course I want you to be happy," he said, gently gruff. "That means everything to me. If it is not with Ivor, then I hope you are happy with the next Earl of Talgarth. It will be a different life from what we lead here. Do you understand that?"

Madelaina nodded seriously. "I do," she said. "But it will not matter so long as Kent is by my side. I can face anything if he is there."

"He shall be there."

Madelaina's face lit up. "Do you mean it?"

"I mean it. Now, get inside and start cleaning up that mess."

Madelaina shrieked and ran back to Kent, throwing her arms around his neck and nearly knocking the wind out of him. He staggered back, keeping his balance as he hugged her more tightly than he'd ever hugged anyone in his life. Truly, it was one of the most momentous moments he'd ever experienced.

With Madelaina still hanging on him, he went over to The Bryn.

"Thank you, great lord," he said sincerely. "I will endeavor to always be worthy of her."

The Bryn nodded, noting the grip Madelaina had on his neck. "Is she choking you?"

"Mostly."

"You deserve it," The Bryn said, motioning to him. "Pry her off and get inside. There is much to do."

With a grin, Kent headed into the cottage with Madelaina still wrapped around his neck. But their departure left The Bryn alone with Bennet and Celyn.

This situation was a little more serious. There was history there. The Bryn was certain they were going to acknowledge that at some point, and quite honestly, he hadn't been prepared to revisit Celyn's past this morning, but here it was. Her past was in front of him.

He forced himself to face it.

"Celyn," The Bryn said. "Go inside and chaperone your daughter. I will speak with de Bermingham in private."

Celyn looked at Bennet fearfully, but the man simply nodded to her. Reluctantly, she headed into the cottage as The Bryn and Bennet faced off against one another.

A moment twenty years in the making.

"I must say that I was surprised to hear that you had come back with Henry's army," The Bryn said. "You've not changed much over the years. Just older."

"The same could be said about you."

The Bryn wondered if that was an insult. It probably was, just as he'd meant his comment as an insult. After a moment, he lifted his eyebrows.

"It would be a simple thing to do verbal battle with you again," he said. "It would be a simple thing to feed on the resentment and dislike I held for you so long ago. Aye, I disliked the man who bedded my daughter so that she became with child. Any father would."

Bennet cleared his throat softly and averted his gaze. "It was wrong of me, I know," he said. "But I do not regret it. I loved Celyn very much. Even after all these years, I still do. My feelings for her have not diminished in any way. The seams have not frayed. The light has not dimmed. She is mine and I am hers. It will always be that way."

The Bryn thought on those rather eloquent words. He knew that Celyn had lived a relatively lonely life. She had never entertained another suitor. She was good to the poor, pious in her prayers, but that wasn't enough to fulfill her. Even The Bryn knew that.

He'd known it all along.

"Years ago, I married an English lass," he said. "I am certain that surprises you, but I did. I do not think you met Celyn's mother, my beautiful Endelyn, but my marriage to her estranged me from my family. I was cast out, to live in shame with the woman I'd chosen. It was difficult to live without my family and my people, but it would have been more difficult to live without Endelyn. I did not realize that when you came into Celyn's life, so casting you out was a simple thing. I did not realize how difficult it was for both you and Celyn until Endelyn died and I was alone. Then I realized what it was like to live without the woman I love."

Bennet was listening to him, but his manner was guarded. "It is not easy."

"Nay, it is not."

"Then you will understand why I am here to ask for Celyn's hand again."

The Bryn nodded, looking at Bennet seriously. "Would you have come had Henry's orders not brought you to our doorstep?"

Bennet shrugged. "Probably, at some point," he said. "But Henry's orders *did* bring me here. I choose to view it as God's will. He has once again put me in front of Celyn because we are meant to be together. I cannot explain it any better than that."

The Bryn accepted that statement. "You were a boy when I last saw you," he said. "But you are a man now. And as a man, I will tell you of something that has changed my mind about you."

"What is that?"

There was warmth in The Bryn's eyes as he spoke. "Your daughter is the finest woman to ever walk this earth," he said. "I have raised her and there are things of importance that I have instilled within her, like loyalty to her family and to her country, and the need to help others, but there are things she possesses that cannot be taught. She is compassionate and kind, and she has a sense of duty and determination that she did not get from her mother. I can only assume she got it from you. I think only a man of great breeding and great character can produce a child like that. You are to be commended."

Bennet hadn't expected to hear that come out of The Bryn's mouth. Slightly confused, but also flattered, he dipped his head in thanks.

"It is kind of you to say so," he said. "I am looking forward to getting to know her for myself, if she will allow it."

The Bryn fell silent for a moment, clearly contemplating his next words. When he finally spoke again, it was quiet and with sincerity.

"Bennet, I know I disrupted your life greatly those years ago," he said. "I hope you understand that it was only in my quest to make Celyn appear incorruptible. What I mean to say is that I wanted people to be sympathetic toward her and did not want anyone condemning her for the situation she found herself in. What I did was in defense of my daughter."

Bennet had known they would touch on this subject at some point and was grateful for the opportunity. For certain, he had much to say on the subject.

"I am a man of patience," he said. "I am a man of understanding, or at least I hope I am. While I understand that you were determined to protect Celyn, as you should have been, your lies had a profound impact on the career of a young knight who was hoping for a great and noble destiny. After you did what you did, I was condemned to the lower ranks. No one wanted me. I ended up serving Henry because the Earl of Hereford knew that you had lied, and told Henry so. Henry sent me to Richmond Castle, where I served for many years. I have always wanted to tell you that your lies changed my life forever. It was not fair what happened. But I want to tell you now, as a father with a daughter, that I understand why you did what you did. In your position, I would have done anything to protect her also."

The Bryn eyed him with a hint of approval in his eyes. "It takes a man of great understanding to say something like that."

"I hope I have grown in character over the years. I hope I am always willing to learn and grow."

"Well said."

"Does that mean I may marry Celyn finally?"

The Bryn snorted softly. "It means that I shall soon be living alone in this cottage because my daughter, and granddaughter, are both to be married," he said. "But… they are marrying fine men. I was a fool not to see that before, Bennet. I hope I may call you Bennet."

"You may."

"You must still call me The Bryn. Call me anything else and I shall take back all of the nice things I have said."

Bennet grinned, not a gesture that usually came from him because he was far more reserved than that. But The Bryn's words, and subtle attempt at humor, had him smiling as he'd never smiled before. But he abruptly closed his eyes and pinched the bridge of his nose as the smile turned into a grimace.

"What's wrong?" The Bryn asked, concerned at what he was seeing. "Are you in pain?"

Bennet shook his head. "Nay," he said quickly. "No pain. But my eyes are watering with joy and I do not want to look like a fool for weeping."

The Bryn chuckled. "You do not look like a fool," he said. "You look like a man who has finally gotten what he wants out of life. Go inside and tell Celyn and see if she does not weep for joy also."

Bennet did.

Now, it was Celyn who attached herself to her man's neck and wouldn't let go. Around them, Ivor and Kent and Madelaina were slowly picking up the pieces from the English raid. Bit by bit, little by little, the cottage was being cleaned up, and as The Bryn stood in the garden, watching the happy people inside his abode, he couldn't help but feel good about it. He couldn't help but think there would be a good future for them all.

And the future gleams like diamonds.

For Kent and Madelaina, and Bennet and Celyn, hopefully it always would.

EPILOGUE

Nine Years Later
Tyr Castle

MOMENTS LIKE THIS were far and few between.
Unfortunately for them.

With four young children in the house and her pregnant with their fifth, Kent and Madelaina had to make time to be together where they could find it.

Like now.

Kent was working his breeches off in a hurry. "You are sure they are with the nurse?" he said. "They were supposed to be the last time, but somehow, Cass escaped the nurse and ended up under our bed."

He looked stricken at the realization that the situation could repeat itself, and, as Madelaina giggled, he went to his knees and peered under the bed to make sure his eldest son wasn't in the same room with his amorous parents.

"Well?" Madelaina said.

Kent's head popped up. "He is not there," he said, standing up and leaving his breeches on the floor. "I love my son dearly. He is clever and bright and talented, like me. But I do not want him in the same chamber with me and his mother as we do what parents like to do."

His warm, big body came down on Madelaina and she wrapped her arms around him, pulling him close. "And we do like to do this."

"Aye, we do."

He nuzzled her neck, gently kissing her as his hand found an engorged breast. She was still breastfeeding their youngest at a little over two years of age, but she was heavily pregnant with their fifth child. As it turned out, Kent and Madelaina had proven quite fertile together, and considering they couldn't keep their hands off one another, the frequent pregnancies were to be expected. But at this stage of her pregnancy, Kent couldn't exactly mount her like he usually did with her enormous belly, so he had to get creative.

As he suckled the tender skin of her neck and shoulder, he could feel her nipple hardening beneath his palm, and he squeezed gently, feeling her twitch beneath him. That was usually a sign that she was ready for him and impatiently waiting for him to join his body to hers. He paused a moment, putting his hand on her belly as he gazed down into that face he loved so well.

"Do you feel well enough for this?" he asked softly. "The physic has said we probably shouldn't because you're near to delivering the child, but if you feel well enough, the midwife says we can do as we please."

She grinned at him. "And you would rather listen to the midwife."

"I would rather listen to my wife."

"Your wife feels quite well and would like for you to finish what you started."

He chuckled, swallowing her up in his big embrace as he kissed her deeply. When he was finished getting her all hot and bothered, he stroked her cheek and continued his tender onslaught by gently taking a nipple in his mouth. He suckled on her, but that drew milk, so he tried not to suckle her too much. Their youngest child still nursed now and then, so he tried to leave some for the lad.

But it was difficult.

Shifting his big body again, he slipped between her supple legs.

There was a soft matting of dark curls down there, something he was very familiar with, and he touched her very carefully as she drew up her knees, groaning in delight. The pink flower was unfurling, doing what nature had intended it should, and he put his fingers into her body, listening to her gasp with pleasure. Kent could hardly hold himself back at that point, and he finally rolled her onto her side so he could enter her from behind.

Madelaina's body was highly attuned to her husband's. She lifted her leg, giving him more room to move, as he thrust into her slick and waiting body. It was pleasure beyond compare as he began to move within her, and she reached between her legs, touching him where he joined with her. But Kent had to move her seeking hand because her touch was a guarantee that he would spill himself prematurely.

And he very much didn't want to.

Forcing her to lift her free arm so she couldn't try to touch him again, he held her from behind, his arms around her, his hands on her pregnant belly, feeling the life that they had created together as he continued to thrust into her. Kent's mouth was on her neck, her cheek, and he tasted of her flesh because she was sweet and delectable. Soft whispers filled her ear, telling her how much he loved her.

How he couldn't live without her.

His pace quickened as his release approached. Usually, he could hold out for quite some time, relishing their coupling, but he didn't trust his children not to interrupt this time together, so he wanted to make this moment mean something. He touched, he kissed, he inhaled. All of her wonderful musk, the scent that drove him mad, filled his nostrils like the most potent aphrodisiac.

It was paradise.

Somehow, Madelaina managed to get her arm down again and put her hand between her legs, feeling her husband's powerful manhood. The flutter of her fingers threw him over the edge and his release came like an explosion, his body tensing until a burst of stars arced through his loins and belly. He released his seed deep into her body, groaning with the satisfaction of it. But even after he climaxed, he continued to move within her because she'd not yet achieved her own release, and he was soon rewarded with the spasms from her body as her climax was achieved.

The air of the chamber was filled with her gasps of pleasure as Madelaina's body twitched and jolted. Kent held her in his arms as she convulsed with pleasure. It was incredibly arousing and incredibly intimate. Tenderly, he put his hands on her big belly as he gently kissed her shoulder.

"How do you feel?" he murmured. "Are you well?"

She sighed heavily. "Very well," she said. "You?"

"Never better."

"Shall we go again?"

He laughed softly. "Give me a few moments," he said. "Let

me lie here with you in my arms and dream of those days when—"

"My lord!" A knocking on the door startled them both. "My lady? I am sorry to interrupt, but there is someone here to see you."

Madelaina groaned, putting her hands over her face, as Kent sat up and answered. "Who is it?" he said.

The person on the other side of the door was a maid who helped keep the family's chambers clean. With four young children, that was no easy feat. Unfortunately, she was terrified of Kent, so hearing his response had her trembling.

"Lord Ivor is here, my lord," she said in a quivering voice. "He has Master Casimir with him."

That had Madelaina struggling to sit up, but with her enlarged belly, Kent had to pull her into a sitting position.

"Cass?" she said, puzzled. "What is our son doing with Ivor?"

"I do not know," Kent said. Then he raised his voice to the servant. "I shall be down in a moment. Show Lord Ivor into my solar."

"Aye, my lord!"

They could hear her scurrying away. Kent got out of bed and went to pull Madelaina over to the edge so she could put her feet on the floor. When she was steady, he went to find his breeches.

"Kent, you really must talk to him about running off," she said as she pulled her shift over her head. "One of these days, he is going to run away and get into real trouble."

"I know."

"He will not have you or your brother or one of your men to save him."

"I *know*, dearest."

"I do not think you do," she said, flustered as she pulled her garment over her head. "You are not his mother. You did not carry him in your body for nine months and spend two days trying to give birth to him. If something happened to him, I would die. I would fade away and die."

She was getting agitated. Kent pulled his tunic on and turned to her, knowing he had to soothe her now before the situation got out of hand.

"Nothing is going to happen to him, my love," he said, turning her around so he could tighten the laces on her dress. "He is a smart lad, and a careful one. When we are in London, he is extremely careful. He even watches his young siblings to ensure they do not come to harm. Cass is a remarkable lad for his age."

With her dress secure, Madelaina ran a quick comb through her hair to smooth it and fixed the bun at the nape of her neck before pointing to her shoes so Kent could put them on her.

"He runs to that old castle, and one of these days, a rock is going to fall on his head," she grumbled, using his shoulder for balance as he bent down and slipped her shoes on. "Honestly, I would think you would be more concerned."

"Of course I am concerned."

"He is your firstborn!"

He stood up and kissed her. "I will speak with him, I promise," he assured her softly. "Now, will you come down with me?"

She was frowning, unhappy at the turn of events as he led her out of their bedchamber and down to the entry to Tyr's big keep. The castle was built on a rise, overlooking the land around it, so anyone approaching it was easy to see for miles.

They descended the stairs together, hearing their children playing somewhere on the entry level.

There were three chambers down there—a solar for Kent, a smaller one for Madelaina, as chatelaine, and then a small hall where the family dined. Madelaina caught sight of the children in the small hall, with their nurse, and made her way over to the chamber to interrogate the nurse about Casimir's appearance with the local Welsh warlord. Arthur was also in the chamber, though in his old age, he mostly slept by the hearth as the children played around him. That left Kent to proceed to his solar, where Ivor should be waiting—but, finding it empty, he headed outside.

He found Ivor in the bailey with a small escort, including Dai, who lifted a hand in greeting to Kent. Kent acknowledged the man, but his focus was more on Ivor and the two small boys at his side.

"Let me guess," Kent said as he approached. "Hen Gastell?"

Ivor smiled ironically. "Hen Gastell."

Kent shook his head reproachfully at his eldest son. Casimir de Poyer received his name because Kent had heard it once, belonging to an envoy from Rome, and liked it. It sounded worldly and sophisticated, a perfect name for a son who would undoubtedly grow up to be a great knight.

If he lived that long.

Casimir looked at his father with as much courage as he could muster. He had dark hair, longer, with half of it over one eye. He was brave to a fault, brilliant, empathetic, and generous. He was also conniving, aggressive, and stubborn.

Kent couldn't have loved the boy more.

"Your mother is very unhappy, Cass," he said grimly. "You were supposed to be with your nurse, yet you clearly escaped her. Lord Ivor had to bring you home. Well? What do you have to say for yourself?"

Casimir indicated his younger, auburn-haired cohort. "Yestin and I were playing, Papa," he said. "It is very important."

"Why?"

"Because I hold Hen Gastell."

"What do you mean, you hold it?"

Casimir sighed, exasperated. "That is what I am trying to tell you," he said. "I have taken it for England. If I do not defend it, Yestin will sack it and take it back for the Welsh. And I cannot allow that to happen."

Kent pursed his lips doubtfully. "Why not?" he said. "What happens then?"

Casimir spoke to his father as if the man knew absolutely nothing about castles or marches or anything else. "*Then* it belongs to Wales and we have to get it back," he said. "Yestin and I have a pact."

"What pact?"

"We meet every seventh day and we fight for the castle," he said. "Yestin had it for a while, but I got it back when I ambushed him."

Kent looked at Ivor, who had his hand over his mouth so the boys couldn't see him smile. That had Kent fighting off a smile as well.

"Ambush him, did you?" he said. "How unkind. Yestin is not our enemy."

"How else am I to get the castle back?"

He had a point. Not knowing what else to say, because he honestly couldn't get angry with his son, Kent motioned toward the stables. "We will discuss this later," he said. "For now, take Yestin over to the stables and show him the puppies. Mayhap his father will let him have one."

Yestin lit up, looking at his father with great hope. Ivor was fully prepared to deny him, to argue the point with him, but he knew sheerly from the expression on the lad's face that, in the end, he would fold. He was an idiot and he knew it.

What a pathetic man he was.

"I suppose one puppy would do no harm," he said. "But only one. And you will be responsible to feed him and bed him. Do you understand me?"

"Aye, Papa!"

The boys took off at a dead run. When they were out of earshot, Kent and Ivor broke down in soft laughter.

"My God," Kent said. "They are just like us. How can I become angry when I did the same thing to my father?"

Ivor shook his head. "I knew where they were," he said. "But Roxhanna is like Madelaina—she worries for them playing in those old stones, fearful one will fall on them, so she sent me out to find them."

"How are Roxhanna and the new babies?"

Ivor puffed up proudly. "They thrive," he said. "Two boys at once, Kent. Not even you and your prolific wife have managed that."

Kent chuckled. "Nay, we have not, at least not yet," he said. "Maddie is due to give birth any time now. She is ready for the child to be born so she can see her feet again."

Ivor grinned. "Well do I remember Roxhanna when she was due to deliver our children," he said. "It is difficult for women. They have my sympathy. And speaking of sympathy, I've not heard from Cheppy lately. How are he and Celyn faring? She was due to give birth, the last I heard."

He used the nickname for Bennet that Orion had started. It

was something that had spread throughout the Six, a name Bennet had once associated with pain, but now a name that he associated with camaraderie and acceptance. Funny how the years had made it something to treasure, much as Orion no longer had a problem with being called Monty.

Something he, too, saw as acceptance.

"They are well," Kent said, motioning for the man to follow him to the keep. "Celyn had another girl."

Ivor laughed softly as he took up stride beside him, heading toward the big, square keep. "A fourth girl," he said. "Poor Cheppy. Surrounded by women."

"I don't mind being surrounded by women."

Ivor continued chuckling. "You do have your share with your wife and daughters," he said. "How long do you intend to stay at Tyr this time?"

"Until Maddie delivers," Kent said. "We'll return to our home in London when the baby is old enough to travel."

"It is wise that your children should be born at your properties," Ivor said. "Henry does not miss you too badly?"

Kent shrugged. "He has Stefan and Orion and Bennet now as part of his personal guard," he said. "Bennet and Celyn's children have been born in London, and they have a good life there. They seem very happy."

"That is good to hear," Ivor said. "And you? Are you still very happy?"

Kent's smile was immediate. "Sometimes I wonder what my life would be like had you not been in it," he said. "You have become part of my fabric. You made it so I could be the happiest man alive with the best wife a man could ask for. Am I still very happy? Maddie has never shown me anything else."

Ivor smiled because Kent was. "And I would not have met

Roxhanna had it not been for you," he said. "Bennet is a great man. I admire him tremendously. But his sister belongs to me. Who knew I would marry a Saesneg?"

Kent chuckled. "It seems strange that Bennet is my father-in-law," he admitted. "Maddie doesn't really treat him as her father, however. More like an uncle. Since he did not raise her, it's a relationship they are both comfortable with. She does, however, treat The Bryn like her father and probably always will."

"I know," Ivor said. "Do not forget that Yestin works with him in the apothecary shop. I do believe my son will be the next apothecary of Penderyn."

"And you are content with that?"

Ivor shrugged. "I want my sons to have a life that makes them happy," he said. "If that makes Yestin happy, then so be it. But the twins—Colin and Garan—mayhap will follow in my footsteps. We have a great legacy to continue, so mayhap it will be continued through them."

They'd come to the stairs of the keep, heading up the steps. "I've offered to let the boys foster here," Kent said. "I would be happy to train them as warriors."

Ivor nodded. "I know," he said. "And I appreciate your offer. But you are not always at Tyr, and I do not want them traveling to London."

"Henry is here," Kent said. "My brother is an excellent knight. He will train them well."

Ivo smiled with gratitude. "I shall think on it," he said. "I will speak to Roxhanna and we shall decide."

"You will let me know."

"Of course. And thank you."

They came to the top of the steps. From this vantage point,

one could see the valley below, the vast green space, the hills as they met the sky. They paused for a moment, looking out over the wide expanse.

"Those years ago when we first met, I never imagined that we would still be friends as adults," Ivor said. He snorted. "Honestly, I did not know if I would reach adulthood. It is still amazing to me that I am a husband, a father. What a great responsibility we have. What a great responsibility our fathers had."

Kent nodded, leaning on the railing as he surveyed his empire. "It is true," he said. "I'm fortunate that my father is still alive. I am so glad he got to see his grandchildren born. But every time Cass runs off to Hen Gastell, I think of those days when you and I would play for hours and hours, pretending to control the world. Those were good days, Ivor."

"I agree," Ivor said fervently. "They were wonderful days. Days that remind me of that song."

"What song?"

Ivor started to sing, off key.

Summer days and summer stars,
And a deep blue sea that glistens like silver.
All at once, the past has turned to shadow,
And the future gleams like diamonds.

When he was finished, Kent looked at him, grinning. "You never could sing very well," he said.

Ivor put his hand over his heart. "I sing it as purely as a song has ever been sung."

Kent chuckled. "True enough," he said. "That's an old song, but when I think on the words, they have a new meaning to me. A past that has turned to shadow and a future that gleams like diamonds. My future with Maddie has never been brighter."

"Kent? Ivor?"

Someone was calling to them. They both turned to see Madelaina through the open door, standing near the entry to the small hall where children were screaming and playing.

"My dearest?" Kent said.

Madelaina waved him in. "Come in, both of you," she said. "I'll send for refreshments."

"Not for me, Lady de Poyer," Ivor called back to her. "I should return to—"

"Inside, both of you!"

Without hesitation, Ivor was the first one through the door. "Aye, my lady."

Kent chuckled, watching the man go inside, threatened by the shout of a pregnant woman. He saw Ivor take Madelaina's hand and kiss it sweetly, grinning at her as she smiled in return. Old friends, dear friends.

Family.

Kent could have never imagined a life like this for himself. Those years ago, when only his career in the Guard of Six mattered, seemed like another lifetime. Part of his past that had indeed turned to shadow. The past where a lonely, focused man lived. Now, for the man who bore *Insurrection*, the only thing for him was a future that gleamed like diamonds, and one diamond in particular.

Madelaina.

The most beautiful diamond he'd ever seen.

And a love that would last for eternity… just like a diamond.

CB THE END BO

Children of Kent and Madelaina
Casimir
Aramantha
Adestan
Endelyn
Gerard
Roderic
Victoriana

Children of Ivor and Roxhanna
Yestin
Colin
Garan
Isabel

Children of Bennet and Celyn
Madelaina
Millicent "Millie"
Marian
Matilda
Marcus

Author's Afterword

I hope you enjoyed Kent and Madelaina's story! Quite involved, wasn't it?

I had to include the children of Ivor and Bennet because their stories were so deeply intertwined with Kent and Madelaina's. And if some of you are wondering just how old Celyn was when she started having children again, I always figured she was about seventeen years old when she had Madelaina. That means in the novel, she's thirty-seven years of age. Plenty of time for her to have more children in her later years.

I also wanted to make mention of something because the book makes sort of a big deal out of it and I didn't want you, as the reader, to think something was deliberately left out or forgotten. I'm talking about Orion Payton-Forrester. We know he has secret parentage, and in this book he doesn't make any discoveries about it and it's never brought up to him, but there will be an Orion Payton-Forrester book as part of this series and everything will be addressed there. What this book has done is sort of lay the groundwork for that. And, yes, Bennet de Birmingham has been added to the Guard of Six, which is now expanding. Unfortunately, he's already had his love story completed with Celyn, so he won't have a novel, but the others will. Remember that Stefan de Lohr has also been added. The names of their swords? You'll read it here first…

Stefan de Lohr—Domination

Orion Payton-Forrester—Liberation

Bennet de Bermingham—Demolition

More great adventures with the Guard of Six! (And, yes, that name will remain.)

Oh—and one more thing. I didn't want to put this in the foreword, but if you've read The Dark Lord series (de Russe Legacy), then you know that de Russe and Wellesbourne are intertwined throughout the history of my world. *The Dark One: Dark Knight* and *The White Lord of Wellesbourne* happen about two hundred years after this book is set, so even though they might have been the antagonists in this tale, they are quite honorable houses, I promise. But every house has a bad apple now and then, eh?

Thank you for reading!

Hugs,
Kathryn

Kathryn Le Veque Novels

Medieval Romance:

De Wolfe Pack Series:
Warwolfe
The Wolfe
Nighthawk
ShadowWolfe
DarkWolfe
A Joyous de Wolfe Christmas
BlackWolfe
Serpent
A Wolfe Among Dragons
Scorpion
StormWolfe
Dark Destroyer
The Lion of the North
Walls of Babylon
The Best Is Yet To Be
BattleWolfe
Castle of Bones

De Wolfe Pack Generations:
WolfeHeart
WolfeStrike
WolfeSword
WolfeBlade
WolfeLord
WolfeShield
Nevermore
WolfeAx
WolfeBorn
WolfeBite

The Executioner Knights:
By the Unholy Hand
The Mountain Dark
Starless
A Time of End
Winter of Solace
Lord of the Sky
The Splendid Hour
The Whispering Night
Netherworld
Lord of the Shadows
Of Mortal Fury
'Twas the Executioner Knight
Before Christmas
Crimson Shield
The Black Dragon

The de Russe Legacy:
The Falls of Erith
Lord of War: Black Angel
The Iron Knight
Beast
The Dark One: Dark Knight
The White Lord of Wellesbourne
Dark Moon
Dark Steel
A de Russe Christmas Miracle
Dark Warrior

The de Lohr Dynasty:
While Angels Slept
Rise of the Defender
Steelheart

Shadowmoor
Silversword
Spectre of the Sword
Unending Love
Archangel
A Blessed de Lohr Christmas
Lion of Twilight
Lion of War
Lion of Hearts
Lion of Steel
Lion of Thunder

The Brothers de Lohr:
The Earl in Winter

Lords of East Anglia:
While Angels Slept
Godspeed
Age of Gods and Mortals

Great Lords of le Bec:
Great Protector

House of de Royans:
Lord of Winter
To the Lady Born
The Centurion

Lords of Eire:
Echoes of Ancient Dreams
Lord of Black Castle
The Darkland

Ancient Kings of Anglecynn:
The Whispering Night
Netherworld

Battle Lords of de Velt:
The Dark Lord
Devil's Dominion
Bay of Fear

The Dark Lord's First Christmas
The Dark Spawn
The Dark Conqueror
The Dark Angel

Reign of the House of de Winter:
Lespada
Swords and Shields

De Reyne Domination:
Guardian of Darkness
The Black Storm
A Cold Wynter's Knight
With Dreams
Master of the Dawn
One Wylde Knight

House of d'Vant:
Tender is the Knight (House of
d'Vant)
The Red Fury (House of d'Vant)

The Dragonblade Series:
Fragments of Grace
Dragonblade
Island of Glass
The Savage Curtain
The Fallen One
The Phantom Bride

Great Marcher Lords of de Lara
Lord of the Shadows
Dragonblade

House of St. Hever
Fragments of Grace
Island of Glass
Queen of Lost Stars

Lords of Pembury:
The Savage Curtain

Lords of Thunder: The de Shera Brotherhood Trilogy
The Thunder Lord
The Thunder Warrior
The Thunder Knight

The Great Knights of de Moray:
Shield of Kronos
The Gorgon

The House of De Nerra:
The Promise
The Falls of Erith
Vestiges of Valor
Realm of Angels

Highland Legion:
Highland Born
Highland Destroyer

Highland Warriors of Munro:
The Red Lion
Deep Into Darkness

The House of de Garr:
Lord of Light
Realm of Angels

Saxon Lords of Hage:
The Crusader
Kingdom Come

High Warriors of Rohan:
High Warrior
High King

The House of Ashbourne:
Upon a Midnight Dream

The House of D'Aurilliac:
Valiant Chaos

The House of De Dere:
Of Love and Legend

St. John and de Gare Clans:
The Warrior Poet

The House of de Bretagne:
The Questing

The House of Summerlin:
The Legend

The Kingdom of Hendocia:
Kingdom by the Sea

The BlackChurch Guild: Shadow Knights:
The Leviathan
The Protector
The Swordsman

Guard of Six:
Absolution
Insurrection

Regency Historical Romance:
Sin Like Flynn: A Regency Historical Romance Duet
The Sin Commandments
Georgina and the Red Charger

Gothic Regency Romance:
Emma

Historical Fiction:
The Girl Made Of Stars

Contemporary Romance:

Kathlyn Trent/Marcus Burton Series:
Valley of the Shadow

The Eden Factor
Canyon of the Sphinx

The Eagle Brotherhood (under the pen name Kat Le Veque):
The Sunset Hour
The Killing Hour
The Secret Hour
The Unholy Hour
The Burning Hour
The Ancient Hour
The Devil's Hour

Sons of Poseidon:
The Immortal Sea

Pirates of Britannia Series (with Eliza Knight):
Savage of the Sea by Eliza Knight
Leader of Titans by Kathryn Le Veque
The Sea Devil by Eliza Knight
Sea Wolfe by Kathryn Le Veque

Note: All Kathryn's novels are designed to be read as stand-alones, although many have cross-over characters or cross-over family groups. Novels that are grouped together have related characters or family groups. You will notice that some series have the same books; that is because they are cross-overs. A hero in one book may be the secondary character in another.

There is NO reading order except by chronology, but even in that case, you can still read the books as stand-alones. No novel is connected to another by a cliff hanger, and every book has an HEA.

Series are clearly marked. All series contain the same characters or family groups except the American Heroes Series, which is an anthology with unrelated characters.

For more information, find it in **A Reader's Guide to the Medieval World of Le Veque**.

ABOUT KATHRYN LE VEQUE

Bringing the Medieval to Romance

KATHRYN LE VEQUE is a critically acclaimed, multiple USA TODAY Bestselling author, an Indie Reader bestseller, a charter Amazon All-Star author, and a #1 bestselling, award-winning, multi-published author in Medieval Historical Romance with over 100 published novels.

Kathryn is a multiple award nominee and winner, including the winner of Uncaged Book Reviews Magazine 2017 and 2018 "Raven Award" for Favorite Medieval Romance. Kathryn is also a multiple RONE nominee (InD'Tale Magazine), holding a record for the number of nominations. In 2018, her novel WARWOLFE was the winner in the Romance category of the Book Excellence Award and in 2019, her novel A WOLFE AMONG DRAGONS won the prestigious RONE award for best pre-16th century romance.

Kathryn is considered one of the top Indie authors in the world with over 2M copies in circulation, and her novels have been translated into several languages. Kathryn recently signed with Sourcebooks Casablanca for a Medieval Fight Club series, first published in 2020.

In addition to her own published works, Kathryn is also the President/CEO of Dragonblade Publishing, a boutique publishing house specializing in Historical Romance. Dragonblade's success has seen it rise in the ranks to become Amazon's #1 e-book publisher of Historical Romance (K-Lytics report July 2020).

Kathryn loves to hear from her readers. Please find Kathryn on Facebook at Kathryn Le Veque, Author, or join her on Twitter @kathrynleveque. Sign up for Kathryn's blog at www.kathrynleveque.com for the latest news and sales.